"Because I full truth. *Please, Tony. If you love me, if I ever meant anything to you, please tell me the truth now."*

Staring into her beautiful green eyes, he felt the moment it happened. He accepted the inevitable. No matter what the street said, no matter what people thought of him, Linda would never believe he had turned so completely dark. Men had threatened her life. A reporter was threatening her career. He couldn't keep her safe if he kept her ignorant.

And whatever he did, he had to keep her safe.

"Are you sure you're ready for this?" he asked, wrapping a strand of her hair around his finger.

Dear Reader,

Alpha males are some of my favorite heroes because they are strong and sexy, but most of all complex. They're also very good at hiding their emotions and vulnerability, which makes their ultimate surrender to love so satisfying. When I first wrote about Tony Cooper in *Dangerous to Her,* I viewed him as a flawed man who, while not classically alpha, was strong enough to fight for others. In *Deadly Charade,* Tony returns to the woman he's always loved, but he does so in shackles, charged with a violent crime. By words and action, he seems to have truly changed. As Linda discovers, however, Tony is still the same loyal, courageous and loving man he's always been. I hope you agree that getting him to admit that, to both himself and Linda, makes for lots of sexy fun.

Wishing you much love and happiness always,

Virna DePaul

VIRNA DEPAUL

Deadly Charade

HARLEQUIN® ROMANTIC SUSPENSE

Recycling programs
for this product may
not exist in your area.

ISBN-13: 978-0-373-27824-4

DEADLY CHARADE

Printed in U.S.A.

Books by Virna DePaul

Harlequin Romantic Suspense

Dangerous to Her #1674
It Started That Night #1706
Deadly Charade #174

HQN Books

Shades of Desire
Shades of Temptation

VIRNA DEPAUL

was an English major in college and, despite a passion for Shakespeare, Broadway musicals and romance novels, somehow ended up with a law degree. For ten years, she was a criminal prosecutor for the state of California. Now she's thrilled to be writing stories about complex individuals (fully human or not) who are willing to overcome incredible odds for love. She can be found on Twitter at @virnadepaul or at www.virnadepaul.com.

For Cyndi, Rochelle and Susan for rooming with me and still thinking I'm fun even when I'm on deadline!

Acknowledgment

Thank you to Rochelle French, Grace Callaway, Vanessa Kier, Karin Tabke, Joyce Lamb, Cyndi Faria, Susan Hatler, Kristin Miller and Sacramento Sheriff's Deputy Paul B., for your help with this one.

Prologue

Linda Delaney woke feeling optimistic about life and love. Even so, the comforting haze of sleep beckoned to her. She pushed it aside, longing for her lover's embrace. Nothing felt as good as being in his arms.

She shifted, intending to burrow closer to Tony under the warm, protective haven of the sheets, but only coldness greeted her. With it came an immediate sense of panic. Dread.

Her eyes popped open and she sat up, alone in her bed. A quick glance at the clock confirmed it was the middle of the night, not even three o'clock. The bedroom door was slightly ajar, allowing tendrils of the illuminated hallway light to sneak inside, much the same way she imagined Tony had snuck out of bed, cautious not to wake her.

For a moment she closed her eyes and fought it off. The suspicion. The feeling of betrayal. The knowledge of what she had to do. But it was no use.

Tony could be watching television. He could be reading. He could be doing a multitude of things, each of them perfectly respectable and ordinary, but deep down she knew he'd snuck away for a more nefarious purpose. To get in touch with his supplier. To exchange money for the painkillers that would take away the man she loved and replace him with a stranger.

According to Tony, the last time he'd used had been a year before they'd ever met. She'd chosen to believe him, but a small part of her had always suspected he wasn't telling the truth. Or that even if he was, it wouldn't last.

And she'd been right.

God, she wished he wasn't using again. But she knew better. She'd seen the signs of his relapse—his restlessness, the sleepless nights, his increasing agitation—but had simply chosen to ignore them. She'd prayed she was wrong. That he'd keep his promises to her in a way her father had never been able to.

She stood and went looking for him. He was in the kitchen, his elbows on the table, his head cradled in his hands, staring down at a plastic bag filled with pills. Hearing her, he looked up, his gaze tortured.

She sat in the chair beside him.

He shook his head. "I haven't taken one."

Not yet. He didn't say it, but she heard it anyway. It was only a matter of time. He'd gotten hold of the drugs, obviously. That evidenced his intent to use them. And he would, no matter how hard he tried not to. He would.

"I know," she said softly. She reached out and touched his arm. Desperately he pulled her toward him and she went willingly, wrapping her arms around him and cradling him close. He was shaking. His body vibrating with need—need for the drugs, she realized sadly. Not her.

His mouth sought hers and she opened it to him as automatically as she opened up her heart. Their tongues surged against one another, and she wished she could infuse him with strength, but his addiction was a dark, monstrous force. It gave him something she never could. An unnatural high. Forgetfulness. Oblivion.

And that's what hurt the most.

They were together. She loved him, more than she'd ever loved anyone. Loved him enough to have stayed with him, despite her job as a criminal prosecutor. But he wanted the drugs more than he wanted her.

Automatically she pulled away, shoring up her courage to ask him to leave.

Obviously sensing that, he pulled her back. "No, not yet," he stated. "Stay with me. You're more important to me than these pills. You know that. Be with me. Please."

One last time. Again, the words went unspoken. And truthfully maybe he didn't even realize that's where this was headed. But he'd inadvertently reminded her what a losing battle this was. Her father had used to say the same thing to them—her, her sister, Kathy and their mother. "You're more important to me than anything. You know that."

In the end it had all been a lie. And that's why they'd had to cut him out of their lives.

Just like she'd have to cut Tony out of hers.

The finality of her thoughts had her panic and despair spiking, so much so that when he cupped her breast in one hand she felt nothing. Given her body's addiction to Tony's touch, that told her more than anything that it was time to let him go. But despite the seeming absence of true desire, her love for him was still there, and she couldn't walk away without telling him—no, showing him—how much she loved him. How much she'd always love him. Even if they couldn't be together.

She led him back to their bed, relieved he went without once looking back at that bag of pills. She straddled him, not wanting to dominate him, but to give to him. Even though it wasn't enough, would never be enough, the desire that had been absent just minutes ago washed over her like a tidal wave.

Her hands caressed him. The strong shoulders so gracefully padded with muscle. The defined grooves in his chest, lightly dusted with hair. The smooth curly locks that had first drawn her to him.

Their breaths grew ragged the longer she touched him, and she was aware of his hands on her hips, lightly gripping her as he arched beneath her. He was hard and she moaned at the sharp spark of pleasure that twisted through her. Frantically she reached down and guided him into her welcoming heat.

She bit her lip at how thoroughly he filled her.

Why, she longed to cry. Why couldn't this be enough for him?

But she kept the words inside. Later, they'd talk. Later, he'd seek to reassure her. To reason with her that he hadn't actually taken a pill. To tell her that he loved her and always would and would never jeopardize what they had together.

He'd mean every single word he said. And she'd be tempted to believe him, even though she couldn't.

All she could have was right now. His body in hers. Her body over his. Loving him enough for a lifetime when all they had left together was tonight.

Chapter 1

Three and a half years later...

Pitting oneself against a drug lord definitely had its downsides, Tony Cooper thought as he sat in his car in front of the Sacramento County Courthouse, watching for any sign of his ex, Linda Delaney.

The first time he'd challenged Mark Guapo, he'd still been reeling from his breakup with Linda some eighteen months before and hoping that by narking on his former drug supplier, he might be able to win her back. The downside? Six months after that, Linda had been lying in a hospital bed, recovering from the wounds that Guapo's men had inflicted on her, and he'd been forced to leave her and accompany his sister Mattie and his niece Jordan into the Witness Security Program.

Now, eighteen months later, he was back, this time to infiltrate Guapo's organization—which despite the other man's prison address, had been steadily expanding—and convince people he was taking over. His main objective? Identify the supplier of a dangerous hybrid bath-salt drug, Rapture. The downside? Too many to list, but the biggest was making sure Linda stayed safe this time and that meant staying the hell away from her.

Yet here he was, hoping for just one glimpse of her. One glimpse to replace his last memory of her, beaten and bruised. One glance to get him through the next few weeks, months and years without her. Then he'd start his car and leave. No one would guess he was here to see her.

Just in case, however, he visually swept the surrounding area, just as he'd done every few minutes for the past half hour.

No one appeared to be watching him, but he knew what they'd see if they were.

What Linda would see.

Would she even recognize him? Sometimes he didn't even recognize himself.

Every detail of his appearance had been chosen with care. Gone was the curly brown hair that had made him look boyish even when he'd been breaking the law. In its place was a shaved head that showed off his eyebrow piercing to its best advantage. The scars on his face, the ones left over from the beatings Michael Sabon, Guapo's brother, had given him, added to the overall look, declaring him to be a badass to the nth degree.

But he didn't feel like one.

He felt like the weakling he was. The same weakling who'd gotten addicted to prescription painkillers in the first place, ultimately losing the love of his life as a result. The same weakling Linda hadn't trusted to refrain from using again.

To some extent she'd been wrong. Just as he'd told her, he hadn't used since before he'd met her, which meant he'd been clean for over five years now. Even so, there had been several close calls, including the night she'd caught him with those damn pills. And there were still plenty of times he doubted his ability to stay clean. Plenty of times his behavior had been affected by his cravings. Plenty of times he felt a hair's breath away from saying to hell with it and giving in.

That was yet another reason to stay away from Linda. Even if physical danger from others wasn't a factor, she'd already made her decision about him. In the end, it hadn't mattered that he'd helped send Guapo to prison. Hell, it probably wouldn't even matter that he'd joined the police academy soon after he and Linda had broken up. Why would it? Just months away from graduating, he'd been too weak to protect Linda or his sister. Guapo's men had beat Linda into a coma and his sister had almost died. Tony had failed everyone he loved.

Again.

Once an addict, always an addict.

And for Linda Delaney, an addict wasn't good enough.

Tony again scanned the street.

His pulse accelerated as he finally spotted her, exiting the courthouse's main entrance. Automatically he stiffened and pain zipped across his back and down his leg. He barely felt it past the mixed joy and longing that squeezed his heart.

As he watched, Linda sat on a bench outside the courthouse and ate a sandwich, watching the antics of a pair of squirrels warring over someone's littered potato chips. It reminded him of the days they'd spent at the local pet store, playfully arguing about what kind of animal they'd adopt someday. He'd wanted a dog. She'd wanted a cat. She'd argued a cat would be less work. They'd ended up getting neither, and it hadn't occurred to Tony until after they'd broken up why Linda would want an animal that was less work to care for—because Tony had been too much work for her as it was.

But that wasn't fair, he thought, willing away the slight taste of bitterness in his mouth. Linda was a busy woman. A successful woman. Just because she hadn't wanted to be tied down to an addict for the rest of her life didn't mean she hadn't given their relationship a fair shot. She had. She'd made him happy. And for a time he'd made her happy, too.

With him out of her life, she appeared to be happy again. Healthy. Safe.

She looked *good*. More like she had when he'd first met her. By the end their relationship had taken a toll on her. She'd lost weight, the light in her beautiful green eyes had dimmed, and worry lines had etched themselves into her skin. That seemed far behind her now. Her blond hair was long and silky. Her body curvy beneath her crisp tailored suit. Her features relaxed and so sweetly familiar that he could almost forget the pain and the years that separated them…

Then a polished, dark-haired man in a suit approached her, causing Linda to smile and Tony to frown. The guy was obviously an attorney, too, dressed in a finely tailored suit with a damned vest and shined shoes. He sat down next to her and handed her something. Their interaction was perfectly respectable, but Tony could tell the man's interest in Linda was far more than professional.

Sweat beaded Tony's forehead and he held his breath. He'd been hoping to see her and he'd been expecting to long for her, but he hadn't expected to see her with another man.

Then another man, this time a blond, stopped to talk to her. He, too, was probably a lawyer given how he was dressed. This man, however, Linda didn't seem to like. Even from across the street Tony saw her smile stiffen and wane. Before it could disappear completely, the blond guy pointed his finger like a gun, cocked it at Linda, then left. Linda immediately shook her head. In response, her dark-haired friend bent his head close to hers, placed his hand on her thigh, and said something that made her laugh.

Jealousy overwhelmed him, making him tremble. A faint buzzing sound filled the car and he vaguely wondered if he was losing it. But then he realized his cell phone was vibrating. With a shaky hand he forced his gaze away from Linda, pulled his phone out of his pocket and saw the number on the screen.

It was Justine, the woman helping him make connections inside Guapo's organization. She'd once dated Guapo's defense attorney, Grant Falcon; Guapo's men had killed him after Guapo had been convicted. Now she was dating another key man in Guapo's organization, Nicco Santos. The man was likely a key component to taking over Guapo's enterprise. He knew things he hadn't told Justine or Tony yet, and Tony was hoping one of those things was the identity of Guapo's Rapture supplier.

He snapped the phone to his ear. "What is it, Justine?"

"Tony!"

He frowned at the note of hysteria in her voice.

"Guapo won his appeal. He'll be out on the streets in the next twenty-four hours and he's going to find out what you've been doing. What *we've* been doing. He probably already knows."

Guapo was getting out of prison? What the hell? Tony's shaking hands went cold. "Does Nicco know?"

"He's the one who told me. He's scared out of his mind. And you know what that means. He's going to give you up. He's going to give *both* of us up."

"Calm down, Justine. Did you try to get the name of the supplier from Nicco again?"

Justine took an audible breath, then said, "He still says he doesn't know. That Guapo's going to take the name to his grave."

How ironic that the tables had turned. At one time Guapo had been desperate to find out the name of the confidential informant who'd sold him out. Now that same informant was just as desperate to get the name of the man only Guapo seemed to know. Sacramento's main supplier of Rapture to kids and soccer moms. The man responsible for killing Rory Maverick, Justine's little brother.

Tony shot another glance at Linda. She was still smiling. The guy beside her reached up, tucking a strand of her hair behind her ear. Swiftly Tony looked away.

It didn't matter. He could still see them together.

He pictured them dancing the way he and Linda had danced. Making love the way he and Linda had made love. Spending their lives together and having a family and building a future together…the way he and Linda never would.

He had no place in her life. Not anymore. Hadn't he just been telling himself that?

Gritting his teeth, he just managed to hang on to his control.

I can't lose it. Not now. I have too much to do.

"Tell Nicco to trust me," Tony told Justine. "And remind him that I've been a much more generous boss than Guapo ever was. I'll be there in five."

Chapter 2

Two weeks later...

Anyone who had ever witnessed a felony arraignment calendar knew it just didn't live up to the grandiose images portrayed on TV. Anyone who'd ever worked in criminal law knew it was a crap assignment. But it was a crap assignment everyone did and, judicial campaign or not, Linda Delaney was no exception. To avoid the arraignment calendar in her office, you had to have risen to the rank of senior assistant, at least.

Loaded down with her files, Linda strode toward Courtroom Five, weaving around the throngs of people waiting for court to begin. Most of them were dressed well in hopes of making a good impression on the judge and gaining leniency for themselves or another. Others just looked pissed or hopeless. There were several kids crying or running around, too. She knew most of them, like the fancier clothes people wore, had been brought along in hopes of eliciting sympathy, as well.

And don't you just sound optimistic about life? one part of her asked.

The other part of her shrugged. The truth was the truth, no matter how unsavory. Didn't mean she was *completely* jaded. In fact, her ability to see things for what they were without letting it affect how she treated others would serve her well as a judge. *If* the citizens of Sacramento County elected her, of course. Although her boss, District Attorney Norman Peterson, believed she was a shoo-in and had finally convinced her to join the judicial race, Linda's past might be more of a sticking point than he believed.

People often asked Linda how she could do her job, day in and day out, and still maintain some level of optimism about the state of humanity. It wasn't easy. Felony arraignment calendar was a morning-long runway show of the most desperate, dangerous and sometimes stupidest human beings possible. It was a constant reminder of the frailty of life and how it could be changed forever by a crackhead in need of a fix or a husband enraged by his wife's relationship with a coworker.

Beatings. Shootings. Robberies. Rapes. Thefts. Gang crimes. Committed every day by everyday people with jobs, friends, families and pets. You learned that the age, gender and the socioeconomic class of victims ran the gamut. No one was safe when it came down to it.

Not Linda's father. And not even Tony, the sweet-faced man she'd once loved to distraction. So much so that she'd stayed with him far longer than she should have.

Linda cursed softly and swiftly shook her head as if doing so would actually keep thoughts of Tony at bay.

It had been difficult to keep him from her mind on his birthday last month. It was even more impossible now.

Mark Guapo, the drug lord Tony had informed on two years ago, the same drug lord whose men had almost beaten Linda to death six months later, had recently been released from prison. The reversal wasn't based on anything that had happened at trial, but on a faulty search warrant. Guapo could still be retried for his crimes, but the tainted evidence would have to be excluded. Linda had already spent the past few days trying to determine if they had enough for a retrial, but understandably, she'd also been plagued with concerns about her own safety.

And that of Tony.

Despite Linda's best attempts to protect Tony, Guapo had still managed to figure out that Tony was the CI who'd helped put him away. They'd gone after not just Tony, but Tony's family, too. Now, Tony, his sister Mattie and his niece Jordan were in hiding in the Witness Security Program; Guapo wouldn't be able to find them.

As for her? Recently free, Guapo would likely be on his best behavior, so chances were she was probably safe, too. Safe but still furious. She'd worked so hard to get Guapo behind bars. And Tony had risked his life, given up so much of it. It seemed the height of unfairness that Guapo had managed to play the system and was now walking the streets as a free man.

Not for long, she thought. Not if she had any say in it.

She paused at the courtroom doors, pushing away thoughts of the past and lost second chances. She'd almost gotten used to lugging around the heavy banker's box filled with files, but opening doors was always tricky. She balanced the box on her hip and reached for the outer courtroom door just as a male hand reached over her shoulder to pull it open.

It was Neil Christoffersen, one of her fellow deputies.

"Good morning," he said with a smile, before taking the box from her. He immediately handed her a cup of coffee. It was the way he normally approached her. He'd proffer her coffee and they'd end up talking about work or debating some legal issue or two. Then he'd try to make things a bit more...personal.

Linda took the cup, wrapped her cold fingers around it and closed her eyes at the heady aromatic smell. The box was heavy and she could use a little treat. No harm done, right?

Well, so long as she discounted the subtle flutter in her stomach. A slight flutter that evidenced her growing attraction to him. She was just thankful the attraction was slight and nothing more. She wasn't open to starting another relationship again. Not when she still dreamed about Tony. Not when she so often second-guessed her decision to break up with him, as well as her failure to reverse that decision even after he'd informed on Guapo, putting his life at risk to do the right thing. She'd been tempted, so tempted, of course. She'd almost convinced herself that she'd been wrong about his inability to change. But then Guapo's men had attacked her and she'd woken in the hospital only to find Tony and his family gone.

He'd left her. For very good reasons, as he'd explained in a goodbye letter, but he'd still left her.

Just like she'd previously left him.

"Good morning," she replied to Neil as she walked deeper into the courtroom.

"So what did you wear?" he asked.

Linda frowned. "Excuse me?"

"To your friend's party. It was the reason you couldn't go out to dinner with me last week, remember?"

His grin and the twinkle in his eyes told her he knew it had been just another excuse to decline his dinner invitation.

He didn't know the half of it. Guilt and shame quivered through her, but she reminded herself that while she'd lied about going to a friend's party, she hadn't done anything worse than that. She'd gone dancing. At a perfectly respectable club. By herself. That wasn't anyone's business, nor was the fact that she liked to go dancing so she could remember how she and Tony used to fit so well together—on the dance floor and off it.

She was entitled to a social life. Dancing at nightclubs wasn't illegal and it wasn't contrary to the judicial position she was seeking. But she had to say something so…

Before she could reply, he said, "I was trying to imagine what you wore. You'd look beautiful in red."

Her skin warmed at the compliment and the accompanying glow of appreciation in Neil's eyes. The urge to tease and flirt back prodded at her, surprising her. She smiled. "Sorry to disappoint you but it was black. A plain black dress."

"Huh," he said, sweeping his gaze down her suit as if he was imagining her wearing a dress instead. "Black's good. Short?"

"Midcalf," she said drolly. "With long sleeves and a high-necked collar."

He looked doubtful. "In June?"

"Hey, I get chilly." She quickly took a sip of coffee to mask her own smile. She pictured the sexy black dress she'd worn. Simple, but by no means puritanical. Linda felt a small thrill, trying to imagine what Neil would have thought of the black lace camisole set she'd worn underneath. Or of the red set she wore today.

But the thrill quickly vanished. She tried—*really* tried to imagine herself disrobing for Neil, but although she once again felt a small flutter inside her, she didn't feel anything else. Instead all she could remember was how Tony had loved buying her sexy lingerie. In fact, he'd loved buying her lots of things, and not necessarily expensive things. Sure, he'd bought her lingerie and jewelry, and often surprised her with dinners out or theater tickets, but he'd just as often written her a poem or sketched her a picture or baked her his famous chocolate-chip cookies with the secret ingredient he'd sworn he'd tell her—but only on their wedding night. Tony had spoiled her in so many ways, big and small, and had never failed to make her feel special. But despite all that, despite his kindness and generosity and sense of humor and the incredible physical connection between them, it hadn't been enough. Because *she* hadn't been enough. Not enough to overcome his cravings for drugs. And even worse, not enough to stop him from getting hold of those same drugs—bringing those very drugs into their *home*—with every intention of using them.

"I'm sensing a fashion intervention is in order," Neil said, jolting her from her thoughts. "But you know what they say," he joked. "Being flawed doesn't mean you're not lovable. I'm sure you looked beautiful," Neil murmured. He watched her steadily. Warmly.

And that warmth eased some of the chill in her bones in a way the coffee hadn't been able to. Linda smiled and seriously reconsidered accepting one of his dinner invitations. What harm could it do?

Maybe she wasn't bowled over by passion right now, but that could change.

They chatted about work for a few minutes longer before court began. As Linda took her seat at the prosecutor's table, she saw movement out of the corner of her eye. Allie Ranch, one of the law-school students interning at the D.A.'s office, smiled and waved to her. Next to her sat Brian Heald, a fellow prosecutor who'd just returned from vacation. Right now Brian seemed to be checking out a brunette across the room. So what else was new? Since his divorce the guy had been chasing everything in skirts, Linda included. She just hoped he had enough sense not to hit on Allie.

Lunch? Allie mouthed.

Allie was only a few years younger than Linda. She'd been an accountant before going back to law school and Linda admired her for being willing to pursue her dream. Linda nodded, confirming they'd have lunch, then turned toward the bench. After routine introductions and instructions to the courtroom audience, the court session began.

"Larry Moser," the court clerk recited. "Charged with assault with a deadly weapon, resisting arrest and assault upon a police dog." Linda opened up Moser's file, reading it quickly as Mr. Moser stood up in the jury box. As was always the case, she didn't know the contents of the files in her box but the notes the charging deputy had left were all she needed to handle this phase of the proceedings. Once things progressed to plea bargaining or trial, she'd obviously know the file inside and out.

Moser's muscular six-foot-eight body dwarfed the inmates seated around him. He grinned wildly at his audience as they gaped at his bald head and the tattoo smack dab in the center of his forehead. A swastika.

According to his file, officers had chased Moser into a nearby residence after he had assaulted a man with a bat. Officers had surrounded the house and sent in one of their K-9 dogs when Moser had refused to come out. To their dismay, Moser had walked out of the house clutching the dog by the throat and laughing like a maniac. Officers had managed to subdue him and save the dog, but Moser had made his point. Unfortunately for him he had a long history of priors, including manufacturing and selling drugs, and if convicted of his current crimes, he'd be facing a three-strikes sentence. As expected, he issued his not guilty plea just like the twenty defendants before him, and the clerk rattled off the date of his next pretrial conference.

For the next hour the calendar progressed and Linda was just about to ask for a bathroom break when the clerk called the next case.

"The next defendant is charged with the first degree murder of Mark Guapo."

Linda's head snapped up. But before she could react any further to the news that Mark Guapo was dead, the clerk gave her another shock.

"The defendant's name is Anthony Cooper."

The name echoed in Linda's head for a moment, disorienting her. She stiffened when she saw the next defendant rise. He was seated in the jury box along with the other in-custody defendants. He sat right next to Moser, and despite the differences in their size, he looked even more ruthless.

Tony.

Her knees jerked up involuntarily, rattling the table and spilling her cup of coffee all over her and her files.

Linda hardly noticed the tepid liquid soaking into her skirt.

Oh, my God, she thought.

She and Tony stared at one another, though she saw none of the same shock she was feeling in his expression. He'd obviously watched her as court had gone on while she hadn't even seen him. Why would she? It wasn't like she spent a lot of time ogling the defendants during arraignment. Quite the opposite. And it wasn't as if he looked anything like the man he'd once been. That man, while desperate enough at times to have taken drugs, had still managed to look boyish. Charming. His inherent kindness had shone in his eyes for all to see.

This man?

Tony's brown hair was shaved, creating a clean frame for his penetratingly dark eyes and sharp cheekbones. Even devoid of expression, he looked hard. Cruel.

Cruel enough to kill even a hardened criminal like Mark Guapo.

Automatically she looked away.

"...all right, Ms. Delaney?"

The judge was calling her name. Shaking, Linda forced herself to her feet, holding on to the table for support. Feeling nauseated, she crossed her arm against her waist. "Excuse me, Your Honor, but could I have a moment?" she asked shakily. The court clerk announced a five minute break and Linda rushed from the courtroom.

As Tony sat in the jury box, chained to two other men in matching orange jumpsuits, he tried to stifle the overwhelming urge to run after Linda. He could feel the audience staring at him, looking at him as if he was part of some freak show in a circus.

Just like Linda had done.

He smirked to cover for the bitter taste in his mouth. He couldn't blame the poor woman for her horror. She had to hate him for what Guapo's men had done to her. Just like part of her had hated Tony for the drug addiction that had caused her to break up with him. Leaving town had been the best thing he could have done for her.

Too bad for both of them he hadn't been able to stay away.

At least Mark Guapo was dead. The man couldn't hurt anyone anymore, and that included Linda. Of course that didn't mean she was safe, especially now that Tony was here, in her world, which made it all the more possible that Tony and all the crap he'd gotten hooked up with lately could be linked to *her*.

Tony closed his eyes, praying no one could see the longing and indecision on his face. No, Guapo's death didn't change anything. Despite Tony's best attempts to get it out of him, the man had indeed taken the name of the Rapture supplier to the grave. That meant Tony still had a job to do, and part of that job included keeping Linda out of harm's way. To do that, he needed people to believe she meant nothing to him. That she never would.

And that included the people she worked with.

According to the men Tony was working for, Guapo had bribed his way not only into police stations and judge's chambers, but into the D.A.'s office, as well. Why else would so many of his men have avoided prosecution or been given such lenient sentences over the past few years? Even though ferreting out those moles wasn't Tony's responsibility, he sure as hell wasn't going to do anything to call their attention to Linda. And if anyone found out about their past, how much she'd once cared about him, or how much he *still* cared about her, it would definitely call attention to her, possibly placing her in danger and making it harder for a drug supplier to trust Tony.

Still…playing his part was hard—so much harder than he'd anticipated—when Linda was almost close enough to touch. To smell and taste.

To love.

In the past year and a half, he'd toughened up. He hadn't magically transformed into the badass he was trying to project, yet the threat of death didn't shake him anymore. Nor did the thought of what various criminal elements would do to him if they ever got the chance.

But the woman who'd just run from the room, averting her gaze and pretending she didn't know him? Didn't see him?

She was a different matter altogether.

Chapter 3

Linda burst into the ladies' room and immediately backed against the swinging door to hold back the demons chasing her. It did her no good. She couldn't erase the horrible image of Tony wearing jail clothes and standing among the other defendants in the courtroom.

As far as she knew, Tony had never been arrested before. Yet now he was being charged with Guapo's murder?

Her heart beating rapidly, Linda stumbled to one of the bathroom sinks. As she stared at her reflection, she automatically touched her hip. She could almost feel the tattoo burning her skin, as if it were about to combust.

Out damned spot! Out. Like Lady Macbeth, she longed to be released from the guilt the symbol caused her. But like Hester Prynne, she'd chosen to keep her brand. As a reminder. In case she ever felt tempted by her impulsive nature. In case she ever started to believe that being with an addict or giving in to a vice herself was okay. In a sense they were one and the same for her. Seeing Tony just now proved it.

Despite the reason he was here, despite knowing he was being charged with Guapo's murder, seeing him had burst open a hunger inside her that she'd barely been managing to keep suppressed. A hunger for him. In comparison the pleasure she'd felt when flirting with Neil seemed laughable.

If Tony had killed Guapo, he had to have been acting in self-defense. Guapo must have gone after Tony, or even Tony's family. But how was that possible? They'd been in the Witness Security Program. They should have been states away from Sacramento. Was Mattie here, too? And if so, why hadn't she—why hadn't Tony himself—called Linda as soon as he'd been arrested?

Because they'd known she wouldn't help? When the only possible reason she'd refuse to help would be…

For just a second Linda's belief in Tony's innocence faltered.

The bathroom door suddenly pushed open. A young woman, a pretty yet world-worn looking brunette with gold highlights and a scowl on her face, walked in. Although Linda kept her gaze averted, she felt the woman staring at her for a few seconds, likely wondering why Linda was upset, before she stepped into a stall and kicked the door shut.

Shakily Linda splashed cool water on her face. It didn't make her feel any better. Her stomach rolled. She bent forward, her hands gripping the cool porcelain sink, and gasped for breath.

He'd changed, she thought again. Not just his hair, but…inside. He'd changed. He'd looked at her with empty eyes when before they'd always been full of life. And love. For her.

Even on the last night they'd been together, even when he'd accepted she wouldn't change her mind about breaking up with him, there'd been a spark behind the desperation and regret. As if there would always be a part of him that would be hers, and that he wouldn't stop trying to convince her. Ever.

But that spark was gone now.

Something cold and hollow had taken its place. She felt it trying to press itself inside her—that same insidious sensation: cold and hollow. And once again she wondered why Tony hadn't called her.

She wondered if he truly had murdered Guapo.

Straightening, Linda swiftly washed her hands. As she did so, she heard sniffing from the stall behind her. Was the woman crying? If so, what a pathetic pair they made. Before she could leave, the other woman stepped out of the stall. Linda turned to look at her.

And barely stopped herself from flinching.

For a split second the woman seemed to look at her with an expression of utter hatred. Then the expression was gone and the woman smiled. She moved to the sink beside Linda and washed her hands.

Was she a friend of one of the defendants Linda was prosecuting? Or a defendant herself, one who'd been released on her own recognizance after her arrest? If that was the case, she was likely being charged with a petty theft, minor assault or drug charge. Given those three options, though she couldn't know for sure, Linda would place bets on the woman being a druggie. Despite her subdued clothing and makeup, the woman had a pinched look to her face and a jittery way of moving. A look in her eyes that seemed all too familiar to Linda. For all she knew, the sniffing she'd heard had been the woman ingesting a controlled substance.

Then again, would she really be so foolish as to do it here? With Linda present?

It didn't matter. Linda hadn't seen her doing anything illegal and she couldn't avoid her own troublesome situation by imagining another one.

Tony had come back into her life with a vengeance. Now she had to deal with it.

The courtroom doors opened and the room quieted as Linda walked back inside. Though Tony stared at her, practically willing her gaze to his, she refused to look at him.

The bailiff called his name, signaling that Tony should stand again. Pain shot through his left thigh, causing him to grit his teeth. Thanks to Guapo and the damage he'd done, Tony now walked with a strong limp that his leg shackles only worsened. But to Tony his physical injuries weren't what hurt the most.

It was the memory of Linda's expression a few minutes ago. The horror and betrayal she hadn't quite been able to hide. Just as she hadn't been able to hide her disappointment on the night she'd woken and found him in the kitchen, staring at that damn bag of drugs.

He was overwhelmed with conflicting feelings of joy and anger. God, he'd tried so hard to put his past behind him. Didn't that count for something? Didn't he deserve to at least tell her the truth, so that he could leave this world knowing she still cared about him? Knowing that she didn't think he was some kind of sick bastard?

But no. It didn't matter that he'd tried. He'd failed. He'd still ended up hurting the people he'd cared about most. His failure could hurt them yet again.

The emotions circling inside him momentarily paralyzed him.

Grief. Confusion. Regret. Longing.

He pushed all of them away. Forced himself to remain impassive as the clerk read the charges against him.

When the judge asked him how he pled, Tony followed the advice of the public defender he'd met with earlier. He lied. "Not guilty, Your Honor."

Chapter 4

As soon as the arraignment calendar was over, Linda rushed back to her office to read Tony's entire file. She'd just reached for it when a voice broke her concentration.

"Hey, are you ready for lunch?"

She looked up to see Allie hovering in the doorway. What was she talking about?

Oh, right. Lunch.

"I'm sorry, Allie, but something's come up. I need to go over a few files so I'll have to skip lunch today."

"No worries," Allie said. "Can I help?"

Linda hesitated. Despite her inexperience, Allie was sharp and had already proven helpful numerous times before. Maybe she could help Linda see beyond her own past and stay objective.

"Sure, take a seat," she said, waving the intern into her office. She flipped open Tony's file. The first things she saw were Tony's booking photos.

At first glance he looked like any other hard-eyed street thug. Defiant. Posturing. But to her he also looked desolate. Empty. Abandoned.

She closed her eyes. Took a deep breath.

I didn't abandon him. I broke up with him because I had to. He wasn't healthy then and he obviously still isn't. So move on.

Aware that Allie was waiting, Linda opened her eyes and forced herself to speak. "Tony Cooper," she said. "Arrested for murder." She handed the photos over to Allie, who took her time perusing the black and whites, no expression on her face.

Linda read the arresting officer's report and said, "Last week the police received an anonymous call that Mark Guapo—"

"That's the drug lord, right?" Allie asked. "The one whose prison conviction was recently overturned?"

Continuing to read, Linda nodded. "Yes. He was released from prison and murdered shortly thereafter. An anonymous caller identified Guapo's killer as a man named 'Coop.' The woman said this 'Coop' had been trying to take over Guapo's criminal endeavors while he'd been in prison." Linda felt her throat close up on her and focused on her breathing. Tony wasn't a criminal. Not the way Guapo had been.

"Bad guy, huh?" Allie asked.

Bad guy? Tony? On paper, it seemed that way. But in real life? Well, besides the drug addiction, Linda couldn't imagine Tony ever being a bad guy. Weak, maybe. But not bad.

Linda flipped through the pages, noting that the charging deputy had been Brian Heald. Ideally Heald should have made the connection that Linda had previously prosecuted Guapo and given her a heads-up about his death, but because Heald had started at the D.A.'s office less than a year ago, long after Guapo's conviction, she wasn't surprised he hadn't. That was especially true given she'd consistently turned down Heald's invitations to go clubbing—he'd been getting snottier and snottier ever since, so the guy was even less likely to do her any favors. Tony's failure to call her when he'd been arrested still ate at her, however.

Searching for possible answers, she summarized the police report for Allie. "When patrol officers reached the location where they'd been directed, a closed car repair shop in West Sacramento, the defendant was passed out near the front door, several feet from Guapo's body. Mr. Cooper was bleeding from an injury to the back of his head and from one leg."

"Did they find the murder weapon?"

Linda licked her finger and turned the page, then nodded. "Police patted him down for a weapon and discovered a bloody wrench tucked inside the waistband of his pants. After that he was transported to the hospital and treated for his injuries. As soon as he'd been well enough, he was transferred to the county jail."

The details of Tony's injuries caught Linda's attention. His left leg, which had always caused him pain anyway, had suffered the most damage, but hadn't been fatal. The infection he'd caught afterward had almost been. He'd fought it for days, but during that time Detective Derek Humphries had interviewed him.

Allie moved behind Linda and read over her shoulder. "Despite his not guilty plea in court, he confessed to the investigating detective," Allie stated. "So he's guilty, right?" She said it with a slight smile, acknowledging that *most* but not all people who confessed were usually being truthful. Though it was rare, people falsely confessed for a variety of reasons, including to protect another. Was that the case here?

"Maybe," Linda said. Tony had admitted killing Mark Guapo, but he'd refused to say anything more. Frustrated, she flipped through the file but found nothing else. That was where the report ended.

Humphries had stopped the investigation at Tony's confession when he should have done far more. He should have asked about motive and the events leading up to the day. He should have asked Tony about his injuries. Sure, Tony hadn't been forthcoming with further information, but he hadn't invoked his right to an attorney yet, either.

She tipped back in her chair, running her fingers across the smooth surface of her wooden desk, letting thoughts run through her mind. It didn't matter that Tony had pled not guilty at his arraignment hearing. Everyone did that as a matter of course and it wouldn't be persuasive evidence against his confession. Still, when he'd said those words, Linda had prayed for them to be true.

She still did.

Standing, she shrugged off her jacket.

"Are we settling in for the long haul?" Allie asked.

"Want to brainstorm?"

At Allie's eager nod, Linda tossed her a yellow legal pad and pen, and asked her to draw a line down the center of one sheet. Over the next few minutes, she and Allie listed on one side the evidence against Tony.

Anonymous call reporting a man named "Coop" had killed Guapo.

Tony Cooper found at the crime scene next to Guapo's dead body.

Tony Cooper found with possible murder weapon, a bloody wrench.

Confession.

Linda hesitated, unsure whether she should add information that she personally knew but that had not been elicited from police. Finally, she told Allie to write down:

Known association with Mark Guapo.

Confirmed drug addict.

Allie raised her eyebrows at the last statement. Nothing in the report had indicated either of those things. Linda pretended she hadn't noticed Allie's questioning expression, and indicated she wanted to look at the list.

Allie handed her the yellow sheet of paper and Linda stared at the items they'd just listed. Humphries's shoddy police work to the contrary, the evidence was more than enough to charge Tony with murder. But this wasn't a completely objective analysis she was conducting.

Linda had once known Tony as intimately as anyone. Previous drug use aside, Tony was a good person. The Tony she'd known? No one could believe he would have murdered Guapo in cold blood.

She couldn't have been so wrong about him and that certainty prompted her to continue with her list.

"What would a defense attorney argue to sway a jury?" she asked Allie.

"The wound on the back of Tony's head suggests an offensive attack," Allie said quickly.

"True. In addition, the use of the wrench against Guapo suggests self-defense or heat of passion rather than premeditation. But what would the defense say about Guapo's knife wound? How would one explain away a stabbing to the chest?"

"By arguing Guapo attacked Tony and things just escalated from there. He grabbed the knife because it was handy?" Allie asked.

"But where did the knife come from? Did Tony bring it with him?"

"Maybe. Or maybe Guapo had it on him."

That was entirely possible. Both scenarios were. Had Tony brought the knife with him, intending to kill Guapo? Did Linda believe Tony could actually commit murder? Given the right circumstances?

Yes, she thought. Good people committed murder all the time, the most obvious reason being self-defense.

It was entirely possible Tony had indeed killed Guapo, if not in self-defense then out of revenge because Guapo had sent his men after Mattie. Maybe even because Guapo's men had hurt Linda.

"Damn it," she muttered. What if that was the case? What if Tony still loved her, just as he'd told her in the letter he'd left her, and had been trying to show her that by killing Guapo? It would still have been wrong, but not as wrong as killing Guapo to protect his stake in the other man's drug business. Not as wrong as killing Guapo for the sheer pleasure of it. And it would mean Linda hadn't loved a man who was so dead inside. So she'd cling to that explanation for now. She'd pray that Tony hadn't killed Guapo at all.

She couldn't escape the truth, however. She'd believed in Tony before. She'd believed in him from the day she'd met him. Yet twice he'd managed to shatter her belief in him. What's to say it wouldn't happen again?

Chapter 5

Years ago Linda had been determined to put her career first. Fate, however, had brought her a friend, Mattie, and then a lover, Tony.

From the second she'd met him, she'd been hooked.

Even after they'd had sex, much earlier than they should have, he'd showed no signs of tiring of her. For the next few months, despite her better judgment, she hadn't been able to stay away from him. He'd unleashed something in her. An inner wildness that had always frightened her but one she had also missed. One that, given who they'd been, had still seemed a little scary but within the bounds of reason. Why shouldn't she have enjoyed it—enjoyed him—at least for a little while?

He hadn't had a lot of ambition. He'd worked as a waiter. Still, he hadn't been lazy. More importantly, he hadn't been like the "bad boys" she'd dated before she'd wised up. Dating him wouldn't have interfered with her job or brought down her reputation.

Instead he'd been sweet. Good.

And he'd made her feel the same way.

One night he came to pick her up at work. She'd had to work late and had missed him terribly. Plus, the evening had marked a celebration of sorts—their third month together.

She felt bad for delaying the festivities. As she went to meet him in the lobby, a thought occurred to her.

The receptionist was long gone.

The office deserted.

Maybe they could do a little celebrating right here…

She told him she needed to grab something from her office and invited him back.

He looked mildly surprised, but followed her.

When they stepped into her windowless office, she shut the door. Locked it.

He raised an eyebrow at her.

High on sheer happiness and feeling bolder than she had in a very long time, she gave her passion free rein. Wanting to surprise him, maybe even shock him, she reached beneath her skirt, pulled down her panties and tossed them to Tony. He caught them and studied the black lace.

Instead of laughing nervously and telling her she was crazy like she half expected, he coolly and calmly put them in his pocket.

Just like that, her desire for him skyrocketed.

She pushed Tony down into her office chair, raised her skirt and straddled him. He caressed her hips.

"So, I take it we're going to be late for dinner?" he said.

"Just something to tide us over." She skimmed her tongue over his lips and into his mouth. He moaned, the sound traveling all the way to the core of her. She felt tendrils of need winding through her body.

She kissed his strong jaw. Then his neck. She unbuttoned his royal blue shirt and kissed each patch of skin as it was exposed. His chest muscles tensed as she toyed with a nipple.

He growled. Arched his hips into hers.

Linda loved the idea that she could do this to him. Make him want her. Make him lose control. And maybe allow herself to release, if only a little, the tight hold she kept on her own.

Linda unbuttoned his pants, slipped her hand inside and cupped the heavy weight of him. Tony closed his eyes and groaned.

With one last kiss she slithered down to kneel between his legs.

He stopped her and pulled her back onto his lap. "Babe, this might not be the best place for this."

Linda leaned back, surprise clearly etched on her face. In the bedroom, at least, he wasn't as mellow as he appeared. He'd been game for pretty much anything up to now. In fact, he'd pushed her own sexual experience to its limits.

He smiled gently at her look of confusion and kissed her lips lightly. "What do you say we continue this at my place? A nice comfy bed. Lots of pillows. Lots and lots of other things, starting with foreplay."

Linda automatically nodded, but it was more to mask her embarrassment than anything else. Had she gone too far? Sure, no one was around, but that could change any second. What was it about her that eventually had to push things over the line? Give herself a little freedom and she went overboard.

Biting her lip, wondering what Tony must be thinking of her, she moved to get off of him. He stopped her.

"Wait. Don't go anywhere yet. Give me a chance to come down."

He kissed her again, and Linda could feel how hard he still was. With his hands guiding her, she slowly rested her head on his shoulder and relished the idea that this man...this glorious, sexy, intelligent man...simply wanted to hold her. He stroked her hair.

"There's another reason I want to go to my place. I—I have something I need to talk to you about. Afterward, if you still want to—"

He shifted slightly, as if he was nervous.

A question formed in her mind. Was he going to propose to her? After such a short time? And if so, what was she going to say?

"How's your day been? Good?"

She automatically nodded at his non sequitur, recognizing full well he was attempting to steer the conversation away from what he'd just brought up.

It didn't matter.

It didn't even matter that he was a waiter and she was an attorney. That just meant she'd be able to support them while he figured out what he really wanted to do with his life.

Yes, she thought. *I want to say yes.*

He took her hand, brought it up to his mouth for a kiss. The tender gesture almost brought tears to her eyes. *I will say yes,* she thought.

He leaned up. Kissed her forehead. Then her nose. Her cheeks. When he tried to move away, she grabbed him and kissed him deeply. She didn't stop for several minutes. When she did, he leaned his head back on the chair, his eyes closed, and tried to catch his breath.

"You're trying my good intentions, woman." Holding her hips, he gently slid her off his lap. He groaned as she rubbed against him, then cupped himself through his coffee-colored trousers. For a moment he caressed himself, sliding the palm of his hand over his erect shaft. Linda watched him, entranced.

"Seriously, you're amazing. You're going to kill me." He didn't sound like he minded.

He stood and wrapped his palm around her neck before plunging his tongue into the warm wet cavern of her mouth. "I want you. I—I love you."

She moaned softly at his words. She'd felt his love, but he'd never voiced it before.

He pulled back. "Ten minutes, babe. Meet me at my place."

When she nodded, he opened the door and checked to see if the coast was clear. He gave her one last heated glance and then disappeared. It was only then that she realized she hadn't said the words back. *I love you.*

She did. She loved him so much it was frightening. She didn't love easy. In fact, the last man, the only man, Linda had ever loved was her father, and her father had hurt her, time and again. She'd never wanted to give another man that same power over her.

But like it or not, Tony already had the power to hurt her.

Because she loved him.

She watched him go with a feeling of dread and excitement. Tony was so much more than she'd expected him to be. If she'd straddled any other guy the way she had him, he would have been inside her in two seconds flat. Tony's hard-on clearly showed he was interested, but he was still able to maintain control.

Unlike her. And that worried her.

He had no idea what kind of emotional baggage she was carrying around. She should be staying as far away as possible from him, not encouraging even the most casual of sexual relationships let alone something more. Something that involved love. But her heart, so starved for masculine attention, for *his* attention, was now operating on overdrive. She couldn't give him up. Not yet. And if he proposed to her, maybe not ever.

As it turned out, Tony hadn't proposed to her that night.

Instead he'd confided in her. About who he really was—a good man with a history of drug abuse. Of addiction.

And she'd loved him enough to stay with him. To try.

Until loving him and trying to help him had no longer been enough.

Chapter 6

Linda stepped inside the special room reserved at the county jail for attorney conferences. Simon Mau, the defense attorney assigned to Tony's case, looked nervous. He'd agreed to let her speak to Tony easily enough. She'd dangled the possibility of a plea bargain in front of him, and the inexperienced attorney, probably secretly delighted at the thought of "winning" a case without having to go to trial, had eagerly jumped at the chance.

Linda nodded to the guard and paused just inside the room. She reminded herself that despite the sick feeling in her stomach, no one knew how nervous she was.

She needed to do this. Needed to talk to Tony.

Had he committed the crimes he'd been arrested for? Did he expect her to help him?

Would she?

Seeing him, even as prepared as she thought she was, hit her hard. His back was to her, and he didn't seem aware that she was so near. She held her breath, waiting…just waiting…and observing. With his hair shorn, Tony couldn't twirl a curl around his index finger the way he used to, but he still was fingering that special spot near his ear. The one she'd loved to kiss. His shoulders, bulked up with more muscle, still formed a solid rectangle, the valley where his spine lay still curved in its familiar path. She'd known that valley like her own body. Once upon a time.

Linda took a calming breath, raised her chin and pushed fully into the room. Tony swung his head around.

He looked tired but met her gaze unwaveringly. "Hello, Linda."

Linda glanced around, but he'd said it so softly that neither the guard nor Mau, who was busy filling out something, had heard him use her first name. She spoke loudly.

"Mr. Cooper, Mr. Mau has given me permission to speak with you about a possible plea bargain. Our office has a few questions about your case, and I was wondering if you would consent to talk to me?"

Tony tilted his head toward the empty chair facing him. "Of course. Anything to help the good guys."

"Thank you," she said.

"Anything for a future judge of Sacramento County."

Her gaze flew to his eyes. "You know about that?" she asked before she could stop the question from leaving her mouth.

"That you threw your name into the hat? Yeah. I always knew you had ambition. And you were always great at passing judgment. I just didn't know you wanted to make the position official."

Fury plunged into her chest but before she could respond. Tony turned to Mau, who had been about to sit down. "I want to talk to her on my own."

Mau understandably balked at Tony's command. "Mr. Cooper, I highly advise you not to do that. You need counsel present. If Ms. Delaney starts to ask—"

Tony cut him off. "You're fired, kid. Beat it. Now."

Linda stared at him. Even his voice was different. Low. Rough. Intimidating in a way she'd never heard him speak before. She tried softening its effect. "It's all right, Mr. Mau. I won't be pulling any tricks. I promise. Thank you for your help. You've been very professional."

Mau looked once more at Tony's set expression. He mumbled, "Whatever" under his breath and fairly raced from the room.

She turned to the guard. "Can we have a few moments alone?"

"You want me to shackle him?"

She shook her head. "That won't be necessary."

The guard looked hesitant, but finally said, "I'll be right outside. Knock on the door when you're ready to go." The guard glanced up at the camera in the corner to remind Linda that he'd be watching.

"Thank you." As he left, Linda walked to the table, taking the chair Tony had offered her.

He leaned back and looked at her from hooded eyes.

"Nice way to treat your lawyer, Tony. He was just trying to protect you."

"I did the kid a favor. He looked like he would freak if he actually had to go to trial."

They stared at each other for at least a minute before he finally spoke again. "It's been a long time, babe."

Babe. He'd used to call her that when they'd been

together and, to her surprise, she'd liked it. But the endearment sounded so different now. So hurtful.

She folded her hands on the table that separated them. Tony did the same. He had scars on his arms as well as his face that she'd never seen before. And one inner wrist still bore the familiar tattoo. An intricate abstract design that hid something more.

"Must've been a hell of a shock to see me," he said.

Her gaze flickered from the tattoo up to his. "To put it mildly."

"I expected you sooner."

"Really? I wasn't sure I'd come."

"Oh, I knew you would. You've read the report, right?"

"Yes." Several times.

"And?"

"And?" she parroted back.

"What do you think? Am I guilty?"

She gave a derisive snort. "Gee, I don't know, Tony. There is the fact that you were caught with a bloody wrench on your person. Oh, and let's see, that's right. You did confess. Sure seems like you're guilty to me."

"Yeah. Sure looks that way, huh?"

She searched his expression and leaned forward. "Are you saying you're *not* guilty?"

Tony didn't answer her.

"I know you had trouble with drugs, Tony, but…"

"But what?"

"But the man I knew—the man I *loved*—could never have killed anyone, even Mark Guapo, in cold blood."

"Huh." He leaned back in his chair, placing his hands behind his head. "And you knew me so well, didn't you, Linda? Probably about as much as you loved me. Probably as well as I knew you, right?"

She frowned. "What's that supposed to mean?"

"The part about knowing you? You never went for the suit type before. Guess that's changed from the way you and that attorney were making goo-goo eyes at each other over a cup of coffee earlier."

So he'd seen her and Neil talking before the calendar had started. So what? She had nothing to feel guilty about. She had a right to a life. A life she'd almost thrown away when she'd fallen in love with Tony.

So why'd she feel guilty?

All she wanted to do was run from the room. Instead she said, "I knew you well enough to know that you loved your sister and niece. That you would have done anything to protect them. Is that what this is about? Did Guapo threaten them again?"

Tony's eyes flashed briefly. "Guapo had no idea where they were. Even I don't."

That surprised her. Almost as much as him not being with Mattie in the first place. Why wasn't he in WIT-SEC? Was it because he really had gone bad? Or did he just want her to believe that? "That doesn't answer my question," she pointed out.

He laughed, lowered his arms and shook his head. "Come on, Linda. You *know* me, remember? I'm weak. You saw it for yourself, that last night we were together in your kitchen. After I started up again, after Guapo's men went after Mattie and I killed Michael Sabon—"

"It was never proved who killed him," Linda interjected, but Tony kept talking over her.

"—I realized the streets just might need a new player. Guapo was still in prison and…" He shrugged. "That's what I've been doing for the past eighteen months. Establishing myself as Sacramento's newest drug kingpin. So no, killing Guapo had nothing to do with protecting

Mattie or Jordan. He tried to reclaim what he thought was still his. I wasn't willing to give it back to him. That's what the evidence indicates, doesn't it?"

She watched him closely. "So you really expect me to believe you took over his organization and then killed him when he got out of prison and threatened to take it back?"

She expected him to look away, but he didn't. His gaze remained steady on hers, his expression blank. "Believe what you want. Right now I'm not sure what my attorney is going to argue."

"You just fired your attorney," she reminded him.

He smirked and she wanted to slap the expression off his face. Instead she stood and turned toward the door. She hadn't gotten the answers she wanted. She hadn't gotten any answers at all. Maybe the only answers were the ones in his file.

Oh, Mattie, she thought, aching for her friend. For the man behind her. For all of them.

"I would think you'd be glad to send me up the river after what I did to you," he called out. "It was because of me that you ended up in the hospital, after all. It was because of me that you almost died."

For a second he didn't sound so tough. The hint of vulnerability in his tone made this man sound like the Tony she'd known. Someone who couldn't stand the idea of causing someone he loved pain. For God's sake, he'd volunteered at homeless shelters and retirement homes. *He* was the reason she did both those things now. She turned back to him. "I never blamed you for those men attacking me, Tony. I know why you informed on Guapo. You were trying to prove something." *To me.* At least in part. But maybe she'd been wrong about that, too.

She waited for him to say something else. To give her another glimpse of the man he'd once been. But he didn't give it to her.

Seconds passed, and she nodded. "Given our previous relationship, I'm not going to be able to work on this case."

He gave her that infuriating smirk again. "Of course not. I should count myself lucky. Every man should be prosecuted by someone he didn't screw…or screw over. But fairness isn't why you're walking away."

She looked genuinely confused. "I don't know what you mean."

"Don't you? I know you're running to be a judge, remember? I have to say, it's a good choice. You've always been obsessed with your reputation. Judge or not, you don't condone failure and you don't abide anyone thinking less of you. Isn't that right, Linda?"

He watched as she contemplated his words before raising her chin defiantly. "So you think I'm recusing myself because I'm worried about my own reputation? Because I don't want our prior relationship to affect my campaign? Believe that if you want, Tony. Either way, if you were hoping for any type of leniency from me—"

"Leniency?" Slowly, he stood. "You dumped me for getting hold of drugs and intending to use them. Now that I'm selling them? No, I'm not expecting leniency. But don't worry. I'm prepared to live with my sins. All of them."

Her stomach churned. His words had been designed to hurt her.

And they did.

Logically, she knew breaking up with him hadn't meant she didn't want to help him. She'd offered her help over and over again. Had been willing to sacrifice so much for him until she'd finally realized how unhealthy that was. "Tony—"

"In fact, maybe I don't mind adding a few more sins to the list," he drawled, walking closer. Closer. "What do you say, Linda? Chances are I'm going to prison for the rest of my life. Want to give me something to remember?" When she said nothing, he grinned and, with one finger, traced her cheek. "Not that I don't have enough memories stored away, but I'm willing to make more."

Her gaze found the camera in the corner of the room. Any moment now and the guard would come barreling in. He had to know that, so why was he taking this risk? Simply to be close to her again? She certainly understood that. Despite everything, she prayed for the guard's inattention, not wanting him to interrupt. Wanting to savor the feel of Tony's touch again, even as she knew how wrong it was.

He obviously sensed what she was thinking. Smirking, he once again took his seat. "I believe this is the time I tell you I want an attorney, Linda. And you're right—I need to call in the big guns. Best that money can buy, you know? After all, I have plenty of money now. Thanks for stopping by."

Tony closed his eyes, tilted his head back and refused to say anything more. The silence pounded at Linda until she couldn't take it anymore. She moved to the door.

Before she could leave, he called out, "Did you ever get rid of it, Linda? The tattoo we got together?"

Once again, she turned around to look at him.

He hadn't opened his eyes. Still, she struggled to keep her face from showing the panic that had suddenly ignited inside of her. "I did," she lied. She lowered her gaze to the inside of his right wrist. Though the letters were disguised by scrollwork, they were there for everyone to see if they cared to look hard enough:

TC + LD

She had the same design marking her skin. She'd been reluctant to get the tattoo on such a visible spot, however, and had instead chosen to put it on her hip. Where chances were the only person who would ever see it was Tony. If they'd stayed together. "You didn't. How come?"

Lifting his head, he stared at her. The chill in his eyes made her shiver. "Why would I? It reminds me what a fool I used to be. Naive. Pathetic. I guess that's the difference between us, Linda. I don't run from my past, not even the nastier parts."

Chapter 7

The day after she talked to Tony, Linda stood in the office across the hall from hers and exhaled in frustration. "Look, Heald, I'm just asking you for a favor. The evidence against the defendant is strong, but it's not foolproof. You like a challenge, don't you?"

Heald crossed his arms across his chest and leaned back in his chair. "So do you. So why are you in such a hurry to hand it off? You lost a case recently, didn't you? Did it make you lose your nerve?"

Jerk, she thought, wondering how many times she would before this conversation was over. He was still pissed that she'd shot him down. Why else would he deliberately mention her recent loss in court?

She didn't like having to ask anyone, let alone Brian Heald, a favor. But, unfortunately, he and Neil were the only two deputies with the time to take Tony's case, and because of their recent flirtations, because Tony had specifically witnessed Neil's flirtation with her, Linda didn't want Neil and Tony getting within speaking distance of one another.

"I told you. I have a scheduling conflict," Linda said. She could do her duty and find another prosecutor to handle Tony's case without revealing the fact they'd used to be intimate. That was nobody's business but their own.

"You never have scheduling conflicts. You'd have to have a life for that. Besides, I heard this guy is a user and has a past connection to Guapo. Along with his confession? Sounds like a pretty foolproof nonchallenging case to me."

She stared at him, struggling to hide her surprise. Damn it, Allie must have been talking about Tony's case with Brian. She hadn't told Allie to keep their discussion about Tony's case a secret, so the other woman hadn't done anything wrong exactly, but Linda should have been more careful about revealing Tony's personal business to anyone. "So that's a no?" she confirmed.

"Unless you'd like to reconsider my invitation to go clubbing? If you promise not to get jealous, I'll show you pics from my vacation."

Ugh. He was an even bigger jerk than she'd thought. Linda smiled stiffly. "No, as tempting as that offer is, I think I'll pass. Thanks a lot."

"Anytime, Linda," he said, pointing his trigger finger at her like a gun, a gesture he often used when he was trying to be cooler than cool.

Barely refraining from rolling her eyes, she turned and walked out the door.

And ran straight into Neil.

He was looking at her with a puzzled frown. "What's

going on, Linda? I heard part of what you were saying to Brian…. You need me to take a case for you?"

She did, but she knew Neil. He'd ask questions and wouldn't relent until he'd gotten some satisfactory answers. Would she give them to him?

She liked and respected him. He seemed to feel the same way, and she believed she had his genuine support when it came to her bid for the open judgeship. Instinctively she felt she could trust him to be discreet about her past with Tony, something she hadn't believed about Brian.

Linda suppressed a sigh of resignation, and then did what she should have done in the first place. She pulled Neil into her office so they'd have some privacy, then explained about Tony.

"To be clear, I'm not asking for special privileges or leniency. I wouldn't want you to handle this case any differently than any other. But as far as my involvement with Tony…I'd rather it not be an issue unless it has to be."

Neil nodded slowly. "I understand why you wouldn't want word of that getting out, especially now. It's irrelevant to your qualifications as a judge anyway. Plus, you obviously knew leaving the guy was the right thing. That must have been hard for you. I can see you still care about him."

She hesitated. "I care about the man I once knew. This man?" She shook her head. "I'm not sure."

"You have to know this already, but if you have personal knowledge about his history with drugs, that could be relevant should he go to trial for Guapo's murder. To establish how they knew each other. And a possible motive."

She swallowed hard. She knew that, and she was

taking a gamble, but she didn't have any other choice. "Read the file. You'll find there's more than enough evidence to prove his guilt without having to delve into his past romantic relationships, even the one he had with me."

It was true, but even so she couldn't help remembering Tony's accusation that the reason she was recusing herself as the prosecutor on his case was because she didn't want her reputation or her judicial campaign tainted by their past. While that wasn't her main motivation, she couldn't deny that he was partially correct. But was that so wrong? To want to protect her future when she knew he could never be a part of it anyway? Swallowing tightly, she returned her attention to Neil.

"In the event Tony recants his confession, you can also move to unseal the confidential court documents proving he acted as a confidential informant against Guapo. But if it comes down to it, if you absolutely need me to testify, I'll do it. I won't ask you to ignore your ethical duty or my own."

Neil stared at her then placed a comforting hand on her shoulder. "Thank you for trusting me with this information, Linda. I'll review the file and let you know if I run into anything troubling."

Twenty minutes later she was alone again. But despite her transparency with Neil and his reassurances, her stomach still felt weighed down with dread.

Tony hadn't given her any reason to believe he deserved her help, yet he'd accused her of abandoning him. Maybe she hadn't done it the first time, but was she doing it now? Was she simply thinking of herself so she wouldn't have to deal with the man she'd once loved?

And to some extent, despite everything, the man she *still* loved?

Just as she'd continued to love her father despite knowing he was a thief.

To her horror, tears of helplessness welled in her eyes. She felt torn. Like she was grieving her childhood and the end of her relationship with Tony all over again. And she knew why. Even years after her mother had finally left her father, she'd always harbored hope that he would turn his life around and choose a relationship with her over his thieving ways. It was the same hope she'd harbored about Tony and his addiction. That someday Tony would return to her. That they'd beat the odds and end up together.

But with each minute that passed, there was more and more evidence being discovered to prove they wouldn't.

She took a long, shaky breath.

She wasn't abandoning Tony, she told herself.

She was doing what was best for both of them.

Neil was a good attorney. He'd be fair. Evaluate the evidence without the baggage of having known Tony in another context. As a lover.

If there was any chance Tony hadn't killed Guapo, Tony would be lucky to have Neil as the prosecuting attorney.

And if the evidence showed otherwise, Neil would do what he was trained to do. What he and Linda and even Brian were compelled to do.

See that justice was done.

No matter how much it broke Linda's heart.

Chapter 8

Despite his somewhat shady past, Tony had never spent time in jail before. Frankly, he could have done without the experience. He had his own cell—a small box with a hard dingy mattress, and welded-together stainless-steel sink and toilet. The thing was so depressing he chose to spend most of his time in the public area where inmates could watch a television controlled by the guards. The current guard on duty was a basketball fan.

Funny thing about sports. So long as you were rooting for the same team, watching a game could bring together men who'd normally be at each other's throats. Didn't matter. Tony's attention wasn't on the game or his fellow cellmates. It was on Linda. How she'd expressed belief in him. And how he'd thrown that belief back in her face, deliberately hurting her.

Once again he told himself he'd had no choice. As

tempted as he'd been to tell her the truth, he couldn't let anyone know he cared about her or allow her to get close to him again. And if she knew the truth? She would get close to him again. She'd feel compelled to intercede. To protect him. Regardless of whether it put her in danger or not.

No, the only thing he could do was convince her that he was a bad man, a druggie and a murderer, so that she'd stay as far away from him as possible. That way if his cover was blown or someone decided they wanted to challenge him for the vacancy left by Guapo's death, Linda wouldn't become a target again.

"Man, what happened to the Kings? They suck," the kid sitting to Tony's left said, jolting him out of his thoughts.

Absently Tony turned his gaze on the televised game just in time to see a Kings player lose the ball. Still he said nothing. As Sacramento's home team, the Kings had a loyal following even in lockup.

The kid snorted with disgust when the visiting team stole the ball. "What a waste of time. Guy couldn't keep hold of the ball if it was glued to him. I—"

"Shut up."

Though he kept his gaze on the game, Tony automatically stiffened. He recognized that voice. It belonged to Larry Moser, a hulk of a man two cells down from him. The one with a swastika tattoo on his forehead and who looked like he ate nails for breakfast. Literally. His teeth, what was left of them, were a mess.

Listen to him, kid, Tony thought. But he wasn't surprised when just the opposite happened.

"You a fan? I didn't think they had any more of those. Like I said, they suck."

Moser stood so suddenly that his chair would have toppled over if it hadn't been bolted to the floor.

"I told you to shut your mouth. I don't have a problem smacking my own kid around when he deserves it. What do you think I'll do to you?"

Tony finally looked up. The kid was trying not to look scared, but his gaze flicked over to the guard's station. The two guards on duty were talking, unaware of the tense situation currently brewing. The kid swallowed hard, then reluctantly stood. Tony understood why. Someone who wasn't willing to stand up for himself in jail soon became victim to a whole new host of problems.

Moser stepped closer.

Tony's pulse revved up. Damn it. He stood and faced the much bigger man. Damn, the guy looked like a bloody mountain. "You don't want to do that," he said quietly. "Even if the kid is an idiot."

Moser laughed. "What do you know about what I want, pretty boy?"

Pretty boy. Not exactly what a man wants to be called when he's locked up in jail with a bunch of other guys.

"Let's just enjoy the game, okay? The kid won't cause any more trouble. Will you?" Turning, Tony glared at the kid. The younger man opened his mouth but Tony never heard his reply.

Moser punched Tony in the face. Hard.

Tony staggered back, slamming into a table that, like the chairs, had no give. Pain shot through his leg, but he quickly straightened. Damn it, he wasn't a natural fighter. Sabon had scarred him up plenty to prove it and, contrary to what he'd told Linda, Mattie had been the one to kill Sabon, not Tony.

Plus, even though he'd packed on weight and muscle

since then, even though he'd trained and was a much better fighter now, better still didn't mean he could go up against a man like Moser and win. Not without some kind of weapon. And by the way the kid had backed up and the other men around them had started cheering, he wasn't going to be getting any help from them. The guards were shouting and moving toward them, but Moser was close enough to get in a couple more shots.

Hell, Tony thought, throwing up an arm and managing to block the man's next punch. Instinctively Tony raised his knee, ramming Moser in the chest, but the guy was so well padded it barely seemed to faze him. He did stagger back a few steps, however, giving Tony time to plan his next move. He danced in place for a second. Then, calling on the recent training he'd had, he kept his bad leg on the ground and struck out with his good one. As he did so, his instructor's words echoed in his head. "Even if a karate kick reaches its target, it will lack destructive power if it is not withdrawn sharply. Think of your leg as a whip."

Tony tried to be a whip, he really did. But although he landed what he thought was a powerful kick to Moser's torso and although Moser again staggered back a few steps, he was on Tony much faster this time.

Moser got Tony into a headlock and mercilessly squeezed. Tony thrashed and rammed his elbow into Moser's gut. Even as the man grunted, a faint buzzing sound rang in Tony's ears and the world began to fade, but he could still hear the guards shouting.

He wondered if they'd get to them before Moser snapped his neck.

Chapter 9

In her office Linda rubbed her eyes tiredly, telling herself for the hundredth time that she needed to get her eyes checked. Or maybe her judgment checked. How could she run for a position on the bench, manage her own caseload and figure out what was going on with Tony all at the same time? She'd always thrived on the adrenaline rush, on the challenge, but she was down to about five hours of sleep a night, if that.

Linda was no longer prosecuting Tony's case, but that didn't stop her from reading his file for about the twentieth time. She reread the preliminary findings of Guapo's autopsy report, once again struck by a feeling that she was missing something. Allie, who'd promised not to share any additional facts about Tony's case with anyone except Neil, was seated in the guest chair in her office, reading the same report.

Dr. John Peluma had conducted the autopsy. "Cause

of death was blood loss, blunt force trauma to the back of the head and a slash to his jugular. According to Peluma, Guapo wouldn't have died right away," Allie said, more to herself than Linda.

"No, he would have died a slow and agonizingly painful death."

"Maybe that's what the defendant wanted. Why else wouldn't he have just brought a gun and gotten it over with? Maybe he wanted Guapo to suffer?"

Linda shuddered, horrified at the thought. But Allie had a point. A wrench or even a knife seemed an impractical way to carry out the deed. That's what kept leading Linda back to the idea that Tony had attacked Guapo in self-defense or in defense of another. But then again, Guapo had suffered, just like Tony, a blow to the back of the head. That pointed to an offensive attack on him as much as it had on Tony.

"Maybe Cooper killed Guapo because of a woman?" Allie asked.

The thought of Tony loving another woman at all, let alone enough to kill for her, made Linda's stomach twist. Of course it was possible—probable, even. After all, he and Linda had broken up years ago. Despite his drug problem Tony had always been a charmer and an amazing lover. It wouldn't have taken a woman long to snatch up what Linda had tossed aside.

"Makes sense," she responded, hating the tension in her voice. "But something else that doesn't make sense are the wounds Guapo sustained. They're contradictory. There's the blow to the back of the head, but also…"

"Right. The autopsy report specified that Guapo's jugular had been slashed with a deep vertical wound."

"Vertical," Linda repeated. "Here, hand me that report," she said, gesturing impatiently.

Allie tossed her the report and she flipped to the front to confirm her suspicions.

"Tony Cooper is at least six inches taller than Guapo. A vertical wound suggests that Guapo's assailant reached up to stab him." She paused. Had Guapo somehow subdued Tony? Gotten him to his knees? Had Tony grabbed the blade from Guapo to protect himself? That made the most sense, otherwise why wouldn't he have grabbed Guapo and slashed his throat with one quick horizontal pull? And why hadn't the blade been found when the wrench had?

Linda rubbed her eyes again and dropped the autopsy report. She grabbed her hair in frustration, making a mental note to talk to Peluma about her concerns. But then she realized she couldn't do that. This wasn't her case anymore.

Talking through the facts with Allie was helpful, but Linda wanted to share her concerns with someone who had as much experience as she with these matters and probably even more. If she confided in Neil, however, he'd realize she was still working the case. Still invested in it. And in Tony.

The fewer people who knew that, the better.

She glanced at Allie. "Thanks for your help on this, but like I told you before, I handed this case off to Neil. If you have any thoughts, you should probably talk them over with him from now on."

Allie nodded and stood. "I'm shadowing him on another case, so no worries. I will."

After Linda thanked her again, Allie left.

No worries.

It was one of Allie's favorite expressions, yet Linda had plenty to worry about.

She didn't want to accept that she had been so wrong

about Tony. Oh, she knew Tony had a temper, even if it was slow to show itself, and he certainly had reason to want revenge against Guapo. But to ruthlessly kill the man to eliminate his competition?

Maybe he'd snapped, an inner voice whispered. Maybe the danger Guapo had wrought upon them all had truly changed him…

She shook her head. She wouldn't go there. If she started thinking that way, she'd be lost for sure. This was a man she'd loved. *Still* loved. And by his comments the last time she'd seen him, he obviously thought that by breaking up with him, she'd heartlessly abandoned him.

One more thing to feel guilty about would send her over the edge for sure. And this time, she knew, she wouldn't be able to pull herself back.

Her phone rang and she answered. "This is Deputy D.A. Linda Delaney."

"Hello, this is Deputy Roskins in the jail. I'm trying to find D.D.A. Neil Christoffersen, but I've been told he's already left. You were the last deputy listed in the file before him and I wanted to make sure your office knows about an in-custody defendant that's been assaulted."

She quickly inhaled. "Who is it?" But she already knew. And part of her knew she'd go to his side. Knew that she had to see him. That even though he might be a bad man, and bad for her in so many ways, he still needed her.

"Tony Cooper."

Tony kept his eyes closed and moaned against the pain. For a minute he remained caught in its nightmarish embrace. His leg and throat burned. Why?

Memory returned in bleak images of jail and basketball games and swastikas. They must have brought him to the hospital. Automatically his hand fumbled for the nurse's call button. He didn't want to think. Didn't want to remember.

He hurt like hell.

All he wanted was drugs. The drugs would bring him relief. They'd make him feel good.

But there was a reason he couldn't have them…

Ah, right.

Because he was an addict.

After his run-in with Guapo, before he was in any kind of shape to tell the hospital staff he was addicted to pain meds, they'd given him Oxy. They'd thought they were being merciful, but all they'd done was feed Tony's addiction so that after years of managing his desire for the drug, he once again felt on the verge of giving in.

He heard a noise and sensed someone beside him. He took a deep breath. He needed to tell them. No drugs. He couldn't—

"Tony."

His eyes blinked open to find a woman leaning over him.

Linda.

He'd dreamed of her so often throughout the past year and dreams were so much better than the cold reality without her. Why was she here now? Looking at him as if she still…cared.

Linda leaned over and touched him, cupping his face and smoothing her palm over his forehead as if she was checking his temperature. Her gaze had that familiar expression she'd often worn around him, despair and affection mixed in one confusing bundle. The times she'd been able to look at him with simple joy, with no doubt, were few and far between, and that was probably the biggest regret of his life. But right now there was no regret. He simply enjoyed her presence, wondering where they were. Why she'd finally come to him…

Once again memory clicked into place, hitting him with the force of a sledgehammer.

She might be here, but they weren't together.

They weren't ever going to be together again.

Hell, she wasn't even going to be the lawyer prosecuting him for Guapo's murder. Good and bad news, that. He wouldn't be so distracted or tempted to tell her the truth. But he wouldn't get the extra time with her, either.

For all he knew, this might be his last opportunity to talk to her.

It almost came rushing out of him then. His love for her. But he reminded himself of what he was doing.

Suddenly their gazes met and she saw he was awake. Swiftly she withdrew her hand.

"Where am I?" he asked.

"Jail infirmary. Do you remember what happened?"

"Yeah. I got into a fight with someone about a basketball game."

"Right."

He narrowed his eyes at her slow drawl. "I'm telling you the truth."

"Just not the whole truth. Rumor is you were protecting someone else from getting coldcocked. Someone younger and with a big mouth."

"I don't know what you're talking about."

"Okay."

"So why are you here? Were you hoping I'd made things easy on you and gotten myself killed?"

She paled and shook her head. Leaned closer, as if to

mesmerize him with the color of her green eyes. "Don't say things like that," she said fiercely. "Now how are you feeling? Are you in pain?"

She sounded so much like herself, so much like the woman who'd jump to his defense if anyone, even himself, dared to put him down, that he couldn't help smiling. She sounded as if she actually still cared about him. That knowledge filled him with a slight sense of unease and he said, "What if I am? You gonna get me some pills? Kiss my 'owies' and make them better?"

She blushed and he remembered how often she'd done just that, sprinkling butterfly kisses across his back and leg to distract him from his pain. He also remembered how thoroughly the distraction had worked.

"Stop trying to pick a fight and just tell me if you need anything," she said softly.

"I need you," he said before he could stop himself. "I always have."

Eyes widening, she sucked in a breath. Then tears filled her eyes before she quickly blinked them away. "Tony," she said on a breath, and it was all there in her voice—the same regret she'd felt on the night she'd broken up with him. So yes, he was right. She did still care about him.

But like always, that didn't change a thing.

Even so, with the light behind her, her hair looked like a halo around her head.

An angel of mercy in a jail infirmary. And as much as he told himself he should take back the words of need he'd just voiced, that he should push her away yet again, he couldn't do it.

Instinctively he reached for her. His angel.

He smoothed his knuckles against her cheek and, to his surprise, she let him. But it shouldn't have surprised him. She was a natural caregiver. As passionate and vivacious and playful as she'd often been with him, she'd never been able to see him in pain without hurting herself. In addition to kissing his "owies," she'd even taken a massage-therapy class so she could help him with his back and leg when they bothered him. But of course what would initially start as a therapeutic massage had almost always transformed into something sensual before too long. When images of their past lovemaking flashed in his head, his hand instinctively moved to cup her neck and pull her down toward him. But before he could, she pulled away.

He forced himself not to reach for her again.

She'd been right to reject him. He was in jail for killing a man! And hadn't he just been wishing for the oblivion the drugs could bring him?

Once an addict, always an addict.

He was a high-maintenance mess. Far more work than caring for a dog ever would be and she'd already voiced her preferences for cats because even a dog would require too much of her.

"You ever get a cat?" he asked, surprising both of them.

She blinked, then laughed. "What?"

"You used to want one. When we were together. I was just wondering…."

Her expression closed up. "No. After what happened with Guapo's men, I had a lot of physical therapy to do. And then catching up with work…well." She shrugged. "I don't have a lot of free time to give a pet."

He stared at her, imagining her participating in hours of painful physical therapy because of him. "Do you still do physical therapy?"

"Occasionally. When something's bothering me.

Mostly…mostly my right knee. One of Guapo's men broke it," she said.

He closed his eyes in horror. "God, Linda. I wouldn't blame you for wishing me dead. A whole lot of lives would be better off if I wasn't around. Everyone knows that."

"Not everyone. Not me. And Mattie would never say that. Not in a million years."

He didn't argue with her. She was right, after all. His sister had stuck by him and though she'd tried to talk him out of coming back to Sacramento, in the end she'd continued to stick by him. If he needed her—correction, if he *asked* for help from her—she'd be by his side in a second. And that's why he couldn't ask for her help.

"Mattie left me a letter telling me about WITSEC." When he said nothing, she gave an exasperated sign. "I know you can't tell me where they are. Or maybe you don't even know. But she was my best friend. Do you know if they're okay?"

He shifted to sit up, and a wave of pain hit him with the strength of one of California's northern coastal waves. Again he could barely stop himself from asking for drugs. From begging Linda to get them for him. But he forced himself to take several deep breaths until the urge passed. Still, she frowned as her gaze swept over him, as if she was trying to assess what part of his body was troubling him the most.

This wasn't good. The fact that she'd told him about her knee injury and had even asked about Mattie was reminding him all too well of how easy it had always been to talk to her. He'd revealed things to her that he'd never told anyone else, some things that he'd been deeply ashamed of. And he'd always felt safe doing so. Until she'd left him.

"Small talk, Linda?" he said finally, knowing he'd get a rise out of her. Knowing she'd be diverted enough to at least not ask about his level of pain.

"So you won't even tell me Mattie and Jordan are safe?"

"The answer is, I don't know. Where they are or *how* they are." Only half of that statement was a lie. He didn't know where they were, but he had no doubt they were safe. Dominic Jeffries, Mattie's husband, would make sure of that.

For months, they'd all been in WITSEC together—Dom, Tony, Mattie, and Jordan. But one of the conditions of him returning to Sacramento was that Dom move them again. And not tell Tony where they went. Just in case. "And it has to stay that way."

"Even though Guapo's dead now?"

God, he wished it wasn't so. "Guapo has plenty of men who are willing to do his dirty work for him. That's going to be especially true now that his drug business is up for grabs."

"But it's not up for grabs now, is it? You've apparently taken it over."

"So long as I'm in jail, there'll be plenty of contenders. But taking over his game? Yes, it was the plan all along, babe."

"Since when?"

He stared at her though hooded eyes. "Since you and I both accepted what I truly am."

"I never accepted that you were a bad man or a criminal, Tony. Just because you make mistakes doesn't mean you're unlovable. I just couldn't be with you. You know why. You know what you are."

As if unable to keep still any longer, she stood and paced beside his bed. He watched her with his heart in his throat. Her long-limbed stride was beautiful. Grace-ful. Agitated.

She suddenly halted and placed her hands on her hips. "Why?"

He dragged his gaze from her hips to her face. "Why what?"

"Why are you trying so hard to convince me you're a bad guy? Why did you confess to murdering Guapo? Given our history, given how susceptible I've always been where you're concerned, why aren't you trying to play me? To gain some leniency? It's what most people would do in your situation."

He forced himself to smirk. "I hear the rumors. I know how hard you're working to be a judge. To get the respectability you've always wanted. Maybe I just don't want to ruin that for you. Or maybe throwing me out of your life finally proved to me how unsusceptible to me you really are."

"Stop trying to make me feel guilty for that, damn it. It wasn't what I wanted. But you gave me no choice."

He scowled and before he could stop himself, he spoke from his heart rather than from his head. "How? By being weak? By being tempted to do something I knew I shouldn't? Making mistakes doesn't mean I'm unworthy of being loved, Linda? Isn't that what you said? What a crock. You kicked me out of your life."

"Not because I didn't love you! Because you got hold of those pills knowing full well you were going to take them, Tony. If not that night, then on another one. You chose them over me and I couldn't trust you anymore."

"Well, we'll never know for sure whether I would have taken them, will we?"

She froze. "What do you mean? It's been years since we broke up…eighteen months since Mattie left…are you trying to tell me you never took those pills? That you've been clean since—"

That's exactly what he'd been implying, but it had been a damn stupid move. Somehow he managed to keep his gaze directly on hers. "I didn't say any such thing. Even if I had, you'd be a fool to believe me, wouldn't you?"

She had nothing to say to that. And he knew she was getting ready to leave.

Desperately, without meaning to, he tried to stop her. "So despite throwing me out of your life, are you saying you *are* still susceptible to me?"

Her mouth pressed into a thin, bitter line. "I really would be a fool to admit that, wouldn't I?"

The way she echoed his own words made him sigh. "Yeah. You would. Because you know who I am, Linda. I don't have to pretend with you. Even when we were together, I always knew what I was."

"You were always a little too willing to think badly of yourself. I suppose I didn't help you with that, did I? Yet aside from the drugs, you always did the right thing, Tony. You were almost too damn perfect, in fact. I saw it most in how you were with Mattie and Jordan. Anything they needed, you were there, even before they could think to ask. You never forgot Jordan's birthday. You were there for every ballet recital. You were there to babysit anytime Mattie needed you. And you didn't just help your family, Tony. You helped total strangers. Do you remember Mrs. Ramsey from the Sunrise Nursing Home? She still asks about you. Still asks about those damn chocolate-chip cookies you used to bring them. You brightened up the day of total strangers and were always putting others first. You did it again a few hours ago by protecting someone more vulnerable than you."

Too perfect? She'd thought he'd been almost too perfect? Hardly, he thought. No matter what he'd done well in her eyes, she'd always seen him as weak. Too weak to take a chance on. But even so, she was making a good argument and suddenly he wanted to cry, Why? Why had she left him if she'd really thought so well of him?

The question was on the tip of his tongue, and he clenched his teeth to keep it inside. Damn it, stopping her from leaving had been a mistake. She needed to go before he made another one. "I told you, I don't know what you're talking about."

"I know. And that makes me sad. Because despite everything we've been through in the past, you never lied to me, Tony. Yet something tells me you're telling a whole bunch of lies now, starting with what happened with Guapo. I can't help but wonder why."

He shrugged. "Wonder all you like, Linda. But as of this morning, I've hired new counsel. Roger Lock. If you want to talk to me further, you'll have to go through him."

Chapter 10

Molly Snow was a professor's wife whose husband devoted himself to his college students during the day but gave himself fully to her at night. It always turned her on to see the transformation in him—in herself—when the day was over. He would shed his conservative wool jackets with the dated leather patches at the elbow. Ruffle the hair that had been ruthlessly smoothed down with gel. And kick off the staid, ugly shoes that reminded her of a traveling salesman's.

It was what kept their marriage strong. Shared secrets. A willingness to stretch boundaries and do anything the other needed. Even if it meant taking the latest street drug to spice things up.

Neither had an aversion to drugs. They didn't do things like acid or heroin, but contented themselves with things that were relatively harmless, like pot or the new "in" thing—bath salts. They added a nice zip to reality. She loved how they made her feel, and how they made him feel, and how, in the morning, he'd kiss her gently, sweetly, as if she was the most precious thing in the world to him.

But at night… Oh, at night… He'd turn to her, just like he had tonight, with heat in his eyes and a wicked grin and she'd shiver at what she knew was in store for her.

"You like this, don't you?"

He squeezed her nipple, pinching it hard through her clothing so that the pain sunk all the way to her core. *Yes, yes,* she thought when he grasped her silk blouse and ripped it from her in three vicious pulls. Her skirt suffered a similar fate. Despite how rough he was with her clothes, his hands were gentle as they roamed over her.

That's why she frowned when she felt the pinch of fear…and anger that washed through her. Anger and fear that was definitely directed toward him.

He leaned in to kiss her. "I love you, baby, I love you so much. Are you going to be a good girl for me? Let me do whatever I want? Say it. Say you'll let me do anything I want."

She almost couldn't speak over the emotions washing through her. She hated him. He was a sick man and he was always trying to drag her down with him. But she forced herself to say yes, which made him smile and kiss her again.

Her eyes flickered to the lit candles that flickered fragrantly beside the bed.

In terms of weapons, they were deceptively harmless.

But she'd just have to be creative.

And she was.

An hour later his hands and feet were bound to the bedposts and she was sprawled on top of him.

She wasn't sure if she hated him now or loved him.

Trying to figure it out made her head hurt, so she stopped trying.

For an instant she thought of the man she'd met at Club Matrix. He hadn't looked like a drug dealer any more than she and her husband looked like users.

Her husband…

She turned back to him.

When she reached for the candles, he laughed, likely thinking she'd repeat the wax play they'd engaged in a few months ago. But that wasn't what she did.

As the bed sheets started to catch fire with her still on top of him, Toby screamed, "Why? Why are you doing this?"

Why? Her brow crinkled when the lick of heat against her skin made her gasp.

Once again she thought of the man who'd sold her the Rapture.

She shrugged. "Why not?"

Chapter 11

Several days after visiting Tony in the jail infirmary, Linda sat in the courtroom audience as Neil handled Tony's preliminary hearing. While Neil questioned one of the responding officers, Tony sat with his defense attorney, Roger Lock, a man who had an impressive reputation for getting his clients off the hook. At this point in the proceedings, however, Lock's skill was hardly necessary. Neil simply had to establish probable cause that Tony committed murder so the court could hold him over for trial. As soon as the judge learned about Tony's confession, that standard would be met.

"Who discovered the weapon on the defendant?" Neil asked.

Scott Anderson, a baby-faced police officer, leaned toward the mic, his gun belt creaking softly. "The EMTs. They were there when my partner and I arrived and were already working on the defendant, who was unconscious. They pointed out the weapon they'd found on the defendant's person."

Linda glanced at Tony. He sat sprawled out and loose limbed in his chair, as if he didn't have a care in the world. Nonetheless he seemed unusually subdued. Was he still feeling the effects of Moser's beating? Was he in unbearable pain? Or was he so high on painkillers that he really was lost in his own world?

"Who took possession of the weapon?"

"I did. I bagged it. Took photos of the defendant before he was transported to the hospital."

Neil had the officer authenticate the wrench and then continued with his direct examination.

"Was anyone besides Mr. Cooper there?"

"There was a dead body. Of a man later identified as Mark Guapo."

Neil stopped to pull out some photographs, which he then marked. "Your Honor, I'd like to mark these photographs as People's Exhibits 7 and 8."

"They will be so marked," the judge said.

"Now, Officer, in Exhibit 7, is this the man, Mark Guapo, you're referring to?"

Anderson studied the picture that Neil held out. Linda knew what that photo looked like—not pretty. "Yes."

"Did you take this photograph?"

"Yes."

"Does this photograph accurately represent the man's condition that night?"

"Yes."

Neil held out another picture. "And in this picture, Exhibit 8, is this the man you found unconscious?"

"Yes."

"Was the man injured?"

"Yes."

"Can you please tell us if those injuries are reflected in the photographs?"

Once again Linda looked to Tony. This time he lifted his chin and stared at her, a tight line in his jaw. But his eyes didn't hold the same anger and insouciance they'd held the first time she'd seen him in court. He looked away again.

The officer pointed out the injuries as he spoke. "He had trauma to his head and leg. He was bleeding from both."

"And it appears you've taken a close-up of those injuries in Exhibit 8, correct?"

"Yes."

"Okay. Now, do you recognize the man in those pictures in the courtroom today?"

"Yes."

"Please identify him for us."

"He's sitting at the table with defense counsel. Wearing the orange jumpsuit."

The officer pointed at Tony. The bruises he'd sustained from the other inmate's attack stood out, adding to the picture of a career criminal in the making.

A twinge of pain passed through Linda as if her body experienced his pain in sympathy.

"Your Honor, may the record reflect that the officer has identified the defendant?" Neil requested.

"The record will so reflect," the judge said.

"Thank you, Your Honor." Neil walked to his table, took a sip of water then turned back to face the witness. "At some point, Officer, did you obtain further information connecting the defendant to Mr. Guapo's death?"

"Yes."

"What was that information?"

"His confession. When Detective Derek Humphries interviewed him."

"Were you present for that confession?"

The officer glanced worriedly at Tony. "No."

"So how do you know about the confession?"

"Detective Humphries relayed the defendant's statements to me."

"What did the defendant tell Detective Humphries?"

Again the officer hesitated, as if waiting for Tony's attorney to object, which of course he didn't. Unlike at trial, hearsay was perfectly admissible at a preliminary hearing. Even if it hadn't been, statements by the defendant fell under a hearsay exception. "The defendant said he'd killed Guapo to protect what was his."

"Thank you, Officer." Neil sat down.

The judge turned to Tony and his defense attorney, Roger Lock. Given the state of the evidence and the way these things normally went, Linda was expecting them to say they didn't have any witnesses. The defense often let the prosecution's evidence speak for itself at preliminary hearing. Even so, she once again willed Tony to look at her. She wanted to know what he was thinking. How he was feeling. She wanted to know if he indeed viewed Neil's appearance as the prosecuting attorney as another abandonment on Linda's part. Or if he was even thinking of her at all.

"We'd like to call Detective Derek Humphries, Your Honor."

Linda stiffened at the defense attorney's words. She'd questioned the thoroughness of Humphries's investigation herself but it was still unusual that the defense was calling him at this point in the proceedings.

She watched as Humphries took the stand.

Linda didn't like him. She didn't like his methods.

Most cops were good ones, and truly cared about finding out the truth, not just scoring an arrest. But despite the rumors of dirty cops still going around, Linda believed Humphries had good intentions. Unfortunately he still lived by the motto that the ends justified the means. If he could walk the line to get a confession, he'd do so. Sometimes it worked to his advantage, sometimes it didn't.

Would it work in this case? She wasn't sure.

"Detective Humphries, you heard the officer tell us that Mr. Cooper confessed to killing Guapo. Was he correct?"

"Yes."

"After Mr. Cooper regained consciousness from his wounds, how long did you wait to start questioning him?"

"I was there within an hour."

"And you read Mr. Cooper his Miranda rights?"

Humphries practically rolled his eyes. "Yes, I did."

"Uh-huh. And he understood his rights?"

"Yes, he did."

"How do you know that?"

"Excuse me?"

Tony's defense attorney walked closer to Humphries. "I said, how do you know that he understood his rights?"

Humphries laughed. "He said he did. He waived them. Voluntarily."

"But he was in severe pain, wasn't he? Was in the midst of fighting off an infection?"

"He seemed uncomfortable. But cognizant."

Roger Lock nodded. "How long did you question him before you got him to confess?"

Neil raised his hand. "I object to counsel's insinuation, Your Honor. There's no evidence that Detective Humphries coerced a confession out of Mr. Cooper."

The judge shook his head. "Well, that's why we're here, isn't it, Mr. Christoffersen? Overruled."

"How long, Detective?"

Humphries shifted in his seat uncomfortably. "Two hours."

The attorney raised his eyebrows dramatically. "Two hours? You questioned Mr. Cooper, who was obviously 'uncomfortable' and probably high as a kite on pain meds, for two hours? Did you offer him a drink? A break?"

Humphries glared at Tony. "No."

"Did you obtain a written confession from him?"

"No."

"Why not? Isn't that standard police procedure?"

"It is. But…"

"But what, Detective?"

Detective Humphries mumbled something unintelligible.

"Speak louder," the judge commanded. "The court reporter needs to get this down."

"He was too weak to write. But I recorded his oral confession."

Linda's eyes widened. "What?" she whispered to Neil. There hadn't been an audio recording in Tony's case file.

Neil stood. "Your Honor, we don't know what tape is being discussed here."

Tony's defense attorney held up a tape. "This is the tape, Your Honor. It's the defendant's oral confession. We learned of its existence after interviewing Detective Humphries. Since Humphries is an agent for the D.A.'s office, I assume the D.A. has no issue with us playing the tape now? Unless, of course, they have doubts about Detective Humphries's…veracity?"

A tense silence pulsated around them. Damn, Lock was good. If Neil questioned Humphries's motivation in providing the tape to Lock, it would be virtually the same thing as challenging the accuracy of the confession he'd taken.

Neil settled back in his chair. "We have no objection to the tape at this time," he clipped out.

"Proceed," the judge said.

Lock smiled. "Thank you, Your Honor." He turned back to Humphries. "You signed this. Just so we're clear, is this the tape you sent to my office?" He handed the tape to Humphries, who studied it carefully.

"Yes, it is."

"Your Honor, with your permission, I'd like to play a portion of the tape."

"Granted."

The defense attorney stuck the tape into a tape recorder he had placed on counsel table. The tape started right where he'd wanted it to.

Humphries's voice warbled distinctly from the machine. "Come on, Cooper, admit it, so we can all get out of here. You killed him!"

Next, Tony's voice. Quite a bit weaker. Shaky.

"The guy came after me," Tony said.

"Don't feed me a line about self-defense. You were taking over his drug business and didn't want to give it back to him."

There was a long pause before Tony spoke again.

"Yes. Okay. I killed him. Killed the bastard so I could take over his business. Now can you leave? Have you gotten what you wanted?"

Tony's defense attorney stopped the tape. Linda shifted in her seat, wishing Tony would look at her.

"That an accurate recording of your conversation with Mr. Cooper?"

Humphries looked decidedly uncomfortable...and all of a sudden Linda wondered if his discomfort was an act. But that couldn't be right. Could it?

"The tape's accurate," Humphries said.

"And Mr. Cooper was correct. You got what you wanted, right?" Tony's defense attorney looked at the judge. "We're done, Your Honor."

"Very well," the judge finally said. "I don't like what I've just heard. I especially don't like that the tape you played came as a surprise to the District Attorney. Even so, given the evidence, I find there's sufficient evidence to hold Mr. Cooper to answer on the offense charged in the information. Is there anything else?"

Despite the fiasco with Humphries, Linda wasn't surprised the judge held Tony over. However, she was surprised when Tony's attorney stood again. "Yes, Your Honor. We've filed a motion asking that Mr. Cooper be released on his own recognizance pending trial."

The judge frowned. "And what supports such a motion? Given he's charged with first-degree murder?"

"He's charged with the first-degree murder of a known drug lord, Your Honor. And there are indications Mr. Cooper was acting in self-defense, just as he told Detective Humphries, since he sustained an injury to the back of his head. Plus, there are court records that will confirm Mr. Cooper acted as a confidential informant against Mr. Guapo, leading to the man's initial incarceration. That's further evidence, not only of Mr. Cooper's willingness to cooperate with authorities, but of Mr. Guapo's motive to attack Mr. Cooper without being provoked."

Linda kept her gaze on Tony, who seemed to be breathing more heavily.

His attorney was making a good argument. It wouldn't have been enough to win the preliminary hearing, but with the issue of bail and Humphries's strong-arm tactics to get Tony to confess when he'd been in the hospital, the judge had a lot more latitude. The motion would probably still fail, but did Tony know that? Or had his attorney raised his hopes? She couldn't tell. He hadn't changed positions. What little she could see of his expression was blank. As if he had no preferences about whether he stayed in jail or was released, even for a short time. She knew Neil would oppose the motion for bail but—

"Your Honor, the prosecution has no objection to Mr. Cooper being released on bail."

Linda's eyes widened and her gaze shot to Neil. What? That was completely contrary to office policy.

Obviously the judge knew this. He raised a brow.

"So you agree with Mr. Lock that the defendant is not a flight risk or a risk to society if released on bail?"

"Based on this record, I do," Neil confirmed.

The judge shrugged. "Very well. I'll release Mr. Cooper on his own recognizance. I hope you know what you're doing, Mr. Christoffersen."

As soon as court was dismissed, Linda asked Neil, "Why didn't you object to bail being granted?"

Neil looked slightly surprised. "I thought I was doing what you wanted me to do. Giving your friend a fair shot at proving his innocence."

Linda shook her head. She hadn't asked any favors

of Neil. Had he misunderstood? "I didn't ask you to bend the rules."

"Not in so many words. But I was reading between the lines. Especially after hearing that recording of Humphries's. You don't think he's guilty, do you?"

She hesitated. In her gut, she still doubted Tony's guilt. But why wouldn't she? She still had lingering feelings for a man who looked nothing like the one now sitting at the defense table. "That's irrelevant," she said, forcing herself to be objective. "I had a prior relationship with him. That's why I asked you to take my place. So that you'd be impartial."

"And that's what I'm being," Neil said. "Everything Lock said was true. Added to that is the fact I have faith in you, Linda. If you're not sure about his guilt, then neither am I."

Tony fought off the nausea bubbling in his stomach and concentrated on a spot on the courtroom carpet a few yards ahead of him. Released on OR? How the hell had that happened? On the one hand he was overjoyed. He wasn't sure he could take living in a crowded jail anymore, not after all his body had gone through in the past few days.

But on the other hand?

Getting out of jail meant once again leaving Linda and immersing himself into a world of drugs and vice. That prospect made jail look like paradise in comparison.

"Unbelievable," Roger Lock, Tony's defense attorney, told him. "I hope you realize just how lucky you are to have been granted bail. Are you friends with the prosecutor or something?"

His gaze automatically landed on Linda, who was talking to Neil Christoffersen.

"No," he said softly, his stomach churning again, only this time the nausea wasn't from the pain in his back and leg. He wasn't friends with Linda and he wasn't friends with Christoffersen. Far from it. He saw the way Christoffersen looked at Linda. If the man hadn't already had her, he was planning on changing that really soon.

Had he failed to object to bail in the hopes of gaining points with Linda? Had she asked Neil to provide the very leniency that she'd told Tony not to expect? And if she had, what did it mean? That she still cared about him? That she didn't believe he was the lost cause he was portraying himself to be?

The thought made hope spark inside him, but he swiftly pushed it aside.

Having her visit him in the jail infirmary had made him soft. His future more uncertain than ever, he'd started to wonder again. Hope again.

That's why this had happened, he realized. That's why he was getting out on bail. It was the universe telling him to get back on track. Away from Linda.

So focus, Tony. He'd copped to killing Guapo to increase his street cred. Maybe that same street cred could help him end this mess once and for all.

He needed Linda to believe he'd turned to the dark side. He needed everyone to believe it if his plan was going to work.

He thought about stopping to talk to her, but that would only create more suspicion about her involvement in the judge's decision. It was best to leave her alone.

He'd use his time out of jail to convince everyone once and for all that he was ruthless. Selfish. Immoral.

The kind of man that Linda would never have anything to do with. The kind of man who'd never care for her.

Then he'd disappear. For good.

Deliberately keeping his gaze away from Linda, Tony turned toward his attorney. As he did so, he caught sight of someone hovering a couple of feet away. The woman stepped forward and they locked gazes.

It was Justine. Damn it, what was she doing here? Was she crazy? She should have been halfway across the country by now.

"Tony?" she whispered, her brown eyes wide and shining with tears.

He sensed Neil and Linda stop talking and knew they'd turned to look at him. Linda had watched him throughout the preliminary hearing, trying, he suspected, to find some evidence of the man she'd once known. He'd wanted so badly to turn to her, profess his innocence and beg her to love him again, but that yearning only proved to him how weak he still was.

That weakness could get her killed.

Now or never, Tony, he thought.

He forced himself to grin. "Justine. Babe. Did you hear what the judge said? He's letting me out on bail." Stepping up to Justine, he wrapped an arm around her waist and pulled her against his body. "Guess what I want to do first?" he said just before he kissed her.

Chapter 12

Being beaten by Guapo's men hadn't hurt Linda nearly as much as seeing Tony kiss another woman. And by the looks of things, kissing wasn't all he was planning on doing with her.

He'd called her "babe"—the same woman Linda had seen in the courtroom bathroom the day of Tony's arraignment. The same one she'd suspected of snorting drugs while inside the stall.

People pushed past her, crowding her against the wooden observation seats, but she remained rooted, her focus on the familiar shoulders of the man she'd once loved, now covered with the languidly draped arms of a woman in a too-tight, too-short black leather miniskirt.

"Looks like he's going to be taking advantage of his freedom sooner than later." Neil's gaze was locked on the kissing couple, too, only his attention seemed more focused on the brunette rather than Tony. "You know who she is?"

Linda quickly glanced away. "No," she said, her voice scratchy but muted. No, no, no, she wanted to scream. Even more so, she wanted to stride up to the kissing couple and shove them apart. She shouldn't care. But more importantly she had no right to.

Turning, she strode toward the courtroom doors, aware that Neil was right beside her. Just before she exited, she couldn't help herself—she glanced back. Tony and his lover had stopped kissing and he was cradling her in his arms as if he never wanted to let her go. But his expression was grim. His gaze locked on Linda for a brief second. Just before he smiled.

That taunting smile did what the evidence itself hadn't been able to do.

It told her Tony really was a changed man. A man who cared nothing for her. One that maybe even hated her. She bit her lip to stifle the sound of her pain, but when Neil laid his hand on her shoulder, she knew she hadn't been successful.

"I'm sorry, Linda," he said quietly.

She shook her head. "Don't be. I'm used to being second best in his eyes. This time, I just happen to be second best to a woman rather than a controlled substance." Who knew it could hurt so much more.

Taking her arm, Neil led her outside. "Come on. Let's get some coffee and talk about something else for a while."

Coffee was the last thing she wanted. And she certainly didn't want to fake pleasant conversation when all she could think about was Tony kissing that woman. But Neil had already witnessed her weakness. Whether they ended up dating or not, she had to work with this man. That meant keeping up pretenses in front of him. She raised her chin. "Fine. But this time I'm buying."

He nodded. "This time, I'll let you."

As they walked toward the downstairs cafeteria at the front of the courthouse, Neil said, "So how'd the two of you meet?"

She visibly stiffened, which caused him to wince.

"Sorry," Neil said. "I know I said we'd talk about something else but you looked so torn up just now. And you only gave me bits of information about your previous relationship."

Sighing, she said, "It's okay. You're doing me a favor by taking his case. It's natural you'd be curious." She hesitated. "I met him through his sister. Mattie Nolan. She was a court reporter here before you started. We—we were friends."

"Were?"

"She left me, too," she said, hearing the bitterness in her voice and mentally wincing. It wasn't a fair accusation, she thought. Mattie had left with her daughter Jordon because she'd had to. Their lives had been in danger because of Guapo, just like hers had been. But why had she left without Tony?

"I'm an idiot," Neil declared, startling her out of her spinning thoughts.

"Wh-what?"

"Obviously a lot of stuff happened between you, Tony and his sister. I shouldn't have brought it up."

"It's okay. Really. It is what it is. I put my trust in the wrong people." She probably looked as dejected as she felt, so she forced a smile. "Can't do that again. Not if I want to win this judgeship."

"You haven't done that with me, Linda. I promise. We'll get through this and then maybe we can get back to the issue of you having dinner with me sometime."

Tilting her head, she studied him. His expression

was earnest. As far from Tony's taunting smile as one could get. She felt her constricted heart loosen slightly. Getting through "this" meant either Tony's freedom or incarceration. Either way, she'd be on her own. She was used to that, but the idea of a dinner date with Neil suddenly seemed like something to truly look forward to.

She took a deep breath. "I'm afraid I've created a conflict between the two of us, haven't I? Having known Tony, I can't exactly date you while you're prosecuting him. As we discussed, the chances of me having to disclose my prior relationship with him are very slim, but still possible. If that happens and I was dating you... But you're right... Afterward..." She nodded, causing him to grin.

"I look forward to afterward," he said. They chatted some more over coffee, deliberately keeping the conversation focused far from Tony's case. When they were done, Neil asked, "You going back to the office or heading out?"

"I'm going to head home."

"You want me to walk you to your car?"

A flash of her assault by Guapo's men in the parking lot swept over her. It did occasionally, but she refused to let it intimidate her. Especially now, she told herself. Eighteen months had passed with no incident and Guapo couldn't hurt anyone anymore. Tony had made sure of that. Or so he claimed.

Man, things were so confusing. She didn't know what to believe and for someone who was used to assessing witnesses and weighing evidence day in and day out, that was truly frustrating.

"I'm good, Neil. Thank you. For everything."

As she made her way to the front of the courthouse steps, she found herself thinking about Neil. Sure, he'd expressed interest in her before, but he was definitely taking extra interest in her now. Because of Tony? Was he afraid that Tony would somehow ruin his chances with her and feeling he'd better stake his claim while he could? But that was ridiculous. Tony was charged with murder. There was—

"Coffee again, Linda?"

Her head jerked up at the familiar voice. Tony leaned against one of the outer walls of the courthouse.

"Honestly, I didn't think you liked the stuff that much. Then again, maybe it's not the coffee you really like, is it?"

She glanced around but saw no sign of the woman he'd been kissing so passionately less than thirty minutes ago. "Where's your girlfriend?"

He frowned. Opened his mouth to speak. Shut it. Then shrugged. "Bathroom," he said.

Yeah, she thought, and she'd place bets on what she was doing in there.

She kept walking toward the garage, the pavement hot under her feet, the sun straight in her face, nearly blinding her. A car idled at the corner, and she coughed on the noxious smoke, but threw over her shoulder, "Did you leave her there? Careful. Getting caught having sex in public while on bail? Could ruin all the work your attorney did to—"

He put a hand on her shoulder. That was all. Fiercely she whipped around, knocking his hand away, not caring that they were on a public sidewalk in front of a crowded courthouse. "Don't touch me."

"Why? Because Neil Christoffersen does that? Are you in love with him?"

She almost laughed. The expression on his face was

dark and thunderous, the jealousy impossible to miss. "Are you crazy? You just kissed another woman—"

"Answer the question, Linda."

"No."

"No, you're not in love with him or no, you're not going to answer the question?"

She shot him a smile as taunting as the one he'd given her earlier. "You figure it out," she said. Turning, she began walking away again.

"Linda, I— Wait!"

It all seemed to happen at once. A car screeched around the corner of the courthouse. Tony yelled and she saw him move out of the corner of her eye. Gunshots fired a split second before she felt something slam against her body.

She hit the concrete so hard the breath was knocked out of her. Pain exploded everywhere and all she could think was that she'd been shot. Then she realized Tony had knocked her down, covering her body with his. Which meant that he might have been shot, too.

She imagined his blood seeping out of him.

She imagined him dead.

Everything that had transpired in the past few years vanished. All she could think was this was Tony.

And he'd been hurt.

Again.

Oh, God. He wasn't moving.

She fought back the gag reflex that suffocated her, and wriggled herself out from under him and onto her knees.

"Tony!" She kneeled over him, her shaking hands tugging at his shoulders.

He groaned.

"Tony! Answer me."

"Linda!" Neil's voice came from behind.

She glanced up, choking back a sob. Neil was scrambling down the steps toward her. Just behind him Tony's girlfriend followed. Her eyes were covered by sunglasses but she appeared to be looking down the street, where the drive-by shooters had disappeared. Several court personnel and officers burst out of the courtroom.

"What the hell happened?" Neil asked, coming down to his knees next to her.

"We were shot at. Tony pushed me out of the way. He's hurt—"

"I'm not hurt," Tony said, his shoulders moving under her hands. He pulled away from her and slowly got to his feet, leaving her kneeling on the ground. For a second he hesitated, as if he was going to reach out a hand to help her, but then his gaze met that of the brunette. His mouth flattened grimly.

She went cold. He'd just saved her life, and now he didn't want anything to do with her? This wasn't a case of male ego—this was Tony's absolute rejection of her because he didn't want his girlfriend getting pissed.

Neil was beside her, helping her up. "Did you see anything? Faces? The car?"

She tore her attention away from Tony. Damn him. "I—I—" She shook her head. "The car was blue. That's all I remember."

"There were two men, a passenger and driver. They were driving a beat-up sedan. Blue," Tony confirmed.

"You recognize them?"

Tony shook his head.

"Were you waiting out here to talk to Linda?" Neil asked.

Eyes narrowing, Tony challenged, "What if I was?"

"If you were, then I'm wondering if you held her up. Just long enough for her to get shot at."

Linda stifled the automatic protest that came to mind and wrestled with that possibility. Had Tony set her up?

"Great theory, but I got shot at, too. Besides, I have no reason to want Linda dead. Why would I? She's not the attorney prosecuting me anymore."

Neil stiffened. "Is that a threat?"

"No. Just an observation. Perhaps you should remember that's what you're doing. Prosecuting me. Yet you made it mighty easy for me to get out on bail, remember?"

Wait—what? How could Tony make such an accusation? "Are you saying Neil's responsible for those men shooting at us?"

Tony finally looked at her. Caught her gaze and held it, challenging her with his stare. "Shooting at *me,* babe. I'm betting you were just in the way. As usual."

Those two words knocked the breath out of her. "Then why push me out of the way? Why protect me at all? Maybe you're not the conscienceless drug dealer you're trying to make everyone believe you are."

"Oh, I am, Linda. Make no mistake about that. As to why I pushed you out of the way?" He shrugged. "You meant something to Mattie once. And yes, you meant something to me. That was worth something. But from now on, you're on your own." He looked at Neil. "Start doing your job and take care of her so I don't have to."

Chapter 13

Tony and Justine were more than a mile away from the courthouse when he said, "Damn it, what am I doing? I can't leave Linda by herself. Not now."

Realistically, he knew he shouldn't go back for her, but he also shouldn't have said anything to her when she'd been walking down those stairs to go to her car. He'd done so anyway. He hadn't been able to help himself. He'd seen the hurt on her face when he'd kissed Justine. How devastated she'd been when he'd smiled at her and called her "babe," as if he hadn't cared one iota for Linda's feelings.

That had been so far from the truth.

Now she'd almost been shot and he'd walked away and all he could think about was how she'd come to see him in the jail infirmary. How concerned she'd been about his pain. His needs. And this was how he was going to repay her?

"We have to go back."

Justine glanced at him from the driver's seat of her car. "And do what? Confess that you're not the heartless criminal you've been pretending to be? You already publicly threw yourself in front of her to take a bullet. Why not advertise to the whole world that you care about her? I'd give her less than twenty-four hours before someone comes after her in order to prove he and not you will be replacing Guapo."

"Maybe she already has someone after her. Despite what I said, I'm not so sure the people who shot at us were after me."

"How can you say that?"

"Why would someone shoot me? Like you said, it would only be to get me out of the picture and get their cut of Guapo's drug ring, but they wouldn't risk shooting me down in front of the county courthouse. Plus, I know who Guapo ran with, and the guys in that car? I didn't recognize them."

"It isn't just the men who were loyal to Guapo who want to take you down. You're open season for every wannabe drug dealer thinking to get in on the action. You made me a promise, Tony. You said you cared about my brother, enough to find the scumbag responsible for getting him hooked on Rapture and to shut him down so another kid doesn't die. Have you changed your mind about that?"

"Damn it, how can you say that after the past few weeks? I did care about your brother. I did everything I could to convince him to get clean and finish high school. To get away from Guapo and turn his life around. And you know I'll do whatever I can to find the Rapture supplier, but—"

"Then be smart. That woman? Linda Delaney? She's

with her friend the prosecutor. He'll protect her in a way you can't."

Like Tony could forget Neil. Asshole. "I don't like him."

She smiled slightly. "No? Good-looking, upstanding guy like him? What's not to like? Other than he's trying to put you in prison, that is." Her smile disappeared. "And all for a crime you didn't even commit," she said softly.

Tony glanced at her. No, he hadn't killed Guapo, but he had a lot of other things he was guilty of. Each one of those things had made him feel like he was lying when he'd pled not guilty in court. He *was* guilty, but he could still do some good. Starting with taking the blame for Guapo's death and making sure Justine didn't have to go through the trauma of a trial. Hell, the woman was still grieving the loss of her younger brother and she'd been helping Tony with his mission any way she could. That was the only reason Guapo had attacked her in the first place, causing Justine to kill him in self-defense.

Plus, Tony copping to killing Guapo had made sense for another reason altogether—once word spread to the streets, it would give more legitimacy to his claims that he was taking over Guapo's drug business and that he was tough enough to do so. Granted, he'd probably also issued a challenge to countless thugs who would try to prove they were even badder than he was, but hopefully word of Guapo's death would keep them away long enough for Tony to find out the identity of the Rapture supplier. "None of that," he told Justine. *I* killed Guapo, remember? Me. That's our story and we're sticking with it. If the man who was supplying Guapo Rapture believes I killed Guapo because I wanted in on their drug partnership, he'll contact me. And we'll be able to shut him down."

"If that's what you still want, then you really can't go back to see that woman, Tony."

Leaning his head back against the seat, Tony closed his eyes. Damn, his entire body ached. And even worse, he really wanted to take something to make the aches go away. Something strong, like Oxy. That, more than Justine's pleas, made up his mind about Linda. "I know."

One thing he didn't know? When the lies would stop. Hell, he hadn't even explained to Justine why he'd kissed her and he could tell she was looking at him with even more interest now. An interest he didn't return.

When was he going to stop hurting those he cared about even as he was trying to do the right thing?

He opened his eyes and straightened. When he'd done the job he was supposed to do, he told himself. When Rapture, the same drug that had killed Rory, Justine's brother, was taken out of the equation.

But despite telling Neil Christoffersen to do his job and take care of Linda, Tony knew he couldn't leave it at that.

He said nothing about his intentions to Justine, but he had to make sure Linda was safe. He was going to learn the identity of the Rapture supplier, but he wasn't going to sacrifice Linda's life to do it.

Justine drove him back to the house where they'd been staying before Tony had been arrested, a dingy dive where Guapo's less loyal acquaintances hung out. There, Tony took a few hours to make the rounds and brag about what he'd done to the man who'd made the mistake of messing with him. Then he went for a walk, bought a disposable cell phone and called Ash Yee, a

Sacramento P.D. detective who used to work with Dominic Jeffries, his sister Mattie's husband.

Though Mattie, Dom and Tony had been in WIT-SEC in Texas, Dom had temporarily come out of hiding to arrange for Tony to work undercover with the Sacramento Police Department. Weeks before, Tony had just graduated from the local police academy, but despite missing Linda desperately, he'd had no intention of ever returning to Sacramento.

Then he'd heard about Rory Maverick's death.

At one time Tony had been close to Rory—at least, as close as anyone could be to a street kid, which wasn't very close at all. The boy had looked up to him and, despite knowing the kid smoked pot and ran drugs for Guapo, Tony, quite simply, had liked him. Had even started to steer him straight. Talk about college.

When Tony had stopped buying drugs from Guapo, he'd likewise cut off any contact he'd had with his associates, and that had included Rory. Again, before he'd moved to Texas, he'd often thought of tracking Rory down, but he hadn't kidded himself. His qualifications as any kind of mentor hadn't improved. Keeping off the drugs was a constant struggle for him and he'd barely been holding things together even before he'd lost Linda. Who was he to interfere in someone else's life and tell him what to do?

Then, just when Tony was set to begin his career as a cop, he'd learned about Rory's death.

And he'd known what he had to do.

He'd talked to Dom, who'd been working as a sheriff's deputy. Dom had made some calls, not to anyone at the Sacramento P.D., but to a few friends of his with the FBI.

It turned out that despite his obvious inexperience,

the FBI had been all for Tony going deep under cover in Sacramento, not only to bring down Guapo's organization but to determine if there were any other corrupt cops in the police department. According to the FBI's contacts, *someone* on the force was still dirty and they suspected someone in the courts was, too. Maybe even the D.A.'s office. It seemed to be the only explanation for how Guapo's men were managing to elude capture or prosecution time and again.

Right now Tony was placing bets on Neil Christoffersen. But he also knew that was probably his jealousy guiding him more than anything else.

So far Tony hadn't caught a whiff of corruption, certainly not from Yee. As far as the Sacramento P.D. was concerned, Yee, his partner, and their boss were the only ones besides Tony who knew he was working undercover and trying to shut down Guapo's operation, but he only kept direct contact with Yee. Yee worked undercover, as well, except he was posing as a Rapture user and, like Tony, was trying to find out the identity of anyone with any connection to Rapture manufacturers, suppliers or dealers.

Tony had no clue what Yee thought about Guapo's death or his participation in it. He hadn't tried to contact him while he'd been in jail, but he was betting they'd had something to do with his grant of bail.

"Where are you?" Yee asked as soon as they were connected, which confirmed he knew Tony had gotten out.

Tony was standing across from Linda's house. He wanted to make sure she'd gotten home all right and it appeared she had. Her car was in the driveway and even now he could see glimpses of her moving around inside. Of course he didn't tell Yee that.

"I'm staying at the house on Tortuga Boulevard." He walked around, canvassing the streets, looking for signs that someone had followed Linda or posed any kind of threat to her.

"What happened with Guapo?"

"He came after me," Tony simply said. "I did what I had to."

Yee remained silent for several seconds, then said, "Word's spread to the street. Even the small-time dealers have heard about it. They're impressed. But they're also wondering whether you'll be able to supply them with the same drugs Guapo did. And if you'll be upping the cost of playing. Any suppliers contact you yet?"

"I just got out of jail, Yee. I'm gonna have to work on reestablishing my contacts. But like you said, word's spread. I'll continue to make it known where potential business associates can find me. But right now I have something else I need to talk to you about," he said.

The house next door to Linda's had a twitchy curtain. Nosy neighbor. Good to know. If anyone suspicious showed up—anyone besides him, he thought—the neighbor would probably notice and likely call the police if there was trouble.

"Did you hear about the shooting at the courthouse earlier?"

Yee sighed. "Yeah. And I heard you saved some woman, too. You both okay?"

Not just any woman, he wanted to shout. Linda. But Yee didn't know about their prior relationship, so he simply said, "Do you have any leads on whether it was one of Guapo's men?"

"Not yet."

"Do you know anything about a D.A. named Neil Christoffersen?"

"I've heard of him. He's supposed to be a straight shooter. Why?"

For a second Yee's use of the phrase *straight shooter* tickled Tony's brain, as if a memory was trying to surface, but the sensation was quickly gone. "He made sure I got out on bail just in time for that drive-by to occur. If the shooters meant to take me down, he certainly had a part in making sure it could happen."

"I'll check him out. See if there's any reason to think he's the mole in the D.A.'s office we've been speculating about. But you said *if* they were meant to take you down? I'd say a bullet is pretty good evidence of their intentions. Why the equivocation?"

"Because I'm not sure I was actually the target. The woman who was with me? She's a prosecutor. District Attorney Linda Delaney."

Yee let out a low whistle. "The one vying to be a judge. The one that Guapo's men attacked? Hell, you were probably both targets, then. Not smart, man. If anyone saw you save her…"

"I know. They'll be more suspicious of me. And more likely to use her to get to me. That's why I need you to protect her."

"In case you didn't know, we're already a little busy over here. You don't ask a lot, do you?"

He fought off a smile. He didn't ask for much at all—not for him.

But he'd ask a lot for Linda Delaney, a woman who grew wisteria over her front porch and sunflowers in her backyard. A woman who didn't own a dog or even a cat to protect her. A woman who lived on a dead end cul-de-sac surrounded by neighbors who were never home, besides the window-twitcher next to her.

And judging by the amount of wooden ducks with

gingham bows around their necks lining the drive, that neighbor was probably a woman in her eighties. Hardly an environment where one could turn to one's neighbors if bad guys started shooting.

"No more than I'd ask of myself. I'd protect her, but I can't do it if I'm trying to find the supplier, now can I. I need Linda taken care of."

"You two…?"

Together? Having sex? Desperately in love with each other? Tony turned on his heel and heavily limped back the way he'd come. "No. We had something going once, but that's over between us."

"But not because you want it to be."

"No, you're wrong," Tony said, trying to backtrack. "She wasn't right for me."

"D.A. Drug addict. Yeah, I'd say that's the understatement of the century. Doesn't mean you don't care about her, though. That's pretty obvious from what you're asking of me."

Why did Yee keep harping on whether he cared about Linda or not?

"It's not merely a request, Yee. I need her protected or I'm pulling out," Tony said softly. What the hell, he decided. Sometimes one had to admit to one's vices. Maybe if Yee knew how much Linda meant to Tony, the cop would take his request for her protection seriously. He gave Yee Linda's home address. "Take care of her for me, Yee."

"Let me talk to some people. We'll put a team on her. But you need to stay away from her, Tony."

"I told you, there's nothing between us. Not anymore."

Even as he said the words, Tony knew they weren't completely true. There *couldn't* be anything between them, but he'd lost his heart to her long ago. For him, she'd always be the one. And he'd regret having lost her until the day he died.

Chapter 14

After giving her statements to the police about the shooting and despite Neil's protests, Linda went back to the office to pick up her files before she headed home. Aching and sore and still troubled by everything that had happened with Tony, however, she decided at the last minute to leave the files on her desk. She didn't want to read any more files. What she wanted was to figure out what was going on with Tony. How he could be so aloof and cruel one minute, and then risk his life to save her in the next.

Linda was still contemplating the question when Cynthia McCall, the receptionist, called her.

"Hey, Linda. You just got a fax."

"I'm heading home in a bit. I'll grab it on my way out."

"Okay...but the fax, it's pretty weird. I think you'll want to take a look at it right away."

What now, Linda thought. She gathered her things and quickly walked to the lobby and receptionist's area that housed the office fax machine. When she got there, she frowned. Brian Heald was inside Cynthia's office, leaning against the doorway and grinning. Cynthia was laughing, obviously pleased by the man's attention. When she saw Linda, however, Cynthia immediately straightened and slid a white piece of paper underneath the receptionist's tellerlike window.

"Thanks," Linda murmured, simultaneously turning away and wincing when she heard Heald murmur something and Cynthia giggle. Heald had to have heard what happened to her, but God forbid he express any concern. Why women kept encouraging the man was beyond her, but she supposed there was someone for everyone.

Linda flipped the cover page of the fax up and frowned.

Tony Cooper is a good man. You know this. Trust your instincts about him, Linda.

Linda looked at the top of the page, searching for information about who had sent the fax and when. She kept her face calm for Cynthia, who was watching her closely. "Thanks, Cynthia. I'll check into this."

She turned around and walked back to her office, her steps keeping time with the pounding beat of her heart. She made several phone calls but still wasn't able to track down who had sent the fax. The outgoing fax number belonged to a copy store in Vacaville and the man on the phone had no idea who had sent it.

Linda struggled once more with indecision.

The fax alluded to her prior relationship with Tony.

Obviously she didn't want that getting out. But the fax verged on being *Brady* material. Nothing about it expressly said Tony was innocent, but she should still tell Neil and Lock about it. Shouldn't she?

If she kept the fax a secret and someone made a stink about it, valid or not, losing her bid as a judge might just be the first step. She could lose her job. Her reputation. Everything she'd worked so hard to protect.

Plus…she didn't just have herself to think about. She needed to think about Tony.

Someone obviously thought he was innocent of what he was being charged with. Coupled with the way he'd saved her earlier, she was more than willing to believe it.

No, she reasoned. She couldn't just think of herself.

She'd show Neil the fax in the morning. But what was she going to do in the meantime?

Undecided, she went home. Paced and worried. After an hour of that, she opened her closet door. She grabbed a banker's box from the top shelf and placed it on the bed. Sitting cross-legged, she pulled out a smaller shoebox, and then a silver-framed picture.

It was of her, Tony, Mattie and Jordan. Tony's hair was as curly as Mattie's and flirted with the collar of his shirt. His eyes reflected a serious quality, but the sheer joy of his smile gave him an undeniably youthful appearance.

This was how she remembered him most of the time. Not as the man who'd sat at her kitchen table looking longingly at those pills. Yet at the same time, it was the second image that had the most power over her. That caused her to feel honor bound not to give in to her feelings for him.

But oh, how she longed to. Her chest ached at seeing not only how happy he'd been, but how happy *she'd* looked. He'd wrapped one of his arms around her from behind, resting his chin on the top of her head. She looked up at him, laughing, her eyes shining with happiness. Linda traced her smile with her finger, then her gaze shifted to Mattie and Jordan.

How she missed them and wished Mattie was here to talk to.

But she wasn't. Linda didn't have anyone but herself. She'd have to figure this out alone.

Linda gently placed the picture back in the box and closed the lid.

Well, maybe not completely alone, she thought.

There was still someone she could talk to. Someone who still had answers, and she couldn't give up until she got them from him. Determined, she changed her clothes, gathered her things and left her house. Instead of taking her car again, she'd walk the two miles to her office. It would give her a chance to clear her head, then she'd get Tony's file and the bail form that should list his address.

She'd walked about four blocks before she froze dead in her tracks.

And stared straight at Tony.

Tony cursed when he saw Linda walking toward him. Instead of one of the suits she'd worn over the past week, she now wore casual clothes. Jeans and a light sweater. Sneakers. The outfit made her seem approachable in a way her professional clothes hadn't. And after having been in jail the past few days, and without her for three-and-a-half years, the picture of her walking toward him in the quiet residential neighborhood seemed surreal.

He literally shook his head to clear it.

Where the hell was she going? And why was she going anywhere, alone and unprotected, after she'd just been shot at?

He supposed she didn't think of it that way, though. He'd told her *he'd* been the one getting shot at. But yet she was still walking toward him.

She stopped a mere five feet away. Close enough for her scent to cling to the slight evening breeze and wrap around him.

He felt his knees weaken and, just as he had when she'd come to visit him in the jail infirmary, he automatically reached for her. This time, however, before his skin could touch hers, he curled his fists and pulled back.

You can't have her, Tony. Not if you want to keep her safe. Wasn't having her shot at today enough to make you remember that, damn it? Knowing he had to keep her at a distance, he forced himself to imagine her with her coworker, Neil. He tortured himself with the image of them together, not just making love, though God knew that was almost too much for him, but growing old together. Of them living years and years together, with not just a cat, but a whole slew of animals and photos of their children and grandchildren. Of them getting to have the life that he'd so badly wanted with Linda. The images flooded through his mind until he almost thought he hated her; only then did he speak. "Well, well. Where are you off to this evening, Linda? Heading out to meet your D.A.?" He made a great show of looking around him, as if Neil would suddenly materialize out of thin air.

Smiling tightly, Linda placed her hands on her hips. "Which one? There's more than one interested in me."

Damn her, he thought, for fueling his jealousy. "I'm not surprised," he forced himself to say. "So besides Neil, who's the lucky guy in the running?"

She stared at him then shook her head. "No one, believe me. So, Tony... You come here often?"

The woman had no sense of self-preservation. Just a steely determined expression on her face that told him quite clearly she intended to pin him down for answers to all her questions.

He turned swiftly, striding away and hoping she'd let him go without a fight.

But, of course, she didn't.

He heard her scampering after him right before she grabbed his arm. "Wait just one second. What are you doing here, Tony? Were you coming to see me?"

Of course she'd jump to that conclusion. It was the only reasonable explanation for being here. But reason and logic had nothing to do with his life anymore. He was pretending to be a hard-core murderer, for God's sake.

He jerked his arm away from her. "Get over yourself, Linda. I was here to see someone else and just had the misfortune of running into you." He looked around. Still didn't see anyone. But that could change at any moment.

She narrowed her eyes at him. "You must really think I'm a fool. When are you going to stop with your ridiculous lies? You saved my life this afternoon, Tony, and I—"

"Then don't have it be for nothing," he clipped out, no longer able to control himself. "Turn around and haul your butt back home, Linda. And stay there. For God's sake, you're a sitting duck out here."

"So are you."

"Yeah, but if I got shot and killed the world would be a better place. If you did—"

Her eyes widened at his inadvertent compliment and he mentally cursed. Shit. He was losing it. Messing things up big time.

"Jesus," he murmured, then gently took her arm and started walking back to her house. "Go home, Linda."

She stopped and wrenched her arm away. "No," she said.

"Damn it!"

"Not unless you come back with me," she challenged.

His eyes widened. "What?"

"I told you when you were still in jail, Tony. I want answers. I need them. Come back to my house. Talk to me. Convince me that you're the baddie you're trying to pretend to be. Only then am I going to let this matter drop."

"This matter, meaning what?"

"This matter, meaning the little charade I think you're playing. I want answers about why you're playing it."

Tony stared at her in frustration, then swept the street again. He'd wanted to make sure her neighborhood was clear of any obvious threats. And he'd wanted to call Yee and make sure Linda got some protection. The last thing he'd wanted—no, the last thing he could allow himself to want—was more alone time with her.

Especially out in the open. Exposed.

If anyone drove by and saw them together...

She'd left him no choice. "Fine," he said. "Let's go back to your house. Ask your questions. I'll give my answers. And believe me, Linda, after that, you'll finally accept I'm exactly who I say I am. Don't blame me if you get all the answers you never wanted to hear."

Chapter 15

Tony was back. Inside her house. Inside the home they'd shared before Linda's life had imploded that evening in her kitchen when she'd found him with that damn bag of pills. Granted, he was only back to convince her he was not just a druggie, but a murderer, but for a moment she relished the picture he made standing in her living room anyway.

"Do you...do you want something to drink?"

"No. I want to answer your questions so you'll leave me alone. I have a girlfriend, Linda. Or have you forgotten that? I don't want to be with you anymore."

The hurt was like a thousand knives piercing her body. The pain unleashed something inside her. Something wild.

She shook her head. He wanted to play dirty? Fine. She was no longer content to simply ask him questions. Now she wanted more.

"That's not why I asked you here and you know it." She stepped closer. Close. And she could see his discomfort on his face. His unease.

His desire for her.

She got to him.

And the only reason she'd get to him was if he still cared about her and still wanted her.

"Ask me your questions, Linda. Or despite having a girlfriend, I'll give you what your body's obviously craving and then walk out of here anyway."

She stared at him. Lost her nerve. In this game, he seemed the expert and she the fledgling player. With a sigh, she backed off.

"Fine." She'd hit him where it would hurt the most first. "Do you even care about Mattie and Jordan anymore?"

He didn't even flinch. "No."

She almost laughed at the ridiculousness of his lie. "So you don't care about me, and you don't care about them, either?"

He glanced away. "It doesn't matter if I care about them. They're gone. Safe."

"Safe. That's an odd way to put it. Do you mean safe from Guapo? Or safe from you?"

When he said nothing, she said, "Fine. Let's get back to me. Why did you save me?"

"That's your next question? Not whether I killed Guapo?"

She shrugged. "I've already asked you that. Multiple times. You've implied you did or dodged my questions altogether—"

"Then let me clarify. I killed Guapo. Clear enough? As to why I saved you? What can I say? It was like a reflex."

She shook her head. "I don't believe you. Not about Guapo and not about why you saved me. On some level you still care about me. You're not the criminal you're trying so hard to pretend you are."

"Really?" As he walked toward her, stalking her, he smiled that same taunting smile he'd shot her in the courtroom. But she'd asked him into her home and she'd be damned if she'd let him intimidate her now.

She held her ground until he stood right in front of her and she had to tilt back her head to hold his gaze. He was wearing jeans, a long-sleeved Henley and a light zippered sweatshirt. He didn't look like Tony, but he smelled like him. His proximity made the air vibrate with her desire, just like it always had. And he made her heart yearn for the one thing she'd once dreamed they'd have together—time. Time to explore, discover and connect.

Time they'd never gotten because she'd had no choice but to let him go.

"What am I?" he asked as he cupped her chin and pressed the pad of his thumb against her lower lip. His eyes sparked with challenge.

She felt an answering spark of anger explode within her.

How dare he taunt her with his touch? His words? How dare he be so close and yet so far, when he'd given her no other option but to end things.

What was he? An answer—a ridiculous, foolish answer popped into her head. One she, a prosecutor and wannabe judge, should have had no problem containing. But she'd always been more than what she showed the world. And these past few days with Tony were reminding her of that.

Instead of pushing him away, she reached up with

one hand, wrapped her fingers around his wrist and nipped at his thumb. He hissed and tried to jerk his wrist away, but she held on and said exactly what she was thinking. "You're what you've always been, whether we could be together or not, Tony. Mine."

His eyes widened with shock and before he could tear himself away, she rose up on her toes and kissed him.

His taste exploded on her lips like the most sinful combination of caramel and chocolate, two things Linda rarely allowed herself because even the smallest taste inevitably had her craving more. She almost always resisted that edgy feeling of being out of control, of being hungry for something more than she could have, but right now she grabbed on to it, letting go of Tony's wrist to clutch at his shirtfront and pull him even closer.

His mouth remained still. Unresponsive.

Disheartened, she almost pulled back. Instead she licked, enticing him to open up and let her in. To let the memory of everything they'd once meant to each other warm and excite him. Kissing him was certainly doing both for her. Heat traveled through her veins, making her skin tingle with pleasure she hadn't felt in almost four long years. Her fingers uncurled and flattened against his chest, stroking him through the fabric of his clothes and finding his small nipples.

He didn't move. Didn't open his mouth. Didn't make a sound.

Thankfully, however, she could feel the hammering of his heart against her palm, telling her he wasn't as unaffected as he seemed.

"Please," she whispered. "Kiss me, Tony. I've missed you so much. You don't know how much I've—"

With a growl, he snapped. His hands buried themselves in her hair as his mouth angled over her own. His tongue sought hers even as he pressed his hips closer, nudging her with the hardened flesh beneath his jeans.

He kissed her as if he was a starving man who'd finally found sustenance. As if he was drowning, and she was air.

Unbelievably she felt a bubble of laughter escape her. Joy. It poured over her, making her want to pump her fists in the air.

Yes! I've finally broken through. This *is Tony. This is the man I love.*

The only man I've ever loved.

She whimpered when Tony suddenly ended the kiss to stare down at her. His expression was fierce, almost tortured, but his hands in her hair were gentle, kneading her scalp, then easing her back for another kiss, this one far more gentle than the first.

This time, instead of kissing her as if he was starving, he kissed her as if he was worshipping her. As if at any moment, she—something precious—would be taken away from him.

Once again he lifted his head. "Linda," he whispered. "We can't do this. I'm not the man you think I am—"

She didn't want to hear it. Refused to listen to anything that would cause these wonderful moments in his arms to stop.

"You're exactly who I think you are, Tony. Mine, remember?"

With that, she stepped back and began pulling off her clothes.

It took Linda mere seconds to strip off her top and bra. She was already working on her jeans when he shook his head. "Linda, no. Damn it, we can't. I'm with Justine—"

Her head snapped up fiercely. "Don't. Don't you dare mention another woman. You're mine, Tony. And I'm yours. Here. Now. I'm yours. Don't you want me?"

He ground his palms into his eyes and barked out with laughter. "Yes. I want you, okay? I've never stopped wanting you. But we've never had problems with sex—"

"Then don't make it a problem. Just give in to it. Give in to *me,* Tony. Just for now, give me back the man I know you to be. Please."

She stared at him, her heart in her eyes, and he felt his own heart expand. A few hours ago she'd been shot at. He'd pushed her out of the way. Now she was offering herself to him without asking for the assurance of tomorrow. That was good because tomorrow wasn't anything he could give her.

But was she right? Could he give her this? Give her himself, right here and right now?

Yes, he decided.

"Finish taking off your pants and come here, Linda."

Amazingly, after everything she'd just begged him for, she blushed. But she didn't balk. She unbuttoned her jeans and swiftly took them off until she was wearing nothing but a pair of miniscule white cotton panties. Looking at her, virtually naked, her creamy skin glowing, Tony almost couldn't breathe.

She was still breathtakingly beautiful, which didn't surprise him in the least.

But what did surprise him? What had his heart clenching with joy?

She'd lied about getting rid of their tattoo.

It still marked her skin, and on some level that meant that despite all the years that had come between them, they'd never been completely separated.

Instinct took over.

He didn't know who he was anymore. Linda's addicted ex. Justine's pretend boyfriend. Guapo's killer. They all faded away to be replaced by a mere man.

A man who wanted Linda and was finally going to have her again.

He walked closer until he stopped in front of her. Until he could feel her breath puffing erratically against him. He stroked her arms, causing her eyes to close and a moan to escape her.

"You're beautiful," he said.

Her eyes popped open and the hint of disbelief there made Tony's heart ache. He caressed her cheek. "You're as beautiful as you always were, Linda. Even more beautiful. And I can't resist you."

She shook her head. "I'm not asking you to," she whispered.

He kissed the side of her neck, inhaling her intoxicating scent that was nothing more than soap and woman, and then moved slowly downward to lick and suck at one of her nipples.

She gasped and arched closer even as she cupped his head, ensuring he didn't leave her.

"Shhh," he said, pulling back to blow on her wet flesh so that her nipple tightened. And then he gave the same treatment to her other breast.

"Tony," she moaned. "Now. I need you now."

He swallowed hard, her urgency spurring on his own. He tucked his hand into her panties and cupped her, hissing at the searing heat against his fingers. "You're so wet. So ready for me."

"I dream about you every night, Tony," she cried. "Please don't make me dream anymore. Take me. Now."

She cupped his erection through his jeans, causing him to curse and his hips to jerk.

Without realizing it, his fingers twisted into the waistband of her panties and tugged until they ripped. It obviously excited her because she moaned and began to claw at the fly of his pants.

"Wait," he said. "A bed. I want you in bed." He swept her up in his arms and though he winced at the pain that flashed through his back and leg, he carried her to the bedroom. It looked so familiar. So comforting, when his body felt inflamed. Seduced. Desperate to have her.

He lowered her onto the bed, where she opened her arms, her thighs, her very body to him. He couldn't bear it any longer. He ripped open his pants and didn't even bother taking them off. Shoving them down, he fell between her legs, cupped her face and kissed her as deeply as he could.

He wanted to crawl inside her and never come out. He wanted this time with her to never end. But even as he breached her body with his, even as their cries of pleasure mingled and their gazes locked, he knew the end was inevitable.

His hips pumped frantically, as if denying his thoughts.

Hers answered in kind, refusing to be passive. Giving everything of herself even as she took everything in him.

And still she looked at him.

Their bodies strained until they shook. As more time passed, he realized they were both holding back, savoring the pleasure they were giving one another while at the same time refusing to give it free rein. Holding back that inevitable end he'd just been thinking of.

But as if they couldn't help themselves, her muscles

fluttered around him. He felt himself get even bigger and harder inside her. Her eyes widened and suddenly the fragile thread of control they'd been holding on to snapped.

Ecstasy contorted the beauty of her face into something even more beautiful. When her climax hit, she didn't scream as she often had in the past. She didn't even say his name. Instead, when she came, she mouthed one word.

Mine.

Tony followed her into pleasure, coming harder than he ever had before. For a few blessed moments his release wiped his mind clean of guilt and regret. When it was over, he collapsed, barely managing to distribute his weight so that he was only partially lying on top of her.

Reality returned so swiftly it was disorienting.

As he struggled to catch his breath, he told himself to get up. To flee. To deny what had just happened between them.

But her hands stroked his back and his hair, prolonging his pleasure. It soothed him. Once again it made all his pain melt away.

Once again he told himself to leave. Once again, he couldn't do it.

His lips sought hers and she kissed him back. With a sigh he burrowed his face in her neck and slept.

Chapter 16

When Linda woke, it was a little after six in the morning and Tony was gone. She wasn't surprised, not by his absence or the pain that filled her because of it. But she was surprised by the depth of her renewed faith in him.

There was no way Tony was dirty.

She'd suspected it when he'd shown up as a defendant in her courtroom. She'd known it after he'd saved her life. And she'd believed it after being in his arms again.

She still believed it.

Now more than ever.

And she wasn't going to let him run away from her again.

She winced at her mental slip. Okay, so he hadn't run from her the first time. She'd pushed him away. She'd had to. And as far as she knew, she still had to. As much as she'd cherished being with him last night, even if she managed to prove he was innocent, she didn't know if they had a future together. He still had his addiction. She was still running to be judge. Those two things didn't go together.

She didn't care. She couldn't predict the future, but she was not going to let Tony destroy his life out of some misguided sense of duty or guilt.

She'd played the words of that fax over and over in her mind.

Listen to your instincts.

Her instincts told her Tony wasn't a killer. And he wasn't a criminal. For some reason he wanted her to believe that, but such a person would have cared more about his own safety than hers. He'd thrown himself on top of her, willing to take a bullet for her.

Tony had acted as a confidential informant once. Whatever game he was playing now, he had to be doing it for some greater purpose.

She lay in bed for several minutes, enjoying the scent of Tony on her sheets and on her body, then she got up. As she did, she felt liquid trickle down her thighs and froze.

He hadn't worn a condom.

And she hadn't even thought about its absence. She'd been too busy savoring the feel of him inside her. The wonder of being in his arms again.

What a fool she'd been.

Slowly she got dressed. While she was on the pill to regulate her cycles, she prayed that by having un-protected sex with her, Tony hadn't risked her health. She couldn't imagine him doing such a thing, even if he had been carried away by passion. But she could never have imagined him killing Guapo, lying to her or kissing a woman in front of her just to hurt her, either. He'd only taken painkillers before, but that could have changed. Maybe he took hard-core drugs now. Used needles. Dirty needles.

She shuddered and pushed her racing thoughts away. She'd let her hunger for him distract her. Now she had more reason than ever to talk to him.

She headed to work, completed the morning calendar, then took her lunch break with Tony's bail receipt in hand.

The receipt listed his current residence. When she pulled up in front of the house, Linda found herself double-checking to make sure there wasn't some mistake. He'd boasted about having money, and Lock, the attorney he'd retained, certainly charged an enormous amount of it. Yet despite his access to a lot of money, he was living in one of the worst neighborhoods in town. She wasn't exactly sure what she was going to find but stalwartly kept moving.

As she made her way up the cracked walkway, she doubted it would be anything good.

There were several people hanging out on the porch of the dilapidated house. They were drinking and smoking joints, but looked relatively harmless. Nonetheless she was comforted by the weight of her Taser gun in her jacket pocket. If any of them made a move for her, she'd zap them without any hesitation. But just as she'd expected, they ignored her, too wasted to care.

She entered the house without knocking. There was a man in a dirty T-shirt staring at the illuminated television set.

"I'm looking for Tony," she said.

He pointed toward the back of the house without even looking at her.

She checked several doors, but didn't see him. Eventually she came to a closed door and knocked. The brunette from the courthouse answered it. Instead of the skirt and jacket she'd worn to court, she wore a tight red T-shirt and frayed cutoffs that showed off her trim body to its best advantage.

The woman laughed humorlessly. "Unbelievable," she said. "The little prosecutor followed you here, Tony. Can you believe it?" She moved to the side so that Linda could see inside the bedroom.

Tony lay in the bed. Though he was halfway covered with a sheet, his chest was bare.

Just as it had when Tony had kissed this woman, pain once again stabbed at her. This time, however, it was multiplied a hundredfold, strong enough that it almost buckled her knees.

He'd gone straight from her bed to this woman's?

Horror ripped a hole right through her until she swayed. That kind of behavior didn't bode well for a woman who'd just had unprotected sex with him. She locked her knees together.

It had been her choice to waltz in here unannounced, but as much as it hurt to see Tony and this woman together again, she'd come for answers. And she was going to get them.

"We need to talk, Tony. Please."

Justine snorted. "Such good manners. But we don't want you here."

Tony contradicted her. "Justine, give us a minute, would you?"

Eyes wide with disbelief, Justine turned to stare at Tony. "You just set up that meeting, Tony. Finally you're close to getting what you want. What we both want. Remember that."

"I remember, Justine. I promise."

With one more look at Linda, Justine left.

Slowly Tony rose and the sheet fell to the floor. He seemed to be favoring his injured leg again, but as she got a quick glimpse of his toned, naked body, all she remembered was the pleasure he'd given her earlier.

"You're blushing, Miss Priss." Reaching down, he picked up the sheet and wrapped it around his waist. "Given what we were doing several hours ago, that's pretty funny don't you think?"

The nickname was something he'd teasingly called her when they'd dated. Then, it had always sounded affectionate. Now? She swore she heard the same affection in his tone. Had their time together impacted him? Softened him? Then what was he doing here? Naked with Justine just mere hours after he'd been naked with her?

"You didn't wear a condom, Tony. I'm on the pill, so I won't get pregnant, but do I need to worry about any other unsavory consequences of our little escape into the past?"

His eyes widened as if he, too, was just now realizing that he'd released inside her. He flushed and his throat convulsed as he swallowed. "You're fine, Linda. I've never forgotten to wear a condom before, and I'm clean. I was just in the hospital, remember? They checked. And thankfully, nothing happened in jail to change that."

Relief swept through her and she gave an audible sigh. "Okay. Thank you for telling me that." She licked her lips, took in the messy, dingy bedroom and forced herself to turn back to him. "So what meeting was Justine talking about? What do you and she want?"

He smiled tightly. "What most people want. Money and even more money. And the meeting she mentioned is the first step in how I'm going to get it. So you see, killing Guapo had the exact effect I was hoping for. His former business associates are lining up to do business with me."

She rolled her eyes. "Right. And you're going along for the ride because obviously money is so important to you." She swept her gaze around the room. "You're living in the lap of luxury, aren't you?"

Tony scowled. "Does Neil know you're here? Or that I was inside your house—inside you—not too long ago?"

"Do you want to be back there? Because I won't lie." She took a deep breath, bracing herself. "I want you there, Tony."

He actually took several steps back, as if he was afraid of her. But she was through playing games. It was best that he know that.

"Then you're a fool. That meant nothing to me, Linda."

She'd braced herself for the cut of his words but they still hurt her anyway. Big deal. She'd hurt before and she'd always picked herself up and kept moving. She'd do it now. "I don't believe that."

He swept the cluttered dresser, shoving its contents—clothes, books, newspapers and a few glasses—to the floor. He stared at what he'd done, then laughed and shook his head. "Like I told you earlier, you're crazy."

"No. You're crazy if you think I'm just going to buy your act when I know who you really are." She gestured at the room around her. At the debris scattered on the floor. "This isn't you, Tony."

"Damn it, stop it. Get it through your head that I don't care about you anymore. That this is the life I want now."

"You touched me as if you cared about me."

"That was sex, Linda. For God's sake, you've never been this full of yourself."

"Guess you're not the only one who's changed, Tony. I'm stronger than I was. Nearly dying can do that to a person. I'm not buying that you killed Guapo. Not when my gut is telling me differently."

"Why not? You assumed I'd start taking drugs again. Granted, you had ample evidence given the pills I was staring so covetously at. Your gut led you in the right direction that night, Linda. It told you I was a loser. Someone you needed to stay away from. Remember that."

He turned, obviously intent on dismissing her, but swayed on his feet. He reached out to steady himself on the wall beside the bed. Linda stepped closer and gasped at how pale he'd turned. A thin film of sweat covered his face and his breaths were shallow and ragged.

"Tony, what's wrong? Are you sick?"

He shook his head. "No. I'm just—I'm just tired. Leave."

She stepped closer, reached out to touch him, but he backed away before she could.

"Damn it, leave me alone. Get out of here!"

He turned away from her, favoring his leg again.

It had always caused him trouble, but he'd hurt it in the fight with Guapo, and he'd hurt it again when he'd pushed her out of the way of gunfire. Yet... She looked around the room for the bottles of painkillers, but saw none. Spying the bathroom door, she pushed through it and checked around the sink and in the medicine cabinet. No pills there, either.

She believed he wasn't a killer, but was it possible he really wasn't a drug user anymore, either? He'd implied as much when they'd talked at the jail, when he'd hinted she'd ended their relationship based solely on suspicion rather than any actual betrayal. What if it was true? What if he hadn't used drugs since before she'd broken up with him?

Despite the fact he was in significant pain?

The thought merely strengthened her belief in his innocence.

But why was he sticking to his charade? Maybe it wasn't to help the greater good, but to help someone specific. Who was he protecting? How bad could the threat be?

She stepped out of the bathroom only to find him sitting on the bed now, his face in his hands. When they'd made love, he'd kept his clothes on. She hadn't gotten to see him au natural or feel him that way, either. Now she stared at him, noting the differences in his body. He'd always been lean with nice muscles but there was a definite toughness that hadn't been there before, and she couldn't help wondering what those bigger muscles would feel like under her fingers, or taste like under her tongue.

Realizing where her thoughts had led her, she jerked her gaze up only to see him staring back at her, his eyes dark and heated rather than in pain. She stepped closer, wanting to take what he was offering, intentionally or not. Wanting to remind herself what it was like to be loved by this man who looked so different but who still inspired the same feelings of peace and pleasure and contentment in her body even as he challenged and frustrated her.

It was Tony's duality that had always drawn her to him, she realized. The darkness she'd sensed under his sweet, affable facade. The darkness that was even more apparent now. As much as she'd hated his addiction, she also felt guilty because it was his layers and complexity that made him who he was.

And that hadn't changed.

"Do you want me to call 911?" she asked. "Get an ambulance for you?"

He shook his head. "I'm fine, Linda. And I'll be even better when you're gone. Get me Justine. She's the one I really want. If you don't believe me, ask her exactly what I did—who I did—after I left you."

He stared at her challengingly and despite the denial on her lips, she hesitated.

He *looked* like he was telling the truth. But it couldn't be. He wouldn't have done that to her.

She sucked in a quick breath, then practically felt her hope and determination deflate. Weariness overcame her.

This was ridiculous. She didn't know what way was up anymore. She couldn't distinguish the truth from lies. Tony didn't want her here. Whatever his reasons were, maybe she just needed to accept that. "Fine," she said. "I won't bother you again."

She left, her movements slow and robotic. She glanced around for Justine so she could deliver Tony's message, but couldn't find her. She was outside by the time she spotted the beautiful brunette, who was talking on the phone in hushed tones, her back to Linda.

"Nicco, now that Guapo's gone, you need to listen to Tony. He's smart. He's going to take us places Guapo never could. He's finally made contact with Guapo's Rapture supplier. That's going to be just the beginning."

Linda's heart pounded, the sound so loud she couldn't hear Justine's next words. She'd been wrong. So very wrong. There it was. Undeniable proof that Tony was working to take over Guapo's place as a drug supplier.

He was right. Whether he still cared about her didn't matter. Just like always, he didn't care nearly enough for it to matter.

She turned away and quickened her steps until she reached the street, wanting only to get out of there. She'd barely rounded the corner of the house when a familiar feeling caused her skin to prickle. It was the exact feeling she'd felt just before Guapo's men had attacked her in the courthouse parking lot.

Chapter 17

Linda's breath seized when a man emerged from the shadow of the house and grinned tauntingly at her.

"Going someplace?"

She averted her gaze, pretended she didn't hear him, and kept walking. He stepped in front of her, blocking her way. Tilting her chin up, she said, "I don't want trouble."

He waggled his brows up and down. "You found it anyway." He reached out to touch her face and she automatically flinched away, hating herself for the involuntary show of fear.

"I'm a friend of Tony's," she said quickly, hoping the lie would help rather than hurt her.

"Is that right?" the man said. He dropped his hand. "You should choose your friends more carefully."

"What do you mean? He runs the show here now, doesn't he?"

"Maybe. For now."

"You planning on changing that? Because he murdered Guapo to keep his territory. What makes you think he won't do the same to you?"

He shrugged then grinned. "Maybe because I know who his friends are now and a man who cares about others is a man with a weakness. You should—"

"Carl, what's going on?"

At the sound of Tony's voice, Linda whirled around and barely managed to suppress a sigh of relief. Tony was wearing a pair of jeans but nothing else, and though she could see he was still slightly unsteady on his feet, he glared at them—at her—with hostility.

"Who the hell is she?" he snapped.

The guy Tony had called Carl laughed, the sound laden with nerves. "She said she was a friend of yours."

"She's no friend of mine. Finish with her fast. I have a delivery for you to make." Without even looking at her again, he turned and stalked back to the house.

She watched him with disbelief. He had to know that Carl had stopped her. And that leaving her in his company could be dangerous to her.

Carl glared at her. "Lying bitch. Who were you here to see?"

"She was here to see me," Justine said. "Our business is over. Let her go, Carl."

"Why'd she say she was a friend of Tony's?"

"She wants to be but he's not interested."

"Hmm…I'm plenty interested."

"You've got a job to do," she reminded him.

He nodded. "I'll come find you when I have some free time, lady."

With a lingering look, he left. Swallowing hard, Linda turned to Justine. "Thank you," she said.

The other woman smiled tightly and shook her head. "Don't thank me. I won't interfere again. I suggest you don't come back here. You're not wanted."

No, she thought, she wasn't. Tony had dismissed her quite easily, leaving her to the hands of one of his lackeys. She'd gladly give him and Justine what they wanted.

She wouldn't be back.

Tony had thought it was the hardest thing he'd ever done—letting Linda walk away from him and out of the dingy house that was now his home. Especially now, after they'd made love. She'd expressed her faith in him and he wasn't being watched by guards. He was a free man. Free to do whatever he wanted. And what he wanted—*who* he wanted—was Linda.

He'd still managed to let her go.

But then Justine had told him that Carl was hassling Linda. He'd had to do something, but, not wanting to make matters worse, he'd forced himself to pretend he didn't care and this time walked away himself. He hadn't wanted to. He'd felt an intense urge to rip Carl away from her. To pound on him. But he'd hung back and waited, ready to move fast if Carl didn't follow him quickly enough. But luckily enough the man had and Tony had sent him off to make some runs.

As for Linda?

He should have been happy with the fact she'd made it past Carl unscathed, but he couldn't leave it at that. She actually believed he'd made love to Justine after leaving her bed.

And even though that's what he'd wanted her to believe, even though driving her away had been exactly what he'd wanted, he'd changed his mind. He couldn't let her believe it. Not that.

At seven that night, almost twenty-four hours after being there and just two hours before he was supposed to meet with the Rapture supplier, Tony drove to Linda's house. Standing outside, he peeked into her living-room window.

She sat on the sofa, her knees drawn up to her chest, the television on. She'd buried her face in her hands and her body shook with sobs.

Damn it.

The sight of her pain, the pain that he'd caused her, filled him with regret. He turned to stride toward the door. To knock. To demand she let him inside. But then her phone rang.

He froze as she wiped her tears, took several deep breaths then picked it up.

Since she'd cracked her window open to let in the breeze, he could just barely make out what she was saying. But he did hear the name "Neil."

He frowned. Neil Christoffersen. The suit who was panting after her.

The man who could offer her so much more than Tony ever could, starting with a clean past and a bright future. Both of which would serve her well as a judge.

Rage and denial filled him, but what could he deny. It was true. Between the two of them, Neil was definitely the better man for her. All he had to do was look at the drying tear streaks on her face to know that.

They made small talk and he was about to turn away and leave when he heard her mention his name.

He stiffened.

"I went to see him. I know, I know. It was stupid of me. I saw his girlfriend, too. She was on the phone when I left. She didn't know I was listening and I…I think Tony was telling the truth about killing Guapo so he could take over his business." She sighed. "Yeah, I know what I heard potentially makes me a witness, but it's hearsay and it doesn't fall into any of the exceptions, so there's no point in putting me on the stand." She paused. "He's said incriminating remarks to me, yes, but…I don't know, Neil. I don't know if I can actually testify against him." She bent her head and Tony's fists clenched at the agony that she must be going through.

"I'll call if I need anything. Thanks."

She hung up the phone and once again stared at the television with a blank face.

He simply watched her. Soaked her in. He stood there, unsure what to do. Should he go in and tell her the truth, or at least part of it, just like he'd planned? Or should he do the right thing and let her get on with her life with a good man?

A faint noise coming from the other side of the house disturbed his mental gymnastics. His first thought was—maybe Yee had sent some cops to check on Linda just like he'd promised. But a cop would be doing a drive-by in a patrol car or would be coming up the walkway to knock on her door, not sneaking around the side of her house.

Unless of course, the cop was a dirty one.

Just because Guapo was dead didn't mean the dirty connections he'd built had died along with him.

Slowly he moved to investigate, tensing when he saw a hulking figure in black clothes and a mask.

Damn it, what was going on? Was this a random break-in? No, that would be too coincidental. This had something to do with the shooting at the courthouse.

The guy was here to hurt Linda. The question was whether it was because of him.

Linda heard the sound of struggling outside and jumped to her feet. She ran to the window, looked out and gasped.

Tony was outside her house, wrestling with a much larger man wearing a freaking ski mask. Quickly she retrieved her Taser and ran outside. She turned the corner just in time to see the larger man punch Tony in the face, then kick his bad leg. Tony crumpled, but even as he did he hung on to the man, refusing to let go. Though she pointed the Taser, she wasn't convinced she could hit the other man and not Tony.

"Stop or I'll shoot," she yelled.

The man looked up before he took off, jumping the side fence.

Linda ran to Tony.

He was bleeding from the nose and mouth, but otherwise his coloring was a pale sickly white. She knelt beside him, cradling his head in her lap. "Tony! What are you doing here? Who was that?"

He closed his eyes, struggled to breathe, then gasped, "Wanted to talk to you. But he was here. Danger."

More dangerous than him? she thought. She really wasn't sure that was possible.

"Let's—" She stopped before inviting him inside. She didn't want to leave him lying here, but it wouldn't be smart to invite him back into her house, either. "Stay here. I'll call the police."

He shook his head. "No. No police."

"Tony, we need to report this. You didn't do anything wrong, so you don't have to worry about being out on bail. I'll explain that you—"

He gripped her arm tighter, which made her gasp. "No police...damn it..."

She wasn't imagining the urgency in his grip or his tone. "Why?"

"He...the man. He—he was here to hurt you. And he might be a cop."

Chapter 18

Tony passed out with his head in her lap. Linda's panic spiked and hysteria threatened to break her control until she realized his breathing was normal, as was his pulse. Whatever was wrong with him wasn't life threatening— at least, not yet. He still needed medical attention. But he'd asked her not to call the police.

Did that mean she shouldn't call an ambulance, either?

She looked around but none of her neighbors had come outside to check on her. Based on the darkened windows, people were asleep and hadn't heard enough to think it was worth investigating. Though he'd always been lean, Tony was still considerably larger and heavier than her. So what was she going to do?

There was only one thing she could do. Get to safety. They couldn't stay here. What if the intruder came back? She needed to get him someplace safe, make sure he would be okay, and think. Only then would she decide whether to call the cops or not.

She bit her lip. Then, despite feeling slightly guilty, she patted him down to make sure he didn't have any weapons or needles on him. He didn't. That didn't necessarily mean he wasn't using or that he'd lied about taking over Guapo's business, but it *was* one more reason to bolster her faith in him.

Getting behind him, she tucked her hands under his armpits and with great effort slowly dragged him an inch at a time toward her car. As she did so, she kept a watchful eye on his face. He was still pale. At one point she reached down to lay her hand on his face and cursed. He was burning up with fever. Whatever he'd been fighting off earlier that evening had taken a firm hold. He'd had an infection in the hospital. She wondered if it had come back.

Inadvertently she glanced down and winced. His pant leg was stained with blood, making her again wonder if the fever was caused by some kind of infection.

She had to stop for a few seconds to catch her breath. As she did, she once more swept her hand over his face, missing the curls that she'd often tangled her fingers in when they were together. But the close-cropped hairdo did more than make him look tough. It made it impossible for him to hide from her. His features stood out and with them every hint of vulnerability that he possessed, especially because he was unconscious and unguarded.

He'd said he'd wanted to talk to her. About what? Had he changed his mind about wanting her help? Had he decided to come clean with her? Decided to trust her with the truth of whatever it was he was doing with the drug ring formerly run by Guapo? And why had he thought the intruder—the man who'd wanted to hurt her, he'd said—was a cop?

She bit her lip, knowing what she did now could have a momentous impact on her life. On her career. Certainly on her bid for a judgeship. Tony was out on bail but he'd been charged with a crime and her office was prosecuting him.

She should ignore what he said. She had no reason to trust him. He'd told her over and over again that he was a changed man. Usually when men said they'd changed, they meant for the better. Tony meant he was worse. A bad man. One who didn't care about her. Yet he'd saved her life once already. And if he was right about that man—whoever he was—being dangerous, he could very well have saved her life again.

And why did she keep thinking he was doing something that needed to be uncovered? Why couldn't she simply accept he was the addicted, opportunistic man he'd tried to convince her he was?

Because she still loved him.

And if she could love a truly bad man, not just a flawed one, then what would that make her?

Linda took Tony to the local E.R. but only because Pamela Dexter, a friend of hers, was the doctor on duty. She'd called beforehand to double-check she'd be there and even then she'd known she was taking a calculated risk. That Tony, if he were conscious, would argue against going. But she couldn't just drive away with him when she didn't know for sure what they were dealing with.

Tony gained consciousness on the way to the hospital, but just barely. As she'd expected, he argued when she told him she was taking him to the E.R., but she simply ignored him, and he was too weak to argue for long. When they got to the hospital, medical staff helped him inside.

Pam owed her a favor and saw Tony right away. At least he hadn't been shot, otherwise Pam would have had to report his injuries to the police. He'd suffered a light concussion and had gotten another infection.

"You said he got into a fight at the jail?"

"Yes."

"That explains the infection, then. A jail's not the most sterile of places and if he'd been bleeding after the assault… We'll get him started on the meds and have him stay overnight—"

"No," Tony said.

"Excuse me?" Pam asked, looking first at Tony and then back at Linda.

"Tony," Linda began. "You need to listen to her. If she wants you to—"

He stood and began to dress. "I'm leaving, Linda. And so are you. We can't stay here." When she remained silent, he paused, taking several deep breaths and obviously struggling to stay focused. Finally he stepped close to her, leaned down and whispered in her ear. "Please. I know I haven't given you any reason to, but please trust me. Take me to a hotel and let me get better before you do anything. I'll explain everything to you then. I promise." He stepped back.

After a second, she nodded. "Okay."

Relief swept over his face.

"Are you taking him home? If so, I'll give him his first round of antibiotics and a prescription for more," Pam said.

Linda nodded. But she didn't say whose home she'd be taking him to.

She wasn't going to take him to a hotel. She had a better place. Someplace more private. Not his home, though. And not even hers.

She was going to take him to the vacation home in Grass Valley. The home her father had deeded to her for some reason.

She hadn't been there in years. During her youth, her family had stayed at the cabin on the creek during the summer, or over winter break. She'd loved the times they'd spent there—sleeping outside under mosquito netting, catching crawdads in the creek, and later, when she was older, hanging out with the neighbor boys who grew a pot patch in the woods and who would take her to the river and get her drunk.

After her father had betrayed her family for the last time, she'd never gone back. She still made sure the taxes were paid and she used a property manager to rent out the property to people wanting to vacation in the idyllic Gold Country. The place was vacant right now, but it would be clean and would have electricity. She figured it would be a while before someone could track her down. That would give her time to think, to plan, without having to worry about whether they were in danger by any of Guapo's men or, if Tony was right, by a dirty cop.

As she drove the winding country highway that would take them to the cabin, she called and left a message for her secretary. Briefly she explained she wasn't feeling well and would need another deputy to take over her caseload for a few days. After a brief hesitation she also asked her secretary to inform Norm that she wouldn't be able to make the fund-raiser tomorrow night, either. "Please give everyone my apologies," she said, even as she winced. Norm would be furious. She'd likely lose votes, too. But she had no choice. There was obviously something more important at stake here.

After hanging up, she kept an eye on Tony, whose head was cradled in the crook of his arm as he leaned against the passenger's side window. Had the man fighting with Tony in front of her house truly been a dirty cop? Dirty cops were a part of life, she knew. Just last year it had been discovered that a cop who'd worked with Dom Jeffries, Mattie's husband, had been working for Guapo. The cop had been charged with everything from assault to kidnapping to murder, then been killed at the hands of a fellow inmate in jail. Though the cop's killer wasn't talking, people pretty much assumed the cop had been killed to prevent him from testifying against Guapo.

It was no wonder the people of Sacramento were feeling shaky about government corruption. There'd even been allegations that Guapo had invaded the District Attorney's Office, though Linda had never believed it. The District Attorney, Norm Peterson, was one of the most honest men she knew. And though Brian Heald wasn't her favorite person in the world, she couldn't even imagine him, let alone any of the others that she worked with, being on the take. That went double for Neil. He enjoyed his job and ambition too much. Plus he had money from a trust fund his grandmother had left him. Assuming what he'd told her about that had been the truth, that is. She had her secrets, after all. It probably stood to reason that others did, too.

She turned off the highway onto a gutted dirt road, wincing with sympathy for Tony as the car bounced over a pothole. Soon, however, she parked the car and stared at the two-story cabin with faded gingham curtains on an isolated plot of land. She'd traveled an hour from Sacramento to this place that would always hold mixed memories for her. And she'd done it for one reason only—to keep them safe. She and Tony.

Watching over him, being his partner at the moment, felt right in a way few things ever had.

She looked over at Tony. He was still unconscious and the silence in the car was the perfect backdrop for doubt to sweep over her.

Was she seriously going to take him into the house she'd once lived in with her father and mother, the one she hadn't been back to, not even after her father had left it to her? Was she going to buy into the paranoid observations of a man that, for all she knew, was having delusional side effects because of the drugs he was taking?

But she had to be fair. She'd concluded at the place he was staying that he might not be taking drugs, after all. He'd seemed genuinely afraid for her safety back at her house. And she couldn't deny the fact that he'd hurt himself trying to protect her. Twice.

So she'd give him the benefit of the doubt and do what she needed to keep them safe. Even if it meant having to face a past she'd hoped never to face again.

Chapter 19

Tony had been jolted to consciousness several minutes
ago and now had to grit his teeth to keep from groaning.
Linda drove slowly over a road full of potholes—moon
craters were more like it—and despite the obvious care
she took not to go too fast and to maneuver around the
biggest dips, every rocking movement of the car caused
pain to zing through him, refusing to let him pass out
again. Instead of telling her he was awake, however,
Tony kept his eyes shut and his head in the crook of
his arm. When Linda finally brought the car to a halt,
set the emergency brake and turned the engine off, he
still didn't open his eyes.

Couldn't open his eyes.

The shooting spears of pain up his back and his leg
was a type of pain he was used to. But the ache in his
head, in his joints, in the very marrow of his bones?
It was the same pain he'd been in in the hospital after

Guapo had been killed. A pain he'd hoped never to experience again. The pain of infection.

Just like it had in the hospital, his blood boiled beneath the surface of his skin, through all arteries and veins, heating him up from the inside out. At some point during their trip he remembered Linda stopping at a pharmacy to pick up antibiotics and codeine. Codeine he wasn't going to take.

The pain was enough to deal with right now. He couldn't risk being doped up, too.

Linda's life had been threatened again. Plus, he'd missed his appointment with the Rapture supplier. If the meeting had been a scam, one meant to ensure he wasn't around when Linda was attacked, then he needed every clearheaded advantage he could get. And if the meeting had been legit, well, he'd have to come up with a damn good excuse for standing the supplier up in hopes of convincing him to give him another chance.

First, however, he needed to figure out where Linda had taken him.

Some out-of-the-way hotel? Given the condition of the road they'd just traveled, Tony wasn't too keen on seeing what the hotel looked like.

"Tony?" Linda whispered his name from the driver's seat.

He couldn't fake unconsciousness any longer. Couldn't stay in the car forever. He forced his eyes open, the mere action of lifting his lids causing another blast of pain. *Oh, God.*

"We're here," she said, her voice still soft.

This time he looked at her, and another ache swarmed through his heart. The concern in her eyes, the deep wrinkles in her forehead, the way she held her body tight and curved in, as if scared for him, made him want to erase his very existence from her life.

He could handle the pain of his injuries and the infection, but he couldn't handle the pain of knowing he was hurting her. Again.

He pulled his gaze off hers and slowly, slowly straightened until he could see out the car window. To his surprise he saw not a hotel but towering pines, filtered moonlight and a faded log cabin. The faint murmur of running water came through the window, which was open a crack. "Where are we?" he asked.

"Just outside Grass Valley," Linda answered, her voice tight.

"Why?"

"My family used to vacation here and now I own the property. Someone could probably track down that fact eventually, but I figure I've bought us a few days, at least."

"A few days for what?" He clenched his teeth to keep in his groan. The pain brought by speaking undulated like waves through his body. Still, his mind imagined spending a few days in paradise with Linda with nothing but time to hold one another and talk. Too bad he couldn't talk about anything that was the truth. Faced with that knowledge and what would be her inevitable questions, all he wanted was to slide back into oblivion.

"We need to get you inside," Linda said. "Can you walk?"

Sure. All he had to do was make his way into her house, then he could find a bed to collapse on. No biggie.

But when he tried to stand, his body betrayed him. The world spun and he closed his eyes. She'd better hurry, or he'd pass out again.

She quickly unclicked her seat belt and came around to his side of the car. "I'm opening your door, Tony. Don't fall out."

It took five minutes, but between Linda's arm around his waist, the flashlight she carried in her other hand to illuminate their path and her murmured words of encouragement, he made it inside the log cabin and onto the bed in some dark back bedroom. There he lay, shaking and sweating profusely.

"Thanks. I'm gonna sleep."

"Only for an hour. I have to wake you up every hour and ask you questions, just like the doctor said. I can also give you some codeine to make you more comfortable. But first…you're soaking, Tony. We need to get your clothes off."

Now weren't those wonderful words to hear? His mind immediately filled with visions of their entwined bodies. Had it been just yesterday that he'd had her? Been loved by her, at least physically? But he knew she viewed him asexually right now. Probably like a child. The thought made his voice harsher than he'd intended. "Leave me alone, Linda," he bit out.

Her expression pinched with hurt and he forced himself to look away.

He needed to be alone.

In the dark.

Fighting off the pain.

He needed her to leave. He didn't deserve her. He was flawed. Had made too many mistakes.

He should leave right now. But he couldn't.

He was suddenly freezing.

Why was he so cold?

Why was Linda's voice so far away?

Why was the world spinning, even though his eyes were closed?

And why, oh, why, couldn't he stop himself from reaching out for her?

Seeing Tony turn and reach for her, as if he couldn't help himself, nearly brought tears to Linda's eyes.

Linda swallowed hard, then pulled off his clothes, even his underwear. She did it to make him comfortable and make sure he got better, but part of her couldn't help but react to his nakedness. She'd felt him inside her when they'd made love. Seen more of his naked body when they'd been at his house on Tortuga. But now he was completely and totally naked, unable to hide from her devouring eyes. She took in the familiar things about his body and the things that had changed.

There was the mole, just above his right nipple, that she loved to kiss.

He was more heavily padded with muscle. The ridges of his abdomen more defined. And below that…

Even soft, Tony was impressive. And familiar. So familiar.

She felt the warmth of arousal but more than that, she felt a pang of deep affection for this man. She wanted to cradle him and tell him everything was going to be okay. But she couldn't know that.

Gently she washed him down with a cool wet cloth. Afterward she took his temperature and did it again every half hour just as her friend Pam had instructed. His temperature hovered between 100 and 102, which was better than the 104 it had been at the hospital.

But she'd continue to keep vigil over him to make sure he didn't relapse.

The evening transformed into dawn and Tony's fever

continued to rage on, causing him to occasionally thrash on the bed. At one point he became so restless that she left the wicker rocking chair to sit on the side of the double bed.

She smoothed her palm over his face and he quieted. As he slept, she let her mind wander to the past. Not their past together, but her past before she'd ever met him.

This had been her parents' room when she was young—she and Kathy had shared the room up on the second story, the one tucked in the eaves, where she'd read books and dreamed through her summer days. That is, until the neighbor boys had noticed her and had taken her under their wing. She'd quickly learned how to ditch a sleeping Kathy by clambering out the window onto the broad-sloped roof and grabbing hold of the oak branch close by, then swinging herself down to the ground.

She'd been twelve the first time she'd snuck out of the house. Fifteen the last time.

The white cotton sheet she'd covered Tony with after removing his sweat-drenched clothes was now tangled between his thighs. She moved to pull the covering up, over his chest, and he shifted.

"God, it hurts," Tony moaned.

Of course he hurt. He'd been beaten by Guapo and then Larry Moser when he'd stuck up for that kid in lockup. Then he'd had the wind knocked out of him when he'd saved her from the drive-by shooting, been attacked at her house and was now feeling the effects of a raging infection. How much pain could one man stand?

"I'm sorry," she murmured, holding his hand in hers. "I know it hurts. I wish I could take your pain away. But you're strong, Tony. You'll get through this." Then she remembered the codeine she'd picked up. Since Pam had administered the first dose at the hospital, Tony wasn't due more antibiotics yet, but she could give him some codeine for the pain. "Let me get your pills, Tony."

He shook his head almost frantically. "Don't go. God, Linda, don't go. I don't need pills. I never did. All I need is you."

A tight knot formed in her belly and pressed upward, under her ribs. He was delirious. Didn't know what he was saying. But yet she knew he was finally speaking the truth to her. At least the truth as he believed it to be at the moment.

He didn't want her to leave him. And that was a really good thing.

Because she wasn't going anywhere.

Her hands shook as she stroked his face with light fingertips. "I won't go, Tony," she whispered. "I'm here. Right here."

Tony moaned, and settled. Linda waited, stroking his head as if reassuring a small child. One more shift in position, then his breathing grew slow and steady. His facial muscles relaxed as he finally fell into a deep sleep. The knot pressing against her heart untied itself.

It was nearly noon when Linda began to feel faint from hunger. After visiting Tony at his house on Tortuga Boulevard, she'd been too upset to eat. And eating had certainly been the last thing on her mind while nursing Tony. Now, however, she needed to take advantage of the fact Tony was sleeping peacefully.

Going to the kitchen, she scrounged in the pantry for something to eat. Instant noodles or pasta with marinara sauce seemed one of the few options. Not exactly what she preferred to eat for breakfast, but she'd have to make do. She put a pot of water on to boil, and then grabbed her gym bag out of the trunk of her car. The clothes in it were old and stale from the last time she'd worked out, but they'd have to do. She hadn't exactly taken time to pack after Tony had warned her a dirty cop was trying to hurt her.

Quickly she showered, threw her dirty clothes into the washer, then went into the kitchen to prepare a meal of rigatoni and marina sauce, with canned marinated artichoke hearts on the side. As she ate, she played the messages that had built up on her cell phone over the morning, taking notes with a pen filled with fake gold flakes—*Welcome to the Gold Country!*—on a pad of yellowed paper she found in one of the kitchen drawers.

Her boss, District Attorney Norman Peterson, had called twice. A deputy from the Sacramento County Sheriff's Department had called. And Neil had called five times.

Lord, what was she going to tell them? Court had already begun and her secretary had likely already scrambled to find another attorney to sub for her. A flood of guilt filled her for her irresponsibility. *Oh, give yourself a break, Linda.*

She'd almost been gunned down yesterday. Seemed like a good excuse to take some time off.

She called Norm and left a message on his work phone, letting him know she needed some down time before returning to work. Then she returned Neil's calls.

He answered on the second ring. "Linda. Where the hell have you been?"

Was that concern or censure she heard in his tone? "I just got your messages, Neil. I'm sorry I didn't call earlier. Something important came up."

"Something more important than getting shot at or

your cases that are set for hearing this morning? Damn it, I thought you were dead. That whoever it was that shot at you had tried again."

Okay, so that was definitely both concern and censure she was hearing. She bit her lip and mentally formulated her words before speaking again. She didn't want Neil to know that she'd gone to see Tony, let alone that they were together. She was treading a thin line between professional standards and reckless behavior, yes, but no matter what Tony had done, no matter what he'd become, he was helpless to defend himself right now. Bottom line, he'd saved her and she was returning the favor.

"Neil," she said, "that shooting affected me more than I expected. I'm still shaky, and I need to take some time away. I've called and left Norm a message and I'm sure he'll understand."

Neil chuffed out a breath. "I'm sure he'll understand, but I'm not sure *I* do. When you didn't return my messages, I went by your place. One of your neighbors told me she saw two men scuffling in your yard, and that you'd hit them with a Taser. Yet you didn't file a report with the police and you certainly haven't said anything at all about that."

Damn. She'd thought no one had seen what had happened.

But nearsighted neighbors aside, there was something else causing her concern. Since when did Neil talk to her in that superior, condescending way? Her first instinct was to call him on his domineering behavior, but since she didn't want to arouse his suspicions any more than she had and because she wanted to get back to Tony… "Was it Mrs. Whitlock?" she asked with a little laugh. "The little old lady in the house to the right of my place? The one with all the wooden ducks?"

"One and the same." She could almost picture Neil rubbing the back of his neck. "And I think those are geese."

"Right. Well, Mrs. Whitlock is retired from the Post Office and has plenty of time to peer out her windows and spread gossip. She's never used this much imagination, though."

"So what she said about two men—"

"There *were* two men in my yard, but they weren't scuffling"—that wasn't quite a lie—"and I can promise you I absolutely did not Taser anybody." Although she had come close, she thought. Given sufficient reason, she knew she wouldn't have hesitated to hit the other man with a thousand volts of electricity to save Tony.

And what did that say about her? About them together?

"Then who were the men, Linda? And where are you? After what happened to you yesterday, I want to make sure you're safe."

His words made her feel better about his high-handed manner earlier. She'd trusted Neil enough to let him handle Tony's case, and she wanted to trust him now…

But Tony's words about dirty cops, along with her own knowledge of them, as well as dirty judges and murdering drug dealers, kept her cautious. "I had a couple of male friends over, that's all. They were goofing off."

"Male friends." More censure in his voice. And a hint of jealousy? "And where are you now?"

Such an innocuous, reasonable question, but it made her nervous. Or was it suspicious? "I'm taking some time off to ground myself. You know how tough it's been for me to see Tony again…and now, with the shooting, well…"

"I don't think you should be alone, Linda. Let me—"

"Please don't worry, Neil. I'm fine. Really. Good-bye."

After she hung up, she thought about what she'd said.

Was she going to be fine?

Not until Tony was healthy again and out of whatever bind he was in.

Not until her heart stopped aching every time she caught a glimpse of him.

Not until her breath stopped whooshing out of her lungs every time he said her name.

No, she wasn't fine, and she didn't know if she'd ever be fine again.

In his dreams, Tony's past, present and future merged into disorienting vignettes that bled into each other. The only constant in them was Linda, and that's what kept him from fighting his way to consciousness. Even when being with Linda caused him pain, it was so much better than the chilling, hollow feeling he felt without her, knowing he was never going to be with her again.

Linda caressed his face. Murmured reassurances. Tucked a blanket around him when he was cold and gave him water when he was hot. She also recognized when he was in pain, and though she didn't promise to take it away, she held his hand and promised him she wouldn't leave. And that was enough.

In his dreams Tony had been granted a second chance to be with the woman he loved, and he wanted nothing more than to stay with her forever.

Only that feeling of blissful oblivion was a little too familiar.

It was the same feelings he'd sought the drugs for.

And those feelings had never lasted. Not only that, but they'd destroyed everything he'd treasured. And something told him that if he wanted Linda, really wanted her outside of his dreams, he couldn't allow himself to luxuriate in a life without constant pain.

As hard as it was, he needed to face reality. For reality always intruded, and if he didn't face it himself, he'd spend it alone again. For an eternity.

Despite how heavy they were, he forced his eyes open.

His vision was hazy. Still dreamlike.

But he could sense her beside him. Feel her hand in his.

He tightened his fingers, holding on to her like a lifeline, and eventually his vision cleared and she came into view.

His breath seized.

He knew he was no longer dreaming, yet she *looked* like a dream. One he'd had on many occasions. It was as if their years apart had never happened.

Her hair was loose, her face bare of makeup and she was wearing a familiar-looking T-shirt, one of his, that she'd often worn to bed.

"I've been looking for that shirt," he murmured.

She blushed, looking slightly guilty, then tipped up her chin. "You left it behind."

"And you didn't burn it. Why?"

"Why would I burn it, Tony? Breaking up with you wasn't what I wanted. It was just what needed to be done."

She tugged her hand away from his. For a second he tightened his grip, wanting to hold on to her, but then he forced himself to let go. Of her. Of their past.

He wanted what was good for her.

He had to remember that.

So what had changed? Why was he—

Memories flooded in. Not of their past, so long ago, but of their *recent* past. The drive-by. Her catching him in her neighborhood and them making love.

God, he still couldn't believe they'd made love. Even in pain, the memory just made him want her more. And he'd wanted her so badly already.

Linda coming to his house. Him following her home. The big man outside her house. A man he suspected might have been sent by Yee. Either way, Linda had been in danger. His gaze flew to hers. "The police. Did you—"

She frowned, then slowly shook her head. "I haven't called anyone. After what you said, after what happened with that dirty cop before, I thought it was best if I waited."

He sighed with relief. For some reason she'd trusted him and done what he'd asked.

She picked up a bottle from the nightstand and poured something into a spoon. "You need to take some antibiotics."

Dutifully, he opened his mouth for the spoon and swallowed down the bitter-tasting medicine, then some water from the glass she offered.

As she fiddled with recapping the bottle, he looked around the room, his vision still coming and going in waves. Knotty pine walls. An old dresser. Red-and-white-checkered curtains fluttered in a gentle breeze that smelled of mint and wet earth. The trickle and hum of a creek sounded nearby.

"This is your folks' old place, right?" he asked, trying to raise himself up in the bed. Dizziness hit, and with it, nausea. He groaned and closed his eyes.

Linda put down another medicine bottle she'd been looking at—the codeine—and helped ease him back down to the bed.

"Yes. You remember me telling you that when we got here?"

He shifted, the cotton sheet cool against his skin. Wait a minute… He pulled the sheet up and peered down. "I remember you driving me here. I don't remember you getting me naked."

He looked up in time to see Linda blush furiously, her cheeks now on fire. If he wasn't so exhausted, he'd grin.

"Your clothes needed to come off. They were covered in sweat and even a little blood. You should be in the hospital, but since you vehemently objected to that option, we're hiding out here, where we're safe. At least, we're safe long enough for you to get back on your feet."

But why had she brought him here? Why had she trusted him when she should be hating him? Running from him?

Because she'd believed what he'd told her.

But was that a good thing or a bad thing? Nothing had changed. It couldn't be coincidence that as soon as he'd shown up, she'd been put in danger.

Yet she refused to give up and walk away. She'd keep digging until she got answers and he was becoming less and less willing to deprive her of them.

Weak, he thought again. He'd always been weak, but especially so where Linda was concerned.

And it didn't matter. He couldn't help thinking about being with her again. In her bed. And maybe in this one. But even if he didn't make love to her again, he was with her.

And that meant everything to him.

He covered his face with a hand. Nausea pounded him from the inside and this time he actually focused on the pain that had been hovering at his subconscious.

"Talk later," he managed to get out.

"Wait. Let me give you some codeine—"

"Later," he repeated and closed his eyes.

"Later," Linda whispered, and then was gone.

Chapter 20

Linda made sure Tony was sleeping again, returned the antibiotics to the fridge, wrote him a note, then drove into town and headed for the little mom and pop grocery store she vaguely remembered from her youth. When she pulled in front, she remembered how the guy behind the counter used to let her and Kathy pick a candy out of the candy display every time their mom took them there.

It was nice to ponder memories from her childhood that weren't so painful.

She slowly maneuvered her cart down the aisles, noticing how familiar even the clientele seemed. Two kids in bathing suits and flip-flops, hair still wet, followed their harried mother up and down the aisles. Just like how she used to follow her mom down the aisles after her mom would pick her up from the local pool.

An elderly woman leaned on her cart in the frozen food aisle, happily chatting with a young New Ager—

the twentysomething woman was clad in a long tie-dyed dress and had an exotic head scarf covering her wild hair. It reminded her of a scarf Kathy had owned at one time.

Linda found herself smiling. Sure, there were a few new stores in town, but not much had changed since she'd stayed here as a kid.

So many things had changed, though.

She'd changed.

And Tony had changed, as well—at least that's what he was claiming.

But had he really?

Automatically she found herself picking out things in the produce aisle that she knew from personal experience he liked. Surely his taste in food hadn't changed. So long as he continued to get better, they'd only be holed up here for a day or two. Just long enough for him to tell her the truth about what was going on.

But then what?

Would he go back to Justine and…

She froze at her mental reminder that Tony had a girlfriend.

She slammed to a stop in front of the pears. Was she crazy? She was buying ingredients to make chicken soup for the man. She was playing Florence Nightingale to an addict and admitted murderer who had a girlfriend, she reminded herself.

And don't forget that she'd slept with him. A man who belonged to another woman, no matter how she still thought of him as hers.

Shame rocked through her. She'd been the one to initiate that kiss with Tony back at her house. That it had exploded into something more than she'd been expecting didn't matter. She'd known he had a girlfriend. She, not Linda, should be here taking care of him.

She maneuvered her cart filled with groceries to the checkout stand with leaden feet. When had things gotten so crazy?

She contemplated the question as she unloaded her groceries onto the conveyer belt, startled when the portly man behind the cash register suddenly said, "Hey, there. You look familiar. You're not Chuck Delaney's kid, are you?"

Her heart picked up its pace at the sudden mention of her father. A man she detested. She stared at the checker, who still held her arugula in one hand, as if frozen in motion until she responded to him. "Excuse me?"

"It's just…well, you're the spitting image of him. Except way prettier. And I know he has daughters. Just wondering if you're one of them."

She hesitated but knew she had no choice. She couldn't very well lie and then hand him a credit card with the last name Delaney, and she didn't have enough in her wallet to pay with cash.

"He was my father," she said stiffly. Though she watched the man carefully, he showed no sign of judgment or pity.

"I thought so. I wasn't sure. The pictures he had of you two were when you were young, but when I saw you…well…" His smile faded as Linda just looked at him, frowning.

Her father had shown this man photos of her and Kathy? How? But more importantly, why?

His daughters had been nothing to her father. He'd proven that time and time again. With every crime he'd committed. Every item he'd stolen. Every time he'd gotten caught and taken away, until he'd been taken away from his family forever.

"How did you see the photographs?" she asked.

The man whose name tag identified him as Fred finally put his attention back on ringing up her groceries. "Your dad sure was proud of you girls. He carried those pictures in his wallet and would show them to me when he was here. He did that practically until the day he—well, you know…"

She did know. Until her father had committed an armed robbery at the bank where her mother had worked.

Yes, she knew what the checker was referring to. Probably everyone in this small town did, too. The bust had been so big it had made the news in Sacramento, and soon thereafter her mother had moved them to Argyle, Texas, to start over.

And despite the fact that Linda had written her dad while he'd been in prison, he'd never bothered writing her back.

Linda went through the motions of paying for the groceries, then loaded the three bags into her car. When she got back to the cabin, she parked the car but didn't get out right away. The man named Fred had talked of her father as if he'd liked him…respected him. And what he'd said about her father carrying pictures of his daughters around? It had to be some kind of mistake, didn't it? Her father was a criminal. One who'd chosen a life of crime over his family. Over her.

Hadn't he?

When she returned from the store, Tony was still sleeping but his brow was once again hot. Frowning, she looked around for the bottle of codeine he'd gotten from the E.R. but she couldn't find it anywhere. She sat beside him. "Tony," she said gently.

He stirred and his eyes flickered open.

"Where's the codeine I picked up for you?"

Instead of answering her, he smiled broadly, looking happy to see her. He tried closing his eyes again.

"No, Tony. Wait." She'd looked everywhere, but couldn't find the damn bottle of pills. She'd put them on the kitchen table. She was certain of it. But whatever... Tony needed something to get his fever down now. She grabbed a glass of water and some Tylenol from the medicine cabinet, returned and shook him gently. "Tony, wake up. You need to take this."

His eyes flickered open and he frowned when his gaze landed on the aspirin she held.

"It's just plain Tylenol. Open your mouth," she whispered. Obediently he did, and she leaned over and placed the pills inside. Then she tipped the water glass to his mouth. He swallowed, but a trail of water spilled down his chin. "Sorry," she said, then dabbed it up with the paper towel she'd brought with her. "Sleep now."

And he did. He conked out for hours. When she went to check on him again, he was awake. Propped up by pillows and sitting up in bed. He didn't look well, but he looked better. More alert. And for some reason that made her nervous.

"Can I have more Tylenol?" he asked. "And maybe some mouthwash to get the cotton out of my mouth?"

She jolted. "Oh. Yes, sure." Like before, she helped him swallow the pills, then gave him some mouthwash, which he spit out in a bowl. But this time when she tried to move away, he gently grabbed her wrist. Holding on with one hand, he took the bowl with his other hand and set it on the nightstand.

"Linda…"

She froze at his touch and took in a breath. She suddenly wondered if he'd asked for the mouthwash because he'd wanted to do more than freshen his breath. He was no longer hot with fever, but his touch affected her as if he was. As if a bolt of lightning had streaked through her. Her abdomen clenched, and she swore she could feel the heat of his touch travel straight through her to land in that throbbing spot between her legs.

They stared at each other as if hypnotized. He swallowed convulsively and her gaze focused on his strong throat. The chin that was shadowed with stubble. The breadth of his bare shoulders. She wanted to lean down and rest her cheek against his chest. Hear the reassuring thud of his strong heartbeat and for a few moments forget that they were adversaries. But until Tony admitted that he'd been lying to her, that's exactly what they were. That hadn't changed simply because they'd made love again or because she was caring for him.

She started to pull away, but Tony's grip tightened.

"Wait. Don't—don't go."

She stilled and remembered the way he'd asked her to stay with him earlier.

Don't go, he'd said. *I don't need pills. I never did. All I need is you.*

"Tony," she began.

"Shhh." He pulled her closer toward him but his grip was gentle, a slight pressure she still couldn't resist.

He drew her down until her lips hovered just a fraction above his. Until she was staring into his beautiful brown eyes, and reacquainting herself with the small gold flecks in them that made them twinkle when he was happy.

Even now they twinkled and she closed her eyes in denial.

This was an impossible situation. His breath was an alluring whisper against her face and she wanted to whimper with the yearning that filled her. He pulled her even closer so that her forehead rested against his but that was all. He didn't kiss her.

But she wanted him to. She wanted him to make love to her again, even though she knew he was too sick to do such a thing right now.

She'd settle for a kiss, then.

Please, she thought. *Kiss me.*

She opened her eyes and blinked.

She hadn't spoken. And neither had he. But staring into his eyes, she heard the words anyway. Her own. But also his.

Kiss me, the look in his eyes begged.

And like a moth drawn to a flame, she couldn't resist the pull of his unspoken desire.

Her lips met his.

Tony knew this was a mistake. A huge mistake. But he didn't care.

Just as he had been at her house less than forty-eight hours ago, he was exactly where he most wanted to be, with his entire world focused on Linda and the feel of her lips on his. Her sweet clean scent wrapped around him in a comforting embrace. With a small whimper that might have come from either one of them, they opened their mouths, their tongues searching for each other's with unerring accuracy. She tasted good enough that he got dizzy and had to close his eyes and grab on to her. But even as his fingers rested on her shoulders, he kept his touch light, careful, not wanting to jar her out of the fantasy of their kiss lest she suddenly realize what they were doing and pull away.

Lest she suddenly remember what he'd said just to push her away—that he'd gone straight from her bed to Justine's.

"So good," he murmured. "You feel so good, Linda. I want you again."

She gave a slight sigh and angled her mouth to get a better taste of him. The kiss quickly turned urgent and Tony couldn't keep his touch gentle anymore. He plunged his fingers into Linda's hair and pulled her closer.

For a few blessed moments their world and their circumstances fell away and they simply reveled in being in each other's arms again.

Reality intruded when his cell phone rang.

Linda jerked away from Tony. Breathing hard, she stared at him, noting how the gold flecks in his eyes had darkened the way they always did when he was turned on. And he was definitely turned on. Pressed against him, she'd been able to feel his chest sucking in air and his body hardening for her. Maybe he wasn't too sick to make love after all.

He reached for her again, but she quickly stood.

She backed away from him, wiping at her mouth as she did so, as if by doing so she could erase the feel of his kiss. Not likely.

She reached into her pocket and pulled out his cell phone. The one she'd taken from him.

His eyes narrowed when she tossed it to him. It landed beside him with a small bounce.

"That's probably your girlfriend. I don't want her knowing about this place. If you want her to pick you up, I'll drive you someplace out of town. But not yet. First we need to talk."

He leaned back against the pillows. The phone's ringing abruptly stopped.

"I don't know what you want me to say."

"About your girlfriend? Nothing. You told me enough when you said you went from me to her. What I want to know is why you think a policeman was trying to break into my home and why that would cause you to fear for my safety. Because you *were* afraid for my safety. And that makes twice that you saved my life. Are you going to keep pretending that you're this big bad drug dealer in the face of that evidence? You're not a bad man, Tony."

"How can you say that? You, more than anyone, know I'm weak, and a weak man easily turns bad."

"Maybe you're not as weak as I thought. You threw the codeine away, didn't you?"

His gaze flickered away. Just for a second, but she saw it. "What makes you say that?"

"And that answers my question loud and clear."

Tony shrugged. "Even if you're right, so what? I don't want to get hooked on painkillers again. It doesn't pay to use drugs when you're dealing them. Cuts into the profits. That doesn't mean I'm not weak. Or bad."

"Whatever the reason, you're not doing it, and that still requires an enormous amount of willpower and strength. I'm glad you're clean."

Surprise and pleasure flashed across his face before he looked away and cleared his throat. "So now what?" he asked. Gingerly he tried sitting up but winced at how difficult it was.

"You want to tell me about what happened earlier?" she challenged.

"I'm much more about action than talking, you know. Why don't you come back here and I'll show you?"

She forced out a disbelieving laugh. "Are you crazy? After what you told me back at the house on Tortuga Boulevard?"

He had the decency to look guilty but quickly recovered. "Maybe you're the one who's crazy. After what I told you, why else would you have kissed me."

"Like you said earlier, we meant something to each other once. And as you know, some habits are harder to break than others. It meant nothing, just like our making love obviously meant nothing to you. Consider it something I gave you for old times' sake. But what I'd rather have right now is some answers. Tell me the truth about what's going on, Tony. There's no reason you can't be honest with me."

"Well now, Linda, that's where you're wrong. Because from what I seem to remember, honesty was never a good idea when I was around you. It made you more likely to abandon me than anything else. Isn't that right?"

"This is ridiculous. If you're not going to give me the answers that I want, then there's no point in us talking. I'm going to fix us something to eat. You rest while I do that. After I eat, I'll drive you back to Sacramento. Back to your real friends. To Justine, who is the woman you're supposed to be kissing, not me."

His lips pressed grimly together. "That's probably what you should do. I'm grateful you've taken care of me, but I've missed a very important meeting and I need to reschedule. Unfortunately I can't stand without falling on my ass. And have you forgotten that someone is trying to kill you? And that someone might be a cop?"

"So you say. But you also say you're a big bad drug

dealer. Either way, I'm not safe. From the dirty cop. Or from you."

With that, she slammed her way out of the room, willing the tears forming to stay at bay.

But they came anyway.

Later, when she'd gathered enough courage, she went in to check with Tony. She told herself that now that he was better, she would indeed drive him back to Sacramento. Only when she stepped into his room, she could tell immediately he'd relapsed. He was lying in bed, but he'd kicked off all his blankets, and before she even reached him she could tell he was shaking.

Once again, he was burning hot.

Helpless. Having to depend on her to take care of him.

And even though she shouldn't have felt relieved by any of that, she was.

Because it meant they'd have more time together. Here. Alone. Without the world or their past to intrude and ruin things.

It wouldn't last long, but for however long it lasted, Linda would enjoy it.

Chapter 21

Tony wasn't sure how much time passed while he fought off his infection. He spent his time sleeping or eating what Linda put in front of him. He vaguely remembered talking to her, even kissing her, but he wasn't sure whether he'd imagined it.

Then he opened his eyes. Feeling infinitely better and clearheaded, he knew his infection was gone. He also knew he hadn't imagined kissing Linda or making love to her at her house. He just wasn't sure what he was supposed to do about any of that now.

One thing he did know, however, was that he wanted to see her. Right now. So despite his stiff limbs and aching muscles, he slowly got out of bed, wrapped a sheet around his waist, and went in search of Linda.

He found her in the kitchen and paused in the doorway to watch her. Damn, she was beautiful, even dressed in running shorts and his old T-shirt, her hair down around her face. In all the time he'd known her, she'd always dressed in a pulled-together fashion at work—perfectly styled hair, perfectly applied makeup and never without lipstick. But at night, when it was just the two of them, she'd let down that perfect hairdo and would let her lipstick get kissed off. She'd end up smudged and smeared and would laugh, uninhibited. He'd always loved the fact that he got to see a side of her that no one else in the world did.

She'd been nursing him nonstop, but his mind kept replaying the last time they'd made love. There'd been something wonderfully familiar yet intoxicatingly new about holding her in his arms. As if they were both the same, yet different. The memory heated his blood, making his fingers curl with the need to hold her and draw her to him again.

As if she sensed where his thoughts had gone, she looked up. She blushed when she saw what he *wasn't* wearing. And then she frowned.

Abandoning the pot she'd been fiddling with, she moved toward him and clucked like a mother hen. "What are you doing out of bed? You should be resting some more."

She went to lay a hand on his forehead, but he stopped her, cradling her hand in his. "I'm feeling a hundred times better. You obviously nursed me back to health. Thank you."

"Oh." She stared at him for a few seconds, then blinked. Pulling her hand out of his, she nodded and took several steps back. "Oh, good. That's good. I'm glad you're feeling better."

"I've lost track of time. How long have we been here?"

"This is our third day here," she said.

He cursed. "That long?"

"That long," she said softly, then walked back to the stove. "We should probably wait to see if you have another relapse, but if you don't…we can head back to Sacramento." She looked at him again, an obvious question in her eyes.

Heading back to Sacramento was exactly what they should do, he thought. The problem was, he didn't want to go back. Not when he had the chance to stay here with Linda. But they'd been here for three days. Justine was probably worried sick about him. Plus, he'd missed his appointment with the Rapture supplier and needed to work on getting that rescheduled. And of course he couldn't forget about the man who'd been lurking outside Linda's house. He'd considered the possibility of a dirty cop, sure, but that wasn't the only possibility.

What a mess.

He didn't know what was going on.

For a second he considered asking for help. Maybe even calling Dom, Mattie's husband. The two of them had set up a way to get in touch in the event of an emergency, and he was thinking it was getting pretty darn close to that. However, calling Dom and bringing him into things meant risking the safety of someone his sister loved. Again. He didn't want that.

Besides, Dom wasn't here right now. Linda was. And she was a prosecutor, for God's sake. Even if someone in her office was dirty, *she* wasn't.

Maybe it was time to confide in her, after all. If he told her the truth, maybe he could convince her to stay at the cabin. Then he could continue his work in Sacramento and—

He shook his head. Right. And do what? Ask her to twiddle her thumbs until he had time to come visit here? Take the risk that someone would still find out about her and somehow get to her? No. Not an option.

So the charade would have to continue.

"I suppose we should head out," he said slowly, wondering if he imagined the disappointment that seemed to briefly flicker in her eyes.

She nodded. "Of course. I'm sure Justine misses you."

He frowned, wanting to shake her for that comment but knowing he had no right. He was the one who'd decided to pretend Justine was his girlfriend. Yet there'd been something he'd been wanting to tell her. Something that had driven him to go to her house before his arranged meeting with the Rapture supplier.

"I didn't sleep with her," he said abruptly. "After we were together. I—I just want you to know that."

Her instant relief was obvious. Licking her lips, she nodded. "Thank you for that, at least. But—but why tell me now?"

He shrugged. "You took care of me. You've always taken care of me. No matter what's happened between us, I owe you that much."

They gazed at one another until he was sure she could see every secret yearning he was harboring for her. With a mental curse, he turned away, mumbling that he was going to shower and dress.

He took his time in the shower, hoping it would wash away not only his lingering aches but the emotional weakness that seemed to have come with them. When he was done, he dressed then eyed the closed bedroom door and the limited floor space around the bed. Reluctant to face Linda again when he was still feeling so needy, he cautiously got down on all fours on the floor.

Before last week he'd been able to do one hundred

push-ups every morning. One hundred in the afternoon. One hundred before bed. Coupled with sit-ups, weight lifting, endurance running and mixed martial arts, all done despite the pain his back and leg caused him, his workout regimen had changed his body. He should be able to do at least a few dozen even now, right?

He managed to do a dozen before his arms caved. He went prone, the muscles in his pecs and biceps quivering.

Damn. He hated being so weak. It reminded him of when Sabon had kidnapped Mattie. How Tony had failed to protect her. How Tony had failed to protect Linda—

"Tony? Are you all right?" Worry filled Linda's voice.

Great. Just what he wanted Linda to see—him flattened by three minutes of working out. "I'm fine," he called. "I'm doing push-ups."

He heard her footsteps and cursed when he couldn't get to his feet quickly enough. For a moment silence filled the air, then he heard a snort. He rolled over and peered at Linda, who stood tall above him.

"Looks more to me like you were making out with the carpet. Maybe you should give your body a chance to heal before you push yourself too hard. Here," she said, coming to stand between his knees and offering him her hand. "I'll help you up."

He let her pull him up to standing but then, despite his best intentions, didn't release her hand even when she tugged it back.

"I wanted to check on you. Your food's waiting for you," she said, her voice breathy all of a sudden.

He swiped the back of her hand with his thumb in a slow caress. "Aren't you going to join me?"

She stared at him. Swallowed hard. Then took a deep measured breath. "No," she said, yanking her hand back with enough force that he automatically let go. "I'm going to go for a long walk. When I get back, we can leave."

He watched her walk away, acutely aware that his heart was racing harder and faster than it had been when he'd been exercising. And wondering how he was going to survive once she walked away from him for good.

Linda left the cabin even though what she really wanted was to stay. She wanted to repeat the kiss they'd shared. She wanted to make love to Tony again. She couldn't think of anything else she wanted more. She left because she didn't trust her own willpower.

She walked around the ten acres surrounding the cabin, bombarded by memories of when she'd been a little girl, and she and Kathy and their father had sometimes played hide-and-seek here. When he'd been around. He'd chase her and Kathy as they ran and giggled. Then he'd catch and tickle them.

Tony had used to tickle her, too. He'd go at her mercilessly until eventually the game turned into something altogether different, and then he'd go at her in the bedroom. They'd go at each other. He'd been the one man she'd felt comfortable letting go of all her inhibitions with. Maybe because he was wounded, like her. Maybe because he wasn't threatened by her professional success. She missed that. She missed reveling in who she really was instead of constantly having to guard against her true nature.

But if she wanted to be a judge—and a young one at that given she was only thirty-three—well, judges were held to a higher standard than even most people.

They couldn't be wild or impetuous or selfish. Quite the opposite, in fact. Judges were impartial and objective and fair. That was what being the woman underneath the robe was all about, right? Being a judge meant she needed to be without prejudice. Blind, like Lady Justice.

Could she be blind to her prejudices against others? To her prejudices about herself?

At one time she had been wild and impetuous and selfish.

Was that what was happening now?

Why else would she so strongly cling to the idea that Tony was innocent? Why would she have made love to him? Kissed him? Brought him here in the first place? Was she blind to the realities of who he really was?

But even as she asked the question, her faith in Tony's innocence didn't waver. Because she *had* kissed him. Tasted who he was now, not just in the past. And he was still sweet. Still good. Still—

Her cell phone rang. When she saw the caller was Neil, she hesitated. He'd called her six times in the past few days, leaving her voice mails every time. The last one he'd left had sounded serious.

With a sigh, she answered.

"Hi, Neil."

Ten minutes later Linda walked swiftly back to the cabin. Neil's words still rang in her ear.

A reporter has linked you and Tony Cooper. He's been asking questions. And implying that you had something to do with Tony being granted bail. He's also questioning the fact that you disappeared soon after he was released. Damn, I'm sorry, Linda. This isn't good. Not for your judicial campaign and not for...

He'd lapsed into silence, but Linda had known what he was about to say.

It's not good for my career as a D.A., either. I might very well lose my job over this, Neil, isn't that right?

Hell, I'm sorry, Linda. But don't worry. I'm on your side and so is Norm. We'll get our comments to the press. Assure them that you only took some time off because of what happened, not because you're with Tony.

She'd swallowed hard. Hesitated. Then said, *But I am with him.*

What?

I mean, I have been with him. Someone tried to hurt me again and he helped me. But he got hurt and...

Dear God, listen to yourself. Someone tried to hurt you and he just happened to be there to help you. Again. *Don't you think that's a little convenient, Linda?*

It wasn't like that, she'd protested.

No? So he wasn't hanging around where he shouldn't have been? At your house maybe?

He *had* been at her house. Even before she'd gone to his place at Tortuga Boulevard. But no, he'd been blocks away. He hadn't even wanted to go into the house with her. She'd practically forced him to.

Hadn't she?

She rubbed her forehead. Of course she hadn't forced him.

She couldn't force Tony to do anything.

Just like she hadn't been able to force him to stop taking the painkillers when they were together.

Linda, he's playing you. Playing on your feelings for him. Trying to convince you he's a good guy so you'll believe he's innocent.

But I wasn't sure of his guilt before...

And he obviously decided to capitalize on that.

It made sense. Everything Neil had said made sense. But it wasn't what her instincts told her.

Listen to your instincts, the fax had instructed her.

But she still didn't know who had sent that fax.

It would have to have been someone who knew both her and Tony. Knew about their previous relationship. But who would—

It hit her then. Mattie.

It could have been Mattie who'd sent her the fax.

Mattie who was in WITSEC and couldn't risk coming out of it because of her daughter, Jordan, but who'd heard of Tony's arrest and wanted to get a message to Linda.

That made sense, too.

And thinking that Mattie had sent that fax, that she still believed in Tony from afar, was a much more palatable option than believing what Neil was saying.

Neil, I heard Justine saying Tony had set up an appointment with someone who sells something called Rapture. Do you know anything about it?

Damn it, Linda, that's the last thing you should be worried about. Where are you? Tell me and I'll—

Neil. Please. Just answer the question.

Rapture is a new street drug. A dangerous one. It's similar to the bath-salt drugs, but it's a hybrid, with an added component that makes the highs more intense, and the withdrawals even worse. It's hard to come by, which is definitely a good thing. It's been linked to mental deterioration in those who use it long enough.

Mental deterioration?

It drives people crazy. Makes them delusional. Makes them dangerous."

"In other words there'd be a reason why someone might want to get to this supplier to stop him from selling these drugs? Someone who was working undercover, maybe?

Neil snorted. *And what? You think the person doing that is Tony Cooper?*

I don't know, Neil. But it's a possibility. As you know, he acted as a confidential informant before. He had lots of reasons to bring Guapo down.

And he sure did, didn't he? He killed him.

At least some of the evidence against him indicates he acted in self-defense.

You're reaching.

No, I'm not. I'm trying to look at all sides. Look at the evidence objectively. That's what a judge would do, right?

You're not a judge yet, Linda. And if you keep this up, you might never be.

I know that, she said softly. *But Tony's isn't just another case I'm prosecuting. I gave that to you, remember? That means I can be a little more objective.*

The reporter we've talked about isn't going to call you objective. And he's not going to stop until he buries you, Linda.

That's a risk I'm willing to take, Neil. If Tony is working undercover to stop this supplier, then...

Then what, Linda? You're going to get back together with him? Stand by him at trial?

I—I don't know. And she didn't. She'd just have figure out the answer when the time came.

Thank you for calling me and warning me about the reporter, Neil. I—I'm sorry I didn't tell you the truth about where I was sooner.

Neil sighed. *I think you're making a mistake, Linda. Be careful. Like I said, the Rapture drug is very dangerous. If Tony's taking it, he can turn on you at any moment. Users are known to snap abruptly, with no warning signs. A few days ago a woman who used Rap-*

*ture with her husband went crazy and ended up burn-
ing both of them during sex. She's in ICU. Even if she
makes it, she's going to have to live with the fact she
killed her husband. I don't want to have to grieve your
death, Linda.*

*And I certainly don't want to die. But I can't believe
Tony would be a threat to me. And I don't think he's
using anything right now.*

*You don't think he is, Linda. But you can't know.
Can you?*

*He hasn't had anything for at least three days. And
he's not experiencing withdrawal symptoms. That tells
me something.* Though in truth, she couldn't know
whether he'd been experiencing withdrawal along with
the negative symptoms of the infection he'd been bat-
tling. She refrained from saying anything about that to
Neil, however.

When will you be back?

*I'm coming back to town in a few hours. I'll check
in with you when I do.*

*Okay. In the meantime I'll try to track down this re-
porter and do some damage control.*

You've been a good friend, Neil. Thank you.

*But that's all you want me to be. A friend. Isn't that
right?*

I'm sorry, she said again. There'd been nothing else
she could say. She didn't know whether she and Tony
would be together in the long run. But she was still in
love with him. She'd been a fool to think she could date
Neil when that was true.

Take care, Linda.

You, too, Neil. She was just about to hang up when
she suddenly remembered what Neil had said about the
woman who'd taken Rapture being in ICU. *Wait! Neil?*

Yeah? I'm here.

Neil, what was the name of the woman who's in ICU? The one who burned herself and her husband?

Snow. Her name's Molly Snow.

After hanging up with Neil, Linda made her way back to the cabin. She wasn't going to ask Tony any more questions. She was going to demand answers and this time he was going to—

She froze as she came around the corner of the cabin. Her spine snapped into place, and betrayal carved an ugly hole in her chest.

He was gone. Tony was gone. He'd taken her car and left her behind.

"No!" she shouted. She kicked the ground, sending gravel spattering across the drive. All the accusations Neil had made about Tony using her echoed nastily in her head.

Why had she trusted him? Angry, she stormed into the house. In the cabin's family room, she stripped off Tony's T-shirt and threw it in the fireplace. She'd burn the damned thing later.

Twenty minutes later, after having run through all the hot water the cabin's old water heater had to offer, she came out off the steaming bathroom, clad only in a towel.

And screamed.

Chapter 22

Linda's scream wasn't one of anger, but sheer terror. She'd gone as white as the towel wrapped around her body.

Tony cursed. "Linda, it's just me!" He held his arms out, palms upright, as if placating a child in the middle of a temper tantrum. "It's just me," he repeated.

Damn it, he'd only meant to clear his head. He hadn't meant to frighten her.

A sob tore out of her chest. "Oh, God, I thought you were him...them."

Them? "Who?"

"I don't know. The men who shot at me. The cop you saw outside my house. Guapo's men...I mean..." Her brow furrowed as she realized she was babbling.

Tony stepped closer. "Linda," he murmured, "you're safe. I'll keep you safe."

She shook her head. "Tony..." Abruptly, her knees buckled.

Damn. She was weak from shock and he was feeling dizzy, as well. The oxygen in the air seemed to evaporate. He swept her up, one arm under her knees, the other cradling her shoulders and head against his chest, and carried her into his room. Gently, with trembling arms, he placed her down on the bed.

"God, Linda. I'm so sorry I scared you." He sat down next to her. She curled into the fetal position and wrapped her arms around her knees. For all her strong exterior, for all her determination in going after a judgeship, Linda was still a wounded woman. A victim. And he'd helped make her that way.

She'd been pounded into oblivion because she hadn't divulged his name to the bastards who demanded she tell them the name of the informant. Him. And they hadn't even talked about the incident. Not really.

Guilt ravaged him from the inside.

"Do you want me to leave you alone?" he asked, ashamed at how tinny and tight his voice sounded.

She hesitated for several seconds. Hell, a whole minute went by and he rose, certain her silence meant she wanted to be alone. But before he could leave...

"Stay," she whispered.

He'd stay. He'd stay by her side until she could pull herself together, and then he'd take off. Get the hell away from Linda. Hitchhike back to Sacramento, if he needed to.

When he heard Linda release a relaxed breath, he looked down and was surprised to see his own hand stroking her hair.

"Where were you?"

"I just went for a drive. I needed to clear my head."

"But you could barely pick yourself up off the floor. Why would you take the car? Where did you go? We had food. Water. You could have called your girlfriend on your cell at any time. Why would you leave without telling me first?"

He saw it in her eyes when she paused. When she swallowed. When she broke his gaze and stared out the window.

"Did you go somewhere to score drugs?" she asked, her voice hollow. "Was Neil right? Have you just been playing me this whole time? Was that man at my house really a dirty cop or someone you hired to break in so you could 'save' me?"

Oh, God, did she really believe that?

He couldn't bear the ache in her voice.

The pain in her eyes.

How long could he keep up this charade? After all she'd sacrificed, didn't Linda deserve to know the truth—at least some of it? His drug addiction had caused her the hell she'd lived through eighteen months ago. The hell she still lived through, given her response to being startled. He couldn't give her everything, but he could give her this.

He took a deep breath and readied himself to speak, hoping the truth would take away some of her pain.

"I took a drive because I'd pushed myself too hard doing those push-ups. I hurt like hell again, and I was afraid if I didn't leave, I'd take the codeine pills the doctor gave me."

"I looked for them. Where—?"

"I stashed them under a loose floorboard under my bed. You were right about me being clean, Linda. And I want to stay that way. I drove a distance away and tossed them over a cliff."

This close, he could see the beat of her heart as the artery in her neck pulsed.

Pulsed.

Pulsed. Her scent covered him, clung to him the way she clung to him when they made love. When their bodies craved and hungered and gave and spent.

"You're really clean? For how long?"

"Like I told you before, since before we ever started dating. I mean, there were plenty of times I almost gave in…"

She nodded, as if it was what she'd expected. And that made sense given what he'd implied earlier. Even when he hadn't meant to, he'd given her the clues she'd needed to believe in him. "I'm so proud of you," she whispered, reaching out to stroke the line of his jaw.

He flinched back. "Please, don't."

She lowered her hand. "Don't touch you?" she asked.

"Don't touch me. Talk to me. Look at me. Just don't."

"Tony, what have you been doing since Mattie and Jordan and Dom left? This drug-lord image you're projecting—it's just an image. I know you've been lying to me about taking over Guapo's operation. You're working with the cops again, right? Serving as an informant again so you can find the supplier of the bath-salt drugs?"

"What the hell do you know about those drugs?"

"I heard Justine talking on the phone with someone named Nicco. She told him that you'd set up a meeting with a Rapture supplier. That you were on your way to taking over Guapo's ring, she said. But that's not the real reason, is it? You want to shut down the supplier because the drugs are so damn dangerous. Because they can drive users crazy…"

A few other things suddenly occurred to her.

The fact that Tony was clean but had only recently admitted to it, and even then, that he still tried to convince her he was "bad." That he'd confessed to Guapo's murder, even though Guapo had been stabbed by someone much shorter than Tony. Someone that was the size of...

"Justine!" she exclaimed. "She killed Guapo, didn't she?"

Tony's eyes widened and though he tried to hide it, she saw the truth in his eyes. He shook his head. "No. What are you—?"

"Justine takes drugs. She took drugs the first day I saw you in court. In the bathroom. I was there. Maybe she even took Rapture. Is that why she killed Guapo? Did she go crazy?"

Tony grabbed her arms. "Whoa. Stop it. You saw Justine taking drugs in the courthouse bathroom?"

"I didn't see her. She was behind the stall. But she was sniffing something."

"You're sure that was the day I was arraigned? I didn't see her there."

"The courthouse was packed, remember? And she looked at me like she hated me. Like she wanted to kill me, Tony."

"That's ridiculous," he said, but he didn't sound so certain. "She knew nothing about you."

"But an observant person would have seen how we reacted to seeing each other that day. Maybe she saw that we cared for each other and was jealous. It would explain—"

"I told you I've been clean off drugs. I haven't told you I didn't kill Guapo. I didn't tell you I'm working undercover to stop a Rapture supplier."

"You don't have to tell me. I can see it written all over your face."

"Damn it, Linda."

She shook her head. "You can't protect me from this, Tony. If that's what you're trying to do, you've already failed."

"I haven't failed at anything. You're alive, aren't you? You're going to be a judge—"

"I'm alive. For now. But forget about me being a judge. I might not have a job in a few days."

"What are you talking about?"

"A reporter has been snooping around. He's connected the two of us. Is claiming I'm the reason you got out on bail."

"How do you know this?"

"Neil called me when I was out for a walk. He told me. So you see, I need you to tell me the truth, Tony. And if there's any way I can help you finish this job you're doing, I need to help you do it. Because in helping you, I'll be helping myself, too."

He didn't look up, not until she reached out and took his hand.

He told himself to pull away, but he couldn't. He wrapped his fingers around hers, wanting so badly to lift them to his lips. To pull her against his chest and just hold her. Instead he forced himself to recall how she'd looked lying in a hospital bed, beaten and broken and fighting for her life.

And that slapped him out of his morbid thoughts faster than he could blink.

Being with her wasn't an option. He had to accept it.

Tony suddenly felt like he couldn't breathe. That he was going to drown in her nearness. He pulled his hand out of hers. "What is this, Linda? Do you get off stringing me along? You're the one who broke off our relationship. You can't have it both ways, so back off."

He heard a sharp intake of breath and looked up,

seeing the hurt there. But Jesus, what did she expect? She'd made her feelings about him clear when she'd kicked him out of her life. Today, last week, the past few freaking years without her, had been a nightmare.

And he hadn't even fallen off the wagon, he thought again. He hadn't slipped up. She'd just assumed he would.

As many times as he told himself she'd had reason to, that she'd been reasonable in protecting herself and her life, it pissed him off.

"You're letting the past skew your thinking, Linda. You're one of the good guys. A prosecutor. A soon-to-be judge. You're getting everything you wanted and you were right to think you wouldn't get it if you had anything to do with me. I'm worthless and would have done nothing but drag you down. Why shouldn't you believe I've done exactly what I've said?"

Her stare was blank. Inscrutable. Time ticked by, marked by croaks of frogs outside the window. The pulse in her neck kept up its furious beat. He waited. He could wait forever.

"You want to know why I can't believe it? Because I loved you, Tony. And I still do. And you know what? I think you still love me, too."

Before he could respond, she kissed him.

As they kissed, Linda was immediately aware of two things.

First, Tony didn't even try to fight their connection this time. Despite the way he'd pushed her away with his words, he refrained from doing it with his body. His mouth opened readily underneath hers, and his arms wrapped around her tightly.

Second, she wasn't going to settle for anything less

than both of them naked this time. Her hands tore at his clothes, refusing to be denied. Buttons flew. Fabric ripped. And he seemed just as frantic to get her naked, too.

Thank you, she thought, when she was completely bare to him. He cupped her breasts and tweaked her nipples. Heat speared between her legs, causing an ache that made her whimper with need.

When he released her breasts, she moaned with disappointment until he replaced his hands with his mouth. He sucked on her strongly, working one nipple until it was red and engorged before moving on to the next. The whole time, her hands roved over his body, relishing the bulge of his muscles and the way they tightened with his need for her.

That was a start, but not good enough. She wanted him trembling. Shaking. Begging for her touch.

This time she pulled away and he moaned in protest. But when she fell to her knees, he tangled his fingers in her hair and urged, "Yes, Linda. Please. Take me in your mouth. I've missed this. Missed you."

He didn't have to ask her again. She didn't reacquaint herself with his length slowly. Instead she drew him into her mouth greedily, as if by doing so she was filling up every empty, lonely spot inside her. She pulled back to flick her tongue over the tip of him, then swallowed him even deeper than before, until he touched the back of her throat.

"I'm going to come if you keep that up," he gritted out.

"That's what I want," she said.

"Me, too. But first..." With a grimace, he pulled away from her and urged her to her feet. "First I want to come inside you again. Here," he said as he cupped her. "It felt so wonderful taking you without a condom. Can we— Will you take me that way again?"

She took a shaky breath and considered his request.

She'd started this knowing where it was going and also knowing they didn't have a condom. She knew she was taking a chance, but hadn't she already risked everything for Tony?

Three and a half years ago she hadn't trusted him enough to stay with him. Did she really trust him enough now to give him this? To give him everything?

She nodded.

He smiled, a big genuine smile that made her feel like she'd hung the moon.

She threw her arms around his neck as he cupped her butt and lifted her onto him. She felt his hard flesh searching between her folds before he sank inside, slowly. Slowly. And so thoroughly that she felt stretched to bursting. His scent enveloped her, as did something else.

His love. She felt it everywhere he touched her. She saw it in his eyes.

He didn't have to say it for her to know.

This man still loved her. She loved him.

But even as she skyrocketed to pleasure, she was sadly aware that loving each other had never been the problem. And it had never been enough.

Chapter 23

Tony watched Linda as she slept. She lay next to him, her body shimmering with sweat, her nipples soft and relaxed. Over the past few days, she'd refused to give up on him. She'd visited him in lockup and then the infirmary, then tracked him to the house on Tortuga Boulevard. Finally, she'd brought him here, to her childhood home, to recuperate in safety.

And she'd done all those thing because, despite everything, she believed in him.

The question was what they were going to do now.

Beside him, Linda stirred. Opened her eyes and looked at him.

"Sleep," Tony whispered.

She smiled, blinked her eyes open and shifted to a sitting position. "I can't."

"Why not?"

"Because I need to hear the truth. The full truth.

Please, Tony. If you love me, if I ever meant anything to you, please tell me the truth now."

Staring into her beautiful green eyes, he felt the moment it happened. He accepted the inevitable. No matter what rumors were spread, no matter what people thought of him, Linda would never believe he had turned so completely dark. Men had threatened her life. A reporter was threatening her career. He couldn't keep her safe if he kept her ignorant.

And whatever he did, he had to keep her safe.

"Are you sure you're ready for this?" he asked, wrapping a strand of her hair around his finger.

"Tell me." Linda's voice was firm. Unrelenting. She wouldn't let go of this, and ultimately, she was right not to. Too much time had passed for this secret to stay between them.

He pressed a brief kiss against her forehead, and then spoke. "After you dumped me—"

She winced and he changed gears. "After we *broke up,* it was so damn hard to know you were close, that you and Mattie were friends, but that I didn't get to be part of your life. It was better than nothing, though. It was some kind of connection with you. Then eighteen months ago, because of what happened with Sabon, Mattie, Dom Jeffries and I entered the WITSEC program. You need to know how hard that was for me. Leaving you so completely. Even though we'd broken up, you were the one good thing besides Mattie I'd ever had."

"Oh, Tony," she said sadly.

He shook his head. "I know you did what you thought you had to. Whether I took the drugs or not afterward, I wanted to that night. You were right about that. It didn't start out that way. I was cocky. Trying to prove something. It was a tough lesson to learn. To accept just how weak I was, when I'd thought I'd gotten stronger. I had the lesson slammed home again when Guapo's men went after you and Mattie. You were hurt. She was hurt."

"That wasn't your fault—"

"Please, Linda. Just let me say this."

"Okay."

"You were both hurt. It wasn't technically my fault, but I didn't do anything to stop it, either. Granted, I wasn't there in the parking lot the night you were attacked, but when Mattie was attacked? That's a different story."

"How?"

"Dom's cop friend, the one that was dirty, took her to Michael Sabon. He wanted her to tell Sabon that I was the informant. I figured out what was happening and called Dom. I figured Sabon would be at this old warehouse by the river, and I was right. I took Dom there. While Dom was fighting with the cop, I had a chance to save Mattie. Only I failed. Michael Sabon overpowered me. He knocked my gun away, the gun Dom had given me to protect myself. And Sabon almost killed Mattie. But first he was going to rape her. Only she didn't let him. She fought back. She was the one who killed Sabon, not me. If she hadn't gotten away and gotten to the gun…if she hadn't shot him…"

"But she did get away. She did shoot him. And you can't blame yourself for what happened. You're a good man. Strong. But you're not a cop. You weren't trained to handle that kind of thing…"

"I'd started the training."

Her expression contorted with confusion. "What do you mean?"

"I'd started the police academy. Before I ever informed on Guapo. I was a few months short of graduating when Sabon attacked Mattie."

"But how? How could Mattie keep something like that a secret from me?"

"She didn't know, Linda. I didn't tell anyone."

"Why?"

"Because I'd failed at so many things before that. I didn't know if I'd fail at that, too. I didn't want to tell any of you. Not until I'd finished. Not until you could be proud of me."

"We—me and Mattie—we've always been proud of you, Tony. Just not the drug addiction. But I knew how hard you tried to fight it."

"But you left me. You left me, Linda."

She obviously heard the hurt in his voice, and her eyes shimmered with tears.

"Shhh," he said. "I'm sorry. I shouldn't have said that. Let me finish what I was saying. Please."

She took a shuddering breath then nodded.

"It would have been easy for me to quit after that. To accept that I was a weakling and give up my dreams of becoming a cop. But when we joined the witness security program, I told Dom and Mattie about what I'd been doing. And they encouraged me to finish what I'd started."

She was holding her breath now, her eyes wide with awareness and anticipation.

"Are you saying—?"

He nodded. "I finished the academy. And after I graduated, I applied to the local sheriff's department to work with Dom. My application was accepted."

In the family room, the grandfather clock chimed. He waited until it quieted.

"Wait a minute. Back up here. You actually graduated from the police academy?"

He nodded. "I graduated at the top of my class."

"They knew about your drug problem?"

"They did. They were reluctant to take a chance at first, but they viewed me as a good risk. It helped that I had Dom's recommendation and that I'd been going to regular NA meetings."

"NA. Narcotics Anonymous meetings. You kept those up."

"Yes. And I've continued to do them. Even after I accepted the job here in Sacramento, I—"

"So wait—" Linda shoved herself to sitting and stared down at him. "Wait just one minute. Are you really telling me that not only have you been clean for the past five years, but that you're a *cop?*"

Linda wasn't sure if reality had ended and fantasy had begun. She stared at the knotty pine wall, heard the trickle of the creek outside, smelled the scent of pine on the breeze that blew in the window, and knew full well she was still in the cabin, sitting close to a naked Tony.

But the world had stopped making sense.

What was Tony saying?

He wasn't a cop.

He was a confidential informant.

He'd used to be a waiter, for goodness sake.

And now he was a drug addict trying to pretend he was climbing to the top of a drug distribution chain.

She'd known in her heart that wasn't true. That he wasn't a murderer. She'd believed him the minute he'd said he wasn't using drugs anymore. But did she believe this?

"You're a police officer," she stated baldly.

"Deputy, actually. Badge, gun and everything. Well, under normal circumstances, I'd have those things. I don't have them now because I've been deep undercover."

"Deep undercover," she echoed.

Linda pulled away from him and lay back down on the bed, one hand on her belly, the other on her forehead. The puzzle pieces were starting to come together—click, click, clicking into place.

She looked at him then. For a moment he looked like his old self again—younger. More vulnerable. More like the Tony she'd fallen in love with, and less like the hardened man he'd become in the past year and a half. But he was a hardened man. One who normally carried around a gun and badge. He was a cop.

"Why didn't you just stay away? You could have had a fresh start. Started as a cop in—in whatever city you were living in without having to worry about Guapo." *Without having to worry about* me.

Only he hadn't really worried about her, had he? He'd stayed away from her for three and a half years. Despite the fact he hadn't been using drugs. Despite the fact he'd been attending the police academy. Despite the fact he'd graduated at the top of his class.

She wanted to ask him why. Why he hadn't come to her? Why he hadn't asked her to go with him?

Because she would have. She would have given up everything, her job, *anything,* to have started a new life with him and Mattie.

Her despair must have shown on her face.

"What is it, Linda? Why are you looking at me like that?"

"Why did you come back to Sacramento, Tony? Because it wasn't for me."

He stared at her. "Not at first, no. But I didn't think you were an option for me, remember? Cop or not, I'm still a recovering drug addict, Linda. I always will be."

His words made sense, but they didn't ease the pain swirling through her. All she could think was that he'd stayed away from her a little too easily. Just like her father had stayed away after her mother had left him.

If he'd cared, if her father had cared, he wouldn't have stayed away. He'd have fought to be with her. To stay with her. Even if all that meant was answering her letters from prison. The fact that he hadn't was like a blade to her throat.

She raised her chin. "So tell me why you came back. Was it because of Justine?"

"No. It was because of Justine's brother. A teenage boy who used to run drugs for Guapo."

Her brow crinkled. Justine's brother? A boy that used to—

Ah, she thought. More puzzle pieces moved into place.

Click, click, click. "Rory," she said.

"You remember him?"

"You talked about him a couple of times. I could tell you adored that kid. You had such hopes for him. You'd thought he could get clean, could even go to college. But that didn't happen, did it?"

"No, it didn't."

So what did? She was about to ask the question when the answer hit her like a ton of bricks. "The bath-salts drug. He took them. And they killed him?"

He nodded. "Yes. And before they killed him, they drove him mad."

"Is that why Justine killed Guapo? Because you'll

never convince me you killed Guapo. *She* did, didn't she?"

After only a brief hesitation, he nodded. "Yeah. She did. She thought she was meeting a friend at that garage but suddenly Guapo was there. She managed to ring me on her cell phone and tell me where she was. I heard Guapo questioning her about me. Before I got there, he'd roughed her up. I pulled him off her and we fought. Guapo injured me pretty bad and turned on Justine again, but by that time she got to the knife Guapo had dropped. She killed him in self-defense."

And Tony had covered it up. Why? Did he really care that much for the woman? The thought made Linda's heart ache. "What about the knife she used?"

"She left with it before the police arrived."

"And she left you there? To take the rap for her?"

"It's what we'd agreed on. And what I owed her. Hell, even with all my training, I hadn't been able to protect her anymore than I'd been able to protect Mattie. I was the cop and I needed to do what was right. What was best for everyone."

Best because he loved Justine? "Why? Why was taking the rap for a murder you didn't commit the best thing to do?" she forced herself to ask.

"It allowed me to protect Justine when I hadn't been able to do so before. Plus, Guapo peddled the Rapture that drove Rory insane before they killed him. Those drugs are still out there, doing the same to countless others. We've penetrated Guapo's organization. What better way to keep me inside than if people believe I was ruthless enough to kill him?"

"What do you mean 'we've' penetrated the organization? Who are you working for? And what's your mission exactly?"

"I'm working in conjunction with the FBI to bring Guapo's drug ring down once and for all, but no one's been able to figure out the identity of the primary Rapture supplier."

"That's why you're trying to set up the meeting with him."

"Yes. And we were going to meet. The time and place were all set up, only…"

"Only you got hurt protecting me…*again*." She shook her head in amazement. "So Justine killed Guapo."

"Like I said, it was in self-defense."

"Are you sure about that?" she said slowly.

Tony frowned. "Yes. I was there, remember? She's a good woman, Linda. She's been helping me, well before Guapo got out of prison. She hates what drugs did to her brother. She wants vengeance as much as I do. Wants the drugs off the streets. She's helping me nail the supplier."

Pain filled her chest, like a cement block had been inserted behind her lungs. "I'll ask again. Are you sure about that, Tony? Don't you remember what I told you about seeing her in the bathroom? About her taking drugs?"

He sat up, the blanket and sheet sliding down to bare his chest. The expression he wore was shuttered, his jawline tight. "I can't know if Justine is using drugs or not," Tony said "Does it really matter that much? Someone who uses drugs isn't inherently evil. But maybe that's exactly what you still believe. Maybe, despite all your claims that you believe in me and how good I am, maybe you think that deep down inside, I'm evil, too."

Chapter 24

Tony's relief at being able to finally tell Linda the truth had morphed into a lump of bitterness. No matter how hard he tried, he just couldn't shake it.

Linda thought Justine was a druggie and, in her mind, that had automatically equated to Justine being a user, a murderer or both. Maybe he wasn't being fair, but all he could think was Linda must see him the same way. Would always see him that way. As flawed. Untrustworthy.

Sure, she believed in him now. But they weren't in a relationship and she hadn't said she wanted that with him again. Hadn't said she'd stay with him once this mess was over, or that she'd stick by him through thick and thin.

And even if she had said it, he wouldn't have believed her.

Tony didn't kid himself. He'd made something of himself. But he was on a dangerous assignment. Even if he made it out alive and accomplished what he wanted, he was *always* going to be a drug addict. There would always be difficult times. And bottom line—he didn't trust Linda to stick by him to get back to the good ones.

Linda was in the kitchen, tidying things up before they left for Sacramento. He finished stripping the linens in the bedroom, carried them into the laundry room, and then went to go get her. She was digging around in the pantry.

"We need to head back. You ready to go?" he asked.

From inside the pantry, she said, "Yes. I'm just looking for a new garbage bag." Her voice was stiff. Quiet. Distant.

The truth had briefly brought them together but it had also torn them apart. He wondered if it would always be that way between them.

This time, however, the distance was his fault, not hers.

Maybe he'd reacted too defensively when she'd expressed suspicion about Justine. She'd just been trying to help, after all.

"Linda, I'm sorry about earlier. About what I said. I guess when you accused Justine of using me, it pushed a button of mine."

She didn't say anything.

"Linda?"

She stepped out of the pantry.

He frowned at the expression on her face. "Hey. What's wrong?"

Her eyes were wide and round and her mouth was slack. Tony noticed she was holding a shoebox in her hands—hands that were trembling.

"What do you have there?"

Linda set the shoebox down on the kitchen table and

lowered herself in a chair. Instead of answering him, she just stared at the box.

Tony flicked the lid off the shoebox and looked at the contents. Envelope after envelope, all stamped. Some were opened, and he could see the childlike loops in the writing of the address on the front. Others were unopened, addressed to Linda and Kathy Delaney in what looked to be a man's handwriting.

"Linda?"

"I wrote him," she whispered. "After we moved to Texas. Despite what had happened. I wrote him all the time. But he never wrote me back. Not once. He never called, never sent birthday cards. It was as if Kathy and I no longer existed for him."

He sat down next to her. "You're talking about your dad?"

She nodded. "I hated him for putting his thieving before his children. We always came second, no matter how he denied it."

Tony pulled out one of the unopened letters addressed to Linda and Kathy. He ripped the envelope open and pulled out the contents and began reading.

My dearest children,
I know that once again your mother will not allow you to read this letter, but I am writing you anyway. I regret the choices I've made in my life. How much I regret losing you two. You both are the light of my life, and I wish so much I could see you grow up. Your mother has her reasons for keeping you from me, and although I don't agree with those reasons, I can understand why she's doing so. Just know that every day, every hour,

I think of you two girls, and I will never stop regretting what I've done.
Love,
Daddy.

Linda swallowed audibly. "Are they all like that?"

He ripped through one unopened letter after another, and read them out loud. They were the words of a father in pain. Their dad had screwed up his life so much he'd lost the only things that mattered to him—his daughters.

After reading the last one, he cleared his throat. "He loved you. Your mom didn't mail your letters and she didn't give you his letters because she was trying to protect you."

Before his eyes her stunned expression hardened. She pressed her lips together and looked at him. "Of course she was protecting me. She knew who he really was. Knew how easily he said he loved us. But if he'd really loved us, he'd have done what was right. He'd have done what it took to stay with us. That's what love is. Action, not just words."

As she spoke, her eyes held condemnation.

For her father.

But somehow, Tony knew they also held condemnation for him.

He tapped one of the envelopes addressed to her dad. "So your father was in prison when you wrote him. You never told me how he died. Had he already been released?"

"My dad was in prison when I wrote him those letters, yeah." She paused. Took a deep breath, then blew it out. "And he still is."

Tony jerked. "You told me your dad's dead. You told everyone your dad was dead."

"You're right. I did. It was easier that way. Since he never wrote or called me, he was as good as dead anyway."

"But what about this reporter who's connected us? Isn't it possible word of your father will get out and be used against you, too?"

Linda shrugged. "I told the D.A. about my father before I ever agreed to run for judge. Considering we're estranged, that I haven't seen him in years, he said it didn't concern him. That my past could actually work in my favor. That I could argue I've been personally exposed to both sides of the law. That I ultimately chose the right one. And that I can make the hard decisions to do what's right."

"Right," Tony said softly. "The hard decisions. Like cutting people from your life that aren't good for you. People like your father. And people like me."

The ride back to Sacramento was just as quiet as the one to Grass Valley. This time, the silence was caused not by Tony's unconsciousness, but by their unwillingness to bring up a sore topic, when all topics between them seemed to fall into that category.

They were about twenty minutes outside the city limits when Linda abruptly spoke.

"I'm going to help you find the Rapture supplier."

For a second, he thought he'd misheard her. When he realized he hadn't, he glared at her. "No way. I don't need your help. I had a meeting set up with him, remember? He'll contact me again. And if he doesn't?" He shrugged. No way in hell would he let Linda help him on this case. No way in hell he'd allow her to be in danger.

"Don't be stubborn, Tony. I can help you. I have connections."

He snorted. "Come on, Linda! You really expect me to rely on you?"

"What does that mean?"

"It means you seem to leave every time the going gets tough. You told people your dad was dead. You left me when you thought I might start taking drugs again. In an operation like this, Linda, you have to trust your partner. You and I may have great sex, but I don't trust you. Not to stick around for the long haul."

He realized he wasn't just saying it to drive her away. He meant it.

His chest ached. They'd had an idyllic time in the woods, but that little cabin in the foothills wasn't real life. In real life, neither of them trusted the other. That wasn't the basis for any kind of relationship, personal or otherwise.

By the look on her face, Linda knew it. But that didn't mean she was going to do what Tony wanted.

"I know what you're thinking, Tony," she said. "I know you're trying to push me away, trying to protect me. But we need to figure this out together. I need to protect my future. My job's on the line here, remember? And my job, whether it's as a D.A. or a judge, is all I have."

Her blunt statement bothered him. She deserved so much more than her job, but she was right. She did important work and it wasn't fair that her association with him was going to get in the way of that. Besides, he knew her. She was going to help him whether he wanted her to or not. Rather than fight it, he should accept her help but limit it as much as possible.

If he controlled the amount of rope she had, at least she wouldn't be able to hang herself.

"Phone calls, Linda. That's all you'll do is make phone calls. And you'll stay with me every minute, you understand? Am I clear?"

She nodded, and the muscle in her jaw flickered.

It was only later, after they'd reached downtown Sacramento, picked up a few of Linda's things and checked into a hotel that he realized he hadn't made her promise him.

Chapter 25

The bar stank of sweat and beer and blood and one hundred moppings hadn't been able to cover it up. Although Tony would much rather be back at the hotel with Linda, he'd left her to do her thing with her laptop while he met with Yee.

"You were supposed to send men to protect Linda," Tony said, his tone accusing.

Yee's brows rose. "I sent men, yes. And they haven't reported anything of interest."

"Anything of interest? Or anything at all? Because Linda hasn't been at her house for the past several days. I'd think you'd have known that if you'd sent men to protect her."

Yee narrowed his eyes and leaned back in his chair. "Several days, huh? And you'd know this…how? No, wait. Let me guess. Because she was the reason you missed your meeting with the supplier?"

"Damn right she was the reason. She probably saved my life. *After* someone tried to hurt her and kill me."

"And you think I had something to do with that? After someone tried to gun one of you down outside the courthouse. Was that my doing, too?"

"I'm just letting you know what my thoughts are. I'm not sure what's going on, but I've given your name to my attorney in a sealed envelope. If something happens to me or Linda, you and your team will be investigated. Do you understand?"

"Oh. I understand all right." Yee sighed. "Damn Cam Blake for his corrupt ways. Our police force is never gonna live it down, are we?" He shrugged. "Do what you need to do, Tony. But I'm telling you. This woman's got you running around in circles. Your head's clearly not in the game."

At that moment Tony's cell phone rang, but he let it go to voice mail and kept his gaze on Yee. As he did so, his suspicion that Yee was dirty evaporated. His instincts told him Yee was on the up and up, but he wasn't ready to tell the other man that. Not yet. Standing, he said, "We've hit a dead end but it doesn't mean I won't be able to find a detour. When I do, I'll let you know. Until then, remember what I said."

Once Tony was outside, his cell rang again. This time he answered. "This is Tony."

"You missed our meeting." The male voice was familiar. It was the same person who'd called Tony before, claiming he'd supplied Guapo with the Rapture drug and that he wanted to do the same for Tony.

"It wasn't intentional," he said, trying to tap down his relief that he might just have another chance to nail this guy. "Someone tried to put me out of commission, but ultimately they failed. Let's try again. I can meet you at the same place—"

"I never meet at the same place twice." He rattled off a location in West Sacramento, then said, "I'll call you next week with the date and time."

"Next week?" Tony said. "No. That's not good enough. We need to meet earlier."

"You're not in a position to be making demands. Mr. Cooper. I said I'd meet you. Don't give me a reason to change my mind."

"Damn it," Tony said. "I—"

But before Tony could finish his sentence, the other man hung up.

After Tony left to meet with his cop contact, Linda called Neil and told him she'd be stopping by the D.A.'s office. "But I won't be reporting for work," she said. "I just need to get a file. The one you have on that woman who burned herself and her husband. Molly Snow. Would you get it for me?"

"What for, damn it? If you're not coming back to work, what the hell are you going to be doing?"

"I just need to look into a few things, Neil. Please. Will you get me the file?"

Several seconds passed and Linda held her breath.

"Fine," Neil said. "I'll get you a copy, but I have to leave for court. Call Allie when you pull into the parking lot. I'll have her bring the file out to you. But then I'm done, Linda. Things have gone too far. Your friend Tony's trial has been set for next Monday. If he doesn't show up, I'm going to ask that the court issue a bench warrant for his arrest, just as I would any other defendant."

"I understand, Neil. And thank you."

When Linda pulled into the D.A.'s parking lot, she called Allie. Less than two minutes later Allie came out with a file.

The younger woman looked concerned. "Hey, Linda. Are you okay?"

"Yes, I'm fine, Allie. I just have some personal things I'm taking care of." Her gaze dropped to the file in Allie's hand. "I'm going to look into a few things when I can though. Catch up on work."

"Sure." Allie bit her lip. "I heard about what happened outside the courthouse. And that Tony Cooper pushed you out of the way. Have you seen him? Where is he now?"

Linda stiffened. Had she seen him? Why would Allie ask her that? And why would she assume Linda knew where Tony was? She stared at Allie, but the other woman's eyes appeared free of guile. "I don't know where he is. Thanks for getting me this, Allie. I appreciate it."

"No worries, Linda. Take care." With a wave and a smile, Allie went back inside.

Linda stared after her for a second, then flipped through the file.

When she was done, she phoned the investigating officer whose number was listed on the police report.

According to Detective Leon, the officer in charge of the case, Molly Snow wasn't near ready to be interviewed, but the woman might be able to lead them to the supplier they were looking for.

Linda drove to the hospital where Molly Snow was being treated. After inquiring at the nurse's desk and flashing her credentials, a nurse escorted her to the appropriate room.

A patrol officer stood guard outside. Linda wasn't surprised. Despite her tragic circumstances, Snow was both victim and suspect. Until they knew whether the District Attorney was going to charge her with a crime, the police needed to insure she stuck around. Linda showed the young officer her identification and stepped inside the room.

Snow was the only person there. She was swathed in bandages. Her eyes were closed, her breathing loud. Linda stood next to her and listened to the repetitive beeping of one of the many machines connected to Snow.

She'd prosecuted a couple of murder-by-fire cases before. She knew that victims who suffered from smoke inhalation were in effect seared from the inside and outside at the same time. God. Linda wondered if Snow even knew her husband was dead.

"Who are you?" The unexpected female voice came from behind her, causing Linda to jolt. At the same time Snow's eyes fluttered open to stare foggily up at her. Snow let out a small moan despite the fact she'd been intubated.

Linda turned to see a middle-aged brunette in a red sweater and jeans rush in. "It's okay, Mol. I'm here. Shhh. Shhh." The woman reached for Molly Snow and rested her hand on a bandaged limb. That's when Linda noticed how short the limb was. She averted her eyes. The doctors had had to amputate Snow's arm.

Snow seemed to calm down at the woman's touch, nodding just the slightest bit before closing her eyes and apparently dozing off again. The woman turned to Linda, saying in a softer voice, "Who are you?"

Linda kept her own voice soft. "My name is Linda Delaney. I'm a deputy district attorney."

The woman's lips tightened. "Are you here to charge her with a crime? Because look at my sister. She's suffering. How can you be so heartless? She's a good person. She would never hurt anyone. Not herself. Not her husband. It was those damn drugs—" Snow's sister sobbed and Linda fought the threat of tears prompted by the other woman's helplessness. How many times had she felt her own helplessness as she'd watched her father destroying his life? And the lives of others, including her own?

"I'm not here to charge Molly with anything. I can't say that won't happen later, but right now…right now I just want to find the person who's really responsible for this. The person who sold her the bath-salt drugs. We don't have much to go on. You are…?"

"I'm Diana Wilson. Molly's younger sister."

Linda nodded in greeting. "Diana, do you know where Molly was getting her drugs?"

"No, no, not at all. I already told the police. They're wonderful. Everyone loved them." The words didn't make sense given Linda's question. Her voice broke on the last word, and she clamped her hand over her mouth to stifle her sobs. She glanced worriedly at Snow.

Linda knew she should leave. The woman didn't need an audience to her grief. Linda turned away, but then hesitated. Turned back. "Diana, do you know if your sister ever mentioned the name Mark Guapo?"

Diana Wilson's reaction was palpable. Her head whipped toward Linda and her eyes widened in shock. Her complexion took on a pasty tone before she shook her head.

"No."

"Diana, please…"

Diana faced her, like a lioness protecting her cub. "You need to leave. You need to leave now."

Linda glanced at Molly Snow, who had begun to stir.

"Okay." She walked toward the door, took out one of her business cards and placed it on a small table on her way out. She then turned to Diana.

"I want to help. Call me if you think of anything. Please."

Diana Wilson didn't respond. But she looked down at Linda's card and stared at it for several long seconds before she turned back to her. "Goodbye, Ms. Delaney."

Tony tried calling the Rapture supplier after the guy had hung up on him but the phone just kept ringing. The man had probably switched cell phones anyway.

A week, he thought. It wasn't ideal, but like the guy had said, at least he was still willing to meet with him.

As he'd done several times since returning to Sacramento, Tony called Justine's cell. Again he got no answer. He thought about driving to the house on Tortuga Boulevard, but he suspected that once he showed his face there again, he'd be delayed far longer than he wanted to be. He'd have to go back eventually. Tomorrow even.

But right now? Right now he wanted to get back to Linda and make sure she was okay. And since he'd already made contact with the Rapture supplier, he felt perfectly justified doing so.

Then again he'd always been particularly good at justifying things when he needed to.

By the time Tony got back to the hotel, Linda was asleep. Exhausted himself, he watched the rise and fall of her breasts as she slept, curled in a tight ball on the corner of the mattress. He'd asked for a suite when they'd checked in, but the best the hotel could do was a room with two double beds. Linda had claimed one, which meant he'd be sleeping in the other.

Alone.

He whispered her name, but Linda remained still. She was dead to the world. Good for her. She needed her sleep.

Tony brought his phone into the bathroom and tried once again to get a hold of Justine. When she didn't pick up he left her yet another message, telling her he was back in town and asking her to call him. He pressed the button to terminate the call and quietly entered the bedroom again. He sat on his bed and looked at Linda.

He looked at her for what seemed like hours.

Then he lay down and went to asleep in his cold bed.

And dreamed about holding her in his arms once more.

Chapter 26

The next morning Linda woke to find Tony had come and gone. He'd left a note, saying he had something important to do and promised to call soon. After eating breakfast, she used her laptop to run a background check on Molly and Toby Snow. Neither of them had had trouble with the law until six months ago, when they'd been cited twice for disorderly conduct outside a local nightclub. She next ran a background check on Molly Snow's sister, Diana Wilson, the woman she'd met at the hospital. Unlike her sister, Diana *did* have an arrest record. She'd been arrested twice for possession of methamphetamine. What was interesting was that she'd been arrested for driving under the influence of a controlled substance after she'd left Club Matrix, the same nightclub where the Snows had gotten their citations.

It was as good a place to start as any.

Linda put in a call to Tony, but only got his voice mail. She left a message telling him she had a lead and asked him to call her back. He called her in less than fifteen minutes.

"Tell me about this lead you're talking about."

"There's a place called Club Matrix. Do you know of it?"

"Yeah," Tony said. "It's an odd place—caters to an eclectic mix of clientele. Straights, gays, professionals looking for a little excitement by being in a dive. Sometimes even bikers go there, but not often."

"I have reason to believe Rapture deals go down at the club. I think we should go there tonight, Tony. Pose as a couple out for a good time and see what we can ferret out."

Silence filled the air. Linda waited, knowing what Tony was thinking. He wanted to protect her. Keep her safe. But her reputation was on the line. And so was Tony's life. Even if he wasn't in physical danger, his ability to move on and get on with his life was at stake. She wanted to help him get past that.

Finally Tony spoke. "There's no need for you to do that, Linda. First, the Rapture supplier contacted me. We're going to set up a meeting next week."

"A week's a long time," she said. "We might be able to find out something useful tonight."

He sighed. "You're right. I've been running around all day trying to find Justine but I'm having no luck. I'm going to check a few more places and then I'll check out the club myself."

"But—"

"I don't want you anywhere near that place, Linda. If drug deals go down there, it's too dangerous. I'll go there tonight. You'll stay in the hotel room. That's the deal we made, remember? You stick to making phone calls and sending emails while I take care of the rest."

"You take on too much, Tony. You need to trust others to help you."

He almost smiled at her scolding. "I trust you more than anyone, Linda."

"Good," she said quietly.

"I'll see you soon," he said before ending the call. Only later did he realize Linda had hung up without agreeing to stay away from Club Matrix.

Several hours later Tony walked into Club Matrix and immediately spotted Linda on the dance floor. Dressed in a tight lace skirt made to look as if it were bare underneath, a bustier and heavy makeup she'd never be seen wearing in court. She looked nothing like herself—not the prosecutor and not even the free-flowing woman who liked to wear T-shirts and jeans when she was at home—which had probably been the point. Now she looked like sex itself.

Of course that image was enhanced by the fact that she was dancing quite provocatively with another woman, a slender blonde. The sight of them together would immediately have men thinking of threesomes, but Tony's attention was focused solely on Linda. And the inevitable hardening of his body as he watched her.

Until a dark-haired man moved behind Linda and put his hands on her hips.

Tony clenched his fists and immediately wanted to rip the guy's head off. He wondered if Linda would... She didn't. Instead she turned, wrapped her arms around his shoulders and tipped her mouth to his ear, whispering.

Tony started toward them then forced himself to stop.

Chances were, if the man knew anything about Rapture, Linda would be able to gather more information with a few well-timed whispers than Tony ever could.

He'd give her exactly three minutes, he thought. After five had passed, Tony caught her eye. She tipped her head toward the man she still had her arms around and waggled her eyebrows up and down. What did that mean? That she'd gotten some good information? Great. Only did she have to keep dancing with the man?

She should be dancing with *him*.

Linda had liked to go dancing at clubs when they'd been together but they'd never frequented a place as hard-core and raunchy as this one. Still, she actually seemed comfortable with the club's alternative crowd. The slender blonde she'd been dancing with had her gaze fastened on Linda and occasionally Linda would catch her eye and smile.

Linda was playing a dangerous game tonight. And the game wasn't just for show. He could tell by her bright eyes and wide smile that she was actually enjoying herself. For some reason she felt safe teasing the crowd—teasing *him*. As fascinating as it was to once again see the more adventurous side of Linda, he wasn't sure he liked it. Right now her behavior smacked of self-destructiveness. They needed to get out of here.

He motioned for her to join him. She shook her head and mouthed the words, "Not yet."

No way. No way would he stand by while another man groped Linda.

He was just about to get up and bodily remove her from the dance floor when he felt a hand on his shoulder. Before he could stop her, a woman dropped into his lap and tried to kiss him. Tony caught her chin and stopped her. She pouted.

"What? You need a group to get it up?" She wiggled, almost causing his eyes to cross. Tony glanced at Linda and saw her scowling at them. Interesting, he thought. Apparently he wasn't the only one who was possessive.

Possessive didn't begin to describe how he felt when the dark-haired man leaned down, kissed Linda's neck and palmed her breast. Rage filled him like mercury speeding its way to the top of a thermometer, rising so quickly and so intensely that he felt like his head was going to explode. He stood up, dumped the woman off him and stalked over to Linda, coming close enough to catch an earful of the conversation.

"So, is life really more fun as a blonde?" The man stroked his hand over Linda's long hair. He pulled her hips up tighter against his. Linda stepped in time with his rhythm but leaned back.

"So, back to Rapture. Do you have any?" Linda asked.

Damn. She wasn't tiptoeing around things, now was she?

The guy tore his gaze from her cleavage and gave her a suspicious look. Tony inwardly swore. They had to get out of here.

She was about to repeat her question when Tony interrupted her. "There you are, baby. I've been looking everywhere for you."

She stiffened at the sound of Tony's voice.

So did the guy she was dancing with. "Hey, man. Buzz off." Linda's partner pulled her closer.

Tony walked calmly up to him and whispered in his ear. The guy gave her a rueful look, dropped his hands and quickly walked away.

Linda's eyebrows snapped together and she crossed her arms over her breasts. "What did you say to him?"

"The truth. That I'd castrate him if he didn't take his filthy hands off you." Tony took her arm and led her off the dance floor. At least he tried to. "Let's go."

She shook her head. "I'm not ready to go yet. I'm learning a lot here. Give me a few more minutes."

She was getting answers to her questions? He didn't care. Not now.

"Don't push me, Linda. Do I need to remind you you're running to be a judge. You get seen here and that's over. Let's go."

Again she shook her head. "Who's going to see me here? You can go if you need to. I'll be fine."

She looked like she actually expected him to obey and leave her here.

The other blonde walked up to them, put her hand on his chest and shouted, "Come on, baby, we can all have a little fun."

Tony studied the blonde, who upon closer inspection looked overly made-up. World-weary. He stepped away from her touch and directed his attention back to Linda. "We're leaving. Now."

Linda narrowed her eyes, clearly pissed at his continued insistence. On some level Tony knew he was being unreasonable, but he just couldn't forget the sight of the man's hands on Linda. The longer they stayed on the dance floor, the more the flashing lights, loud music and bumping bodies grated on the raw feeling of jealousy threatening to suffocate him.

Linda's next words acted like an accelerant to his already-inflamed emotions.

"Stop acting like a caveman and let me go, Tony. I'll leave when I'm ready to leave."

Tony lost it. "Caveman, huh? All right, if that's what you think…" He spun her around and picked her up over his shoulder. She squawked in surprise and then started struggling.

"What the…! Are you crazy? Put me down!"

The blonde and the dark-haired man watched them leave with a regretful shrug.

Tony headed for an unoccupied corner of the room and then slipped into a shadowed corridor that clearly led to the restrooms. Looking for more privacy, he found a side corridor with two doors. Neither opened, but at least now they were out of view of the crowd. One of her knees connected with his stomach, and Tony slipped, almost dropping her. He set her on her feet with a jarring thud. "What is wrong with you?"

"Me?" she yelled. "Since when do you have the right to manhandle me?"

"Since when do you have the right to tease me?"

Her mouth hung open in shock and her cheeks suffused with color. "What?"

"That's what you've been doing, right? Trying to get a rise? What, did you get a thrill, letting that bastard touch you? Were you trying to make me jealous?"

Linda gave him a look of disbelief. "I was *working,* Tony. Remember? Trying to get information. And it was working until you dragged me away."

Tony crossed his arms, refusing to apologize. "You shouldn't have let him touch you. I didn't like it."

Linda frowned, hearing only the censure in Tony's comment, not the emotion behind it. "Well, get over it, Tony."

Like hell he would, he thought. She was his. He'd be damned if he'd let some other man touch her, even if it was only to further their investigation. Grabbing her hand, Tony pressed her palm against his crotch. Her fingers curled around him, making him impossibly harder. "I've been inside you. I think that gives me a say."

She jerked her hand away but Tony immediately backed her into the wall. And did what he'd been wanting to do all night. Kissed her.

She fought him. For about two seconds.

Then she kissed him back. Opened her mouth wide and rubbed her tongue sinuously against his. She tasted sweet, like she'd been sipping Shirley Temples all night. The thought was so incongruent with where they were, how she was dressed, what they were doing. Yet it managed to turn him on even more.

He tried to slow down the kiss. Gentled the touch of his mouth on hers.

She wouldn't let him. "This way," she said.

He felt her hands at his pants.

"Linda…" He looked around. They were alone in the corridor, hidden by shadows, but that could change any second. "Let's get out of here."

"No, I want you now."

She kneeled in front of him, her frantic fingers working his zipper, pulling his erection free and then moving to take him in her mouth. He grabbed her and forced her up. He knew what she was doing. Usually he wouldn't say no. But he wasn't going to let her get away with it now. He saw the excitement in her eyes. The thrill of where they were.

"Then we're doing it my way," he growled. "I want you to look at me when I have you."

Tony pulled her to standing, then pushed her up against the opposite wall and slowly lifted her skirt. With one hand he tugged her panties down and off. He grabbed the backs of her thighs and lifted her up until her legs wound around his hips. He didn't look away as he entered her. When a couple stumbled down the adjoining corridor, laughing drunkenly, he shifted to ensure she was hidden and grabbed her face. "Look at me," he said. "Just me."

Tony kissed her as he began moving his hips in slow shallow thrusts.

Linda bit her lip to control her moans, but cried out when he hit a particularly sensitive spot. He spread her thighs even wider.

A loud noise sounded to her left, causing her to flinch.

"Look at me, Linda," he said.

She did, looking stunned. At what they were doing. And what she was feeling. Yet desire danced in her eyes, opening its arms and beckoning him on.

And so did love.

Tony lowered Linda to her feet and gently straightened her clothing.

She couldn't even look at him. God, what must he think of her? She'd just let him have sex with her in public. No, she hadn't just *let* him.

She'd demanded it.

Even now quivers of lingering pleasure ran through her, threatening to overshadow her guilt and uncertainty.

But then she saw the two people ten feet away and staring at them.

Linda gasped and felt her face heat with shame.

Tony frowned. "What is it? Who—?"

He turned and saw them.

Neil and Allie.

Chapter 27

When Tony and Linda got back to the hotel, she was a completely different woman than the one he'd found in that nightclub. All of her spirit and passion and yes, recklessness, had dissipated. In her place was a woman who was withdrawn and troubled.

Was she regretting what they'd done? And if so, was it because Neil and Allie had caught them, because of what she'd done, because of who she'd done it with or all of the above?

Anger still throbbed through him at the memory of what Neil had said to them, a sneer of disdain on his face. "I hope you've had fun, Linda. Because what you have to face in the morning? It's going to be anything but."

Tony had immediately stepped forward to push the man away, to warn him that threatening Linda was not a good idea, especially in front of Tony, but Linda had put a hand on his chest, staying him. She'd looked from Neil to the woman he was with but that woman had refused to look at Linda.

Linda had opened her mouth to say something to Neil, but then she'd shut it. She'd reached down, taken Tony's hand and said, "Let's go, Tony." That physical connection had hit him like a punch in the gut. It had told him she was choosing him over her career or her reputation—at least for now. And he'd wanted to pump his fist in the air in victory.

But after they'd left and started driving, the air had been supercharged with tension and any sense of satisfaction on his part had quickly cooled.

Now Linda kicked off her heels and sank into the corner of the hotel sofa. He perched a hip on the edge of the table, shoved his fingertips into the pockets of his jeans and kept his eyes on her face. Something was bothering her. Something more than embarrassment because they'd gotten caught having sex in a public place.

"Do you want to talk about it? Him? Neil?"

Her eyes jerked to his. "What? No. There's nothing to talk about. He's a colleague of mine. We were becoming friends. That's all."

"You're not—you're not upset because he was there with another woman?"

"No. At least not for the reason you think. Allie is a law-school student, but she's an adult. Late twenties. I just—I just don't think it's a good idea to mix business and pleasure." She grimaced. "But I guess that's exactly what we did."

"Because you consider trying to help me find the supplier part of your job?"

She just shrugged, and that vague gesture pissed him off.

Easy, he told himself. She's embarrassed because of what happened and that's completely understandable. Focus on something else. Like maybe the fact she'd put herself in danger when she'd agreed not to do so?

No, not a good topic to discuss right now, either. Not if he wanted her to open up to him. So…

"What did the guy you were dancing with say?" he managed to ask.

Linda shrugged and plucked at the lace on her skirt. "He said he knew someone who knew someone who could get Rapture. Someone that might surprise me. I suppose I'll have to go back, since you dragged me off him before I could get more information—"

Her casually stated intention to go back to the club made him blink in disbelief. "No," Tony snapped out. "I pulled you off him before he got suspicious—" And before he could rub his hands all over her damn body. "If you'd kept pushing, he would've known something was up. He would have assumed you were undercover."

"I doubt we'll ever know now. You dragging me off—"

"Will make him think you're a challenge. His pride will make you irresistible to him. You're not going back to that club." Not without me.

Linda didn't respond. She just curled her knees up to her chest, wrapped her arms around her shins and rested her chin in the cup made by her knees. She still wouldn't meet his gaze.

"What the hell is going on here?" Tony asked. "A half hour ago you were clawing your way across my body, now you won't even look at me."

"It's nothing," Linda murmured.

"Don't give me that, Linda," Tony snapped out. "I know you a hell of a lot better than you think. There's something you're not telling me. Something you're hiding, and I think it has less to do with this case than it has to do with you."

She refused to speak and simply closed her eyes. The lack of strength in her spine, the way her shoulders seemed to cave in on themselves, the dead look in her eyes, all told Tony her mind was churning something over. Something deep. Something dark.

Or maybe she was just feeling regret. Regret because he'd come back into her life and ruined it.

Yeah, that just might be it.

He sighed. "Are you thinking about your father? About the judgeship?"

The nod of her head was almost infinitesimal, but the motion showed him everything he needed to know. He came off the table, crossed the short expanse of carpet and came to sit next to her. He wrapped an arm around her shoulders, and although she remained stiff and unbending, he kept his arm there. Whatever was going on in her head, she needed him.

"Tell me," he said simply.

She hesitated. She'd already shared her body with him at the club, but she was obviously reluctant to share the most important part of her. He swallowed hard, closing his eyes in disappointment. But then she spoke.

"I never told you about my father, about how he was still living, because I was ashamed. But it was more than that. Much more. I'm not just ashamed of him. I'm ashamed of myself."

"But why?"

"My mom used to say how much I looked like him. How much I was like him. But she didn't even know about what I did. How bad I used to be."

His first thought was that she was exaggerating. Linda Delaney? Bad? It didn't compute.

"You don't believe me? My father was a bad man. He had bad genes. And I inherited those genes."

Tony stirred next to her. She really believed what she was saying, but he didn't. Sure, genetics could pass down the color of eyes, a cleft chin, even a propensity for alcoholism, but he did not believe genetics could make someone bad. Even so, Linda was on a roll, and he wasn't about to stop her from continuing.

"The first time I got drunk was on my twelfth birthday. After all of my friends went home from my birthday party, I snuck out and crawled through the window of the neighbor boy's house. I drank a quarter bottle of vodka before I threw up and passed out. After that I continued to sneak out at night. Got myself a fake ID and would go by myself to nightclubs. I'd dance and drink and smoke. My mom never knew, although Kathy suspected. It continued after my dad went to prison and we moved to Texas. I was a teen beauty queen, top of my class, presented this perfect exterior, but underneath I was boiling. It was like I couldn't stay within my skin."

"You were leading a double life," Tony said. He could smell the scent of her hair, feel her soft skin under his thumb, the warmth of her body pressed against him.

"I fooled around, too, Tony," she said. "I wasn't doing it for the booze or the cigarettes or anything like that. I just really liked the way my body felt when someone touched me. Alive, aroused, like what lived beneath my skin was finally able to break free." Linda covered her eyes. Her shoulders shook, and for a moment he wasn't sure what was happening. Then he realized she was crying, barely able to hold back her sobs.

He wanted to cry himself. She was breaking his heart.

None of what she said mattered. It surprised him, but it also made her seem more real to him. He still respected her more than any woman he'd ever met.

"You don't know me," she finally said. "You think I'm so good. Everyone thinks that. But I'm not. The judicial position? I don't deserve it. Just like I didn't deserve to be happy with you. The way I got off on making love with you in public just proves it. I'm as bad as my father." She sounded desperate to convince him and herself.

Tony refused to believe that. "He was an armed robber, Linda. That's not the same thing as liking the thrill of public sex now and again. You're beautiful. And smart. Funny. And kind. Yes, you're human. You've made mistakes. But we all do. It doesn't matter." He shook her lightly. "No matter what you say. No matter what you do. You're the best person I know."

She didn't seem convinced. "You should be thankful I kicked you out of my life, Tony. I blamed our breakup on you, but the truth is, I'm no catch. I'm a bad person, Tony. You don't know about what I've done. Who I used to be, even before you and I were together. I judged you, but the truth is, I don't deserve anything good. I don't deserve you."

With those words, Linda pulled herself to standing, and walked to the bathroom.

Tony sat there, stunned and frozen.

Was that really how she saw herself?

As someone undeserving of good things, things like love, simply because she'd made mistakes? This was not the cool, collected D.D.A. primed to become a judge. This was a woman with more baggage than he'd ever imagined—a woman wounded during childhood, who hadn't healed from her wounds.

Damn her father for making her believe she wasn't lovable. Damn himself for unintentionally making her feel the same.

He shoved to his feet and stormed over to the door. "Linda, come out. We need to finish talking." He turned the handle and found it locked.

"Leave me alone. Please!" Her voice had risen, almost as if in panic.

"I can't do that, Linda. I'm sorry. Now please, baby. Please let me in."

He waited.

And waited.

And forced himself not to speak again. He was about to lose the battle when he heard a slight click as she unlocked the door.

Gently he pushed the door open to see her curled in a tight ball on the floor. She seemed to shrink into herself, her face twisting in grief. He bent down, stroked her hair back then curled his arms around her to lift her. She didn't resist as he picked her up, carried her into the bedroom, sat down on the bed and cradled her in his lap.

Her body shook as she choked back her sobs, the stifled sounds somehow more tragic than if she'd let out her grief in a wail of agony. Each sound was a fist around his heart, killing him with the knowledge that he had brought her to this place where she clearly believed she wasn't worthy of love.

"Oh, baby," he whispered, "you're breaking my heart." He kissed her temple. Her cheek. Then her lips. Soft, closemouthed kisses meant to comfort more than arouse, but it didn't matter what he intended. Linda reared up, clinging to him, opening her mouth and kissing him with obvious desperation.

Tony cupped her jaw and tried to take control of the kiss, but she wouldn't let him. She straddled his lap, wrapping her arms and legs around him, rubbing herself against him as if she'd suddenly caught fire and he was the only thing that could extinguish the flames.

"Slow down, baby."

"No," she whimpered, tearing at his clothes and then her own. "Not slow. I want it like before. I want you to take me, just like you did in the club."

Her words set off alarm bells inside him and he pulled back, frowning. "Linda, no—" His words dissolved into a low groan when she cupped him in her hand and began stroking him with the exact pressure he liked. If that wasn't enough, she kissed a path down his throat and laved one of his nipples.

"Please, Tony. I need you. I need this. Please."

"This isn't what you need. We need to talk."

"I don't want to talk. I want you to show me. If you really think I'm good, if you ever loved me, Tony. Show me, now. Please."

"You are *so* good. And I couldn't love you more but—"

"Then prove it to me."

Damn it. He didn't know what to do. At least his brain didn't. But his body did.

He stood with her legs still wrapped around his torso, his bad leg almost buckling under him, but he pushed forward.

She'd shoved his pants down his legs so that they tangled around his ankles, hobbling him. "Like this. Right here." She reached down and grasped him, then rubbed him against herself.

Tony's knees wobbled and he struggled to stay standing. He gripped her ass tightly, lifted her up and down, and groaned when she sank onto him several inches.

With her hands braced on his shoulders, she immediately rose up and then sank down on him again. One more time and he was all the way inside her, shaking and gritting his teeth to keep from screaming.

He lifted her, controlling her movements so that she took him in deep slow thrusts. "Look at me," he whispered, but she shook her head and buried her face against his neck. "Linda, please—"

She was hiding from him. He didn't want her to hide. He tried to pull her head back, but she tightened her hold on him at the same time her internal muscles clamped down.

"You don't have to be ashamed of your darker side, Linda. It makes you human. That your body loves to touch and be touched this way is how nature made you. Passion is as much a part of you as your mind. Be proud of who you are. Because I'm so damn proud of you, baby. I always have been and that hasn't changed."

Linda looked at him. Finally, she really, truly looked at him, as if she saw into his soul. As if she finally was allowing herself to believe his words. His hands smoothed a path from her hips to her upper back and back down again. When she didn't protest, his hands swept her sides, lingering on the soft swell of her breasts.

"Be proud, Linda," he whispered.

A hint of a smile teased the corner of her lips. She let her eyes drift shut, then said, "Tony, I want you so much. Please. Please."

He shook his head but she grabbed his face and kissed him hard. She ground herself against him, moaning and closing her eyes when she dragged against his abs. "Tony. Please let me come. Please."

Her begging combined with the telltale trembling in her limbs undid him. With a guttural moan, he turned, stumbled into the bedroom and followed her down onto the bed, never breaking their connection. Grasping her thighs, he spread her wide and pounded into her. This time she didn't hide. She stared at him, her eyes mirroring the ecstasy he felt in his own expression, until the pleasure became too much. With a scream, she came, her body shaking, her core gripping him, her arms embracing him.

He followed right after her, roaring her name.

The ecstasy of an orgasm may be short-lived, but for Linda, the aftereffects lingered long after her body had found its release. She luxuriated in Tony's arms, tracing the bulge of new muscles covering him everywhere. Tony had changed in so many ways from the man she'd fallen in love with. This man, so familiar to her, was also almost a stranger.

The one thing that hadn't changed was the issues that stood between them.

"Want to tell me what's going on in that head of yours?" Tony asked. He shifted, coming up on an elbow and leaning his chin against his fist. With slow and deliberate movements, he brushed a strand of hair off her forehead and behind her ear. His eyes stayed focused on his fingertips, as if he didn't want to pressure her into answering.

"There have always been too many things that stood between you and me. Things that blocked any chance we could have had."

"My addiction, first and foremost," Tony said as his

gaze met hers. A muscle jumped in his jaw, but he kept his eyes soft.

"I didn't trust you to stay clean. Not really. When I saw those pills…" Linda averted her gaze and stared at the drapes blocking the window. At this time of night the streets of Sacramento were quiet. Most activities were taking place in the bedroom. Some slept, but lovers made love, children woke from nightmares and called for their daddies, and teenagers huddled under covers to text friends and hash out all the latest gossip. Some, like her, obsessed about their problems and worries and the imperfection in their lives.

"When you saw the pills," Tony finished for her, "you automatically assumed that once an addict, always an addict. But you had a good reason. I didn't intend to take those pills, but I forgot that when I actually had them. I was tempted, Linda, and you saw that. What else could you do? Live in fear your whole life that I'd slip up? Addiction isn't something you can erase from your life."

Linda pulled back, startled by Tony's understanding. His eyes caught hers, and this time he didn't look away. Instead he stared at her, his irises so full she felt she was swimming in a sea of golden-brown. His intensity didn't scare her. There was a gentleness about him, a reminder of the good man she'd once known. She trusted this intensity, and opened herself to hearing what Tony had to say.

"Once an addict, always an addict. But there's a difference between being a user and being a recovering addict." Tony's voice pitched deeper. "I was tempted to use that night, Linda, but I didn't. My foolishness was in thinking I had to prove to you just how strong I was, and that plan backfired."

"I don't understand. What do you mean?"

"I brought those drugs into the house to prove something to you. To show you how strong I was. To show you that no matter how much I wanted them—and yes, I wanted those drugs—I still wouldn't use. I wanted to ask you something, and I felt I didn't have the right to ask you until I proved why you could have faith in me."

"What were you going to ask me?" But even as she asked, she knew.

"I was going to ask you to marry me."

Chapter 28

At his words, Linda had closed her eyes.

The shakiness in Tony's chest rose. Had he pushed things too far? Shared too much of himself? He hadn't been going to tell Linda about wanting to marry her, but she'd been feeling so vulnerable. So unsure of herself. She'd trusted him enough to confide in him, and he'd wanted to give her a piece of himself in return.

He shouldn't have piled so much on her at once. He wasn't just a drug addict but a cop. Not just a former boyfriend but a man who'd wanted to marry her. Not just a man she'd once loved, but a man who was virtually a stranger to her.

To himself. He leaned back against the bed, breaking his contact with her, and swiped a hand over his face. Christ. Did he even know who he was anymore?

"You were going to propose to me?" Linda whispered. "And you thought that bag of pills would make me say yes?"

"It sounds stupid now, but at the time I was feeling cocky. And desperate. I knew you hated your father for being weak. And even though we were trying to make things work, I knew you thought I was weak, too. How else could I prove that I deserved you? So much for that plan, right?"

She crossed an arm over her eyes, hiding herself from him, then spoke. "I blamed the disintegration of our family on my father. Blamed him for everything. He put his addiction and his lawless lifestyle before his family. I wasn't going to see that happen again."

"Yeah," Tony said, "you made that clear."

Linda turned her back to him, and for a moment Tony thought she was leaving. Getting up off the bed. But instead she snuggled close against him, nestling her bottom against his crotch. She reached behind her, felt for his hand, and wrapped his arm around her waist, settling his hand on her breast.

Hope fluttered to life but he ruthlessly squashed it down. This was good, but it was a stasis of sorts. He was neither coming nor going. Neither happy nor sad. The future was full of unknown possibilities, including more disappointment. She wasn't kicking him out. But he wasn't willing to allow himself to hope.

Not yet.

"Am I just another girl with daddy issues?" she whispered. "And are they issues of my own making?"

"A father in prison? I don't think you're making anything up. But after finding that box of letters from him, you must be feeling…confused. Unsettled. In a matter of days you found out two people you were close to weren't what you thought. First me, then your dad."

For several minutes the only sound in the room was the low hum of the air conditioner and Linda's tight breath.

"I've judged both of you when I had no right. How's that for irony?"

"Of course you had a right. We hurt you. That's not what we wanted, but we did, and you wanted to protect yourself."

"But I hurt you, too. And all you did was protect me. And even my father, he deeded me the property in Grass Valley when I hadn't seen or heard from him in years."

"You're his daughter. He knows you loved him. You just didn't get the benefit of knowing he loved you. Not through his letters."

"My mother didn't tell me about them."

"She wanted to protect you."

"I need to see him, don't I?"

"It might do you good. Someday. But don't ask too much of yourself."

She shifted to face him. "How can you say that? Look how much you ask of yourself? You're endangering your own life, living without those you love, because you're trying to do the right thing. But when do you get to be happy, Tony?"

He stiffened. "When I've done enough to make up for my past."

"What past? You never hurt anyone on purpose. You have nothing to make up for. But you don't believe that, do you?"

"Do you believe it about yourself?" he countered.

She nodded, the movement sending her silken hair sliding across the pillow to rest on his cheek. He breathed in deep, taking in the scent of her shampoo. The scent of her. Instinctively he knew she wasn't answering in the affirmative, but rather agreeing with the point he was making. He pulled her in closer to his body.

"What a pair we make," she said with a sigh. "Speaking of which, we're still a team in this. We're going to find the supplier of that drug, Tony. And when we do, we'll revisit this conversation about what we each deserve and what we have to make up for. Deal?"

He smiled. "Deal." When he kissed the back of her neck, she let out a deep, shuddering sigh of contentment. He felt that same contentment. And right now, for a few hours at least, he was going to enjoy it.

The next morning Justine still hadn't answered any of his calls so he went looking for her again. He couldn't deny it anymore—he was worried about her. Where the hell could she be? Had something happened to her? Had someone found out she was helping Tony and decided to do something about it?

As he drove around town, he battled the mother of all headaches. Sex with Linda last night had been beyond amazing, but for a man who'd been pounded like a piece of brisket and had just battled an infection, the aftereffects were rather painful. For the past few days he'd been swallowing ibuprofen along with the antibiotics, but the meds were doing little for the sledgehammer going at it in his head.

As he grew more and more panicked about Justine, Tony told himself to think logically. If something had happened to her, he'd have heard about it by now. Maybe she didn't want him to find her. Maybe Linda was right and she didn't really care about Tony's mission to find the supplier and was happily getting high somewhere.

Yet he knew she'd genuinely loved Rory. And she'd

done a lot to give Tony the credibility he needed to win over Guapo's supporters. He was indebted to her. And for that, whether she used drugs or not, he owed her.

But for now there was little he could do if Justine wasn't picking up her phone or situated anywhere he could find her. Tony drove to the beat-up house that served as his headquarters. When he arrived, Carl was passed out on the living-room couch, beer bottles at his feet and drug paraphernalia littering the scarred coffee table in front of him. With a snarl of disgust, Tony shoved Carl to the floor.

After some fumbling and swearing Carl shoved himself up on his hands and knees, and stared at the stained shag carpet in front of him. Then he raised foggy eyes to Tony, blinked and grinned. "Hey, man. Where you been? You are in some serious trouble, dude. Justine's been on a warpath since you disappeared. Thinks you ran off with some other woman."

Tony swallowed hard, knowing perfectly well that Justine would know he'd been with Linda. But right now he was still undercover and as such he played his part. "You know what the rules are," Tony said, his voice low and filled with venom. "Drink all you want, screw all you want, but do not bring drugs in here. I do not want anything at this house that could link us to the business. Are you a moron, Carl?"

This pretense was exhausting. He hated playing the tough guy. Having to be tough. Constantly on alert. Suspicious. It was becoming more reality than fantasy.

Except when he was with Linda. With Linda, he could be himself. Relax. Be gentle. Soft.

Well, not quite soft, he thought with a completely inappropriate spurt of amusement.

Carl sat back on his haunches, his hands resting

lightly on his thighs. "I'm sorry, but I couldn't resist. Justine's been MIA the past few days, too. She showed up last night, stoned out of her mind and going on and on about having hit the mother lode. Said she understood why her brother had gotten hooked on Rapture. Said you were an idiot for trying to stop the supplier from selling more." Carl's eyes narrowed. "Wonder what she meant by that?"

Tony shrugged, though inside he was reeling from Justine's betrayal. "Who the hell knows? You just said she was stoned out of her mind. Is that what you're high on? Rapture?"

"No," Carl whined. "She said she didn't have any more, so I had to make do with what I could."

"Did she say where she got the Rapture?" And whether this was the first time she'd tried it, Tony thought. Had she been using Rapture the entire time they'd been working together?

"Some place with lots of traffic. A club."

"What club?" Tony snapped even as suspicion made his heart pick up speed. He gripped Carl's hair and yanked his head back, making the man wince.

"Quit it, man, or I'm going to hurl."

Looking around, Tony spotted an empty beer bottle, grabbed it and broke it against the wall. Yanking Carl's head back even farther, he held the jagged glass threateningly close to Carl's throat. "What club?" he asked again.

Carl's eyes were as wide as saucers and it took him several attempts to speak. "A place called Club Matrix."

After taking evasive precautions to make sure he wasn't followed, Tony drove back to the hotel where Linda was staying. "You might be right about Justine,"

Tony told her. "She's been going to Club Matrix. She might even have been there last night. More important, she went there to score Rapture and she's been getting high on the stuff." Pacing, he ran his hands through his hair. "But why? I don't understand. Why would she take the drug that killed Rory?"

"She might have already been using the stuff when Rory was killed. Who knows? Even if she hadn't been, she was using something. Plus…well…women will do crazy things out of jealousy."

Tony stopped pacing. "But who would Justine be jealous of?"

Linda stared at him as if he was an idiot. "Of me, Tony. She was obviously in love with you."

"What? No. I mean, I know I deliberately misled you about our relationship, and maybe I haven't been explicit with her about my feelings, but…but…"

"But you kissed her in court, remember? Even if it was to hurt me…"

He winced and swiped his hands over his face.

Despite his obvious discomfort, Linda forced herself to continue. "If she loves you, how do you think she felt when you disappeared for days without contacting her? Especially knowing how you feel about me?"

"I never told her about us or how I felt about you—" Tony said quickly.

"You wouldn't have to. She would have seen the way you looked at me. A woman who loves a man would recognize his desire for another woman. And you know what they say about a woman scorned." She snorted. "For all we know she's the person behind the attempts on my life—" Her eyes widened as the truth of her own words sunk in.

He felt his own eyes widen, as well. "No," he whispered. "I can't have been that wrong about her. Can't have brought that kind of sicko danger into your life simply because some woman…some woman…"

"Cares about you, Tony. It might be in some kind of twisted way, but she does care about you."

His face tightened. "If she's responsible for the threats on your life, that's not going to stop me from—"

His cell phone rang. When he looked at the screen, he cursed. "It's her. But why now? Carl must have told her I came by."

Linda nudged him as the phone continued to ring. "Aren't you going to answer?"

"I—I don't know. Damn it, if what you just said is true, what am I going to do? Confront her? Risk her blowing my cover and ruining everything I've worked for?"

Linda cupped his face in her hands and urged him to look at her. As he gazed at her, his accelerated heartbeat slowed slightly.

"You're going to do what you need to do, Tony. And if there's any way you can help Justine while doing it, you will. Because you're you."

He swallowed hard. Basked in the pleasure of her faith in him. At least in this, right here and right now, she had faith in him.

"Answer the phone," she said softly.

He did.

Several minutes later, he hung up and looked back at Linda. Anger. Fear. Dread. They swirled through him like a tornado, making him shake and breathe hard. He shook his head in disbelief. "She said she set up a meeting between me and the guy she's been buying Rapture from. I have no idea whether it's the same man who contacted me or not, and I didn't tell her about that. I'm supposed to meet her at the club tonight."

"But," she prompted.

"But...she knows I've been seeing you. And she doesn't like it. She says she'll make sure the meeting goes through. But only if I meet her at a motel before the designated time. Take some of the Rapture drugs. And have sex with her."

Chapter 29

"No," Linda whispered. She didn't know what horrified her more. Tony being forced to take drugs or being forced to have sex with Justine.

No, that wasn't quite true, she thought. The sex definitely horrified her the most, and what kind of hypocrite did that make her given she'd left him because of the drugs in the first place. Either option was unbearable. "You can't, Tony. Please don't—"

He gave a sharp bark of laughter, startling her. "Of course I can't. I'm not about to let someone blackmail me into doing drugs or having sex with her."

Relief swept through Linda even as she wondered… wasn't some part of him tempted by the drugs? By the possibility of sex with a woman as beautiful as Justine?

It was if he could read her mind. He glared at her, held her away from him and said, "No amount of money or drugs could persuade me to sleep with Justine. I want to avenge Rory and help others, but I'm not going to do it that way."

She suddenly couldn't help herself… She flung her arms around his waist and hugged him close. "I'm so glad."

His laugh this time was softer. Exasperated yet full of affection. As he lapsed into silence, however, she could practically feel him struggling to adapt to the weird turn of events.

They held each other for several minutes before she said, "So what are you going to do?"

Tony pulled back and released her. "I'm still not completely sure whether the cops I've been working with are clean, but I have no choice but to trust them. They're the lesser of several evils as far as I'm concerned. I'm going to call Yee. Tell him what I know about Club Matrix. And hope the Rapture supplier we're looking for shows tonight whether Justine gives him the go-ahead or not. I'll go in with a wire and ask some questions and—"

She started to speak, but he cut her off. "—and *no,* you aren't coming with me, Linda. Please. As much as I love the memory of our last visit there, don't fight me on this. This is *my* job. Let me do it. *Trust me* to do it."

He knew her so well. She *had* been going to suggest she go with him.

"Okay," she nodded. "But I think we should do something together. Before you leave for Club Matrix."

He wiggled his eyebrows up and down. "And what's that?"

She swatted at him, relieved that he could keep his sense of humor despite his despair over Justine. "Obviously not what you're thinking. Well, not *just* that," she amended. "I think we should see Justine together and try to reason with her."

"Uh, what makes you think that's a good idea? Given the nature of her demands, she's obviously jealous of you and willing to play hardball. I'm completely willing to believe at this point that she's the one that's been causing us—causing *you*—problems. I don't want you near that kind of danger. Any kind of danger."

He was willing to risk himself, yet never wavered from his determination to protect her. At that moment his selflessness made her fall even more in love with him. But she had to help him somehow. She couldn't just sit here and let him take all the risks. She opened her mouth to argue, but he tapped a finger against her lips.

"While I'm gone, you're going to stay here, Linda, where you'll be safe. But about that other thing you suggested we do before I leave? I happen to think that was a very, very good idea."

Smiling, she nudged his finger aside and moved to kiss him. There was still time before he had to leave. She'd love to spend it in his arms, and if she could manage to convince him during that time to let her help, then all the better.

To her surprise, however, he evaded her touch and said, "Let's go for a drive."

After donning a baseball cap and sunglasses, Tony brought Linda to the nearby Discovery Park, a swath of nature and wildlife following the American River as it coursed through the heart of Sacramento. She was confused and, understandably so, a little annoyed by Tony's lack of romantic follow-through. But Tony kept smiling mysteriously at her, and periodically kissing her—long wet kisses that kept her blood set to a constant simmer until she finally realized that's exactly what he wanted. He'd decided to take her on some kind of adventure be-

fore he had to leave for Club Matrix, and despite everything, she was going to give herself over to it. To him.

Surrounded by the river on one side and overgrown
brush, trees and grasses on the other, Linda realized
that the sound of the city had faded to nothing. That the
acrid smell of exhaust and smog had been replaced by
the earthy scent of the river and a hint of mint.

"Look," Tony said, his voice eager and excited. He
pointed down the pathway.

Linda traced the arc his finger made and saw a pair
of deer trotting in the bushes. She let out a gasp and
stopped, freezing in place.

"I've seen them out here before," Tony said. "These
may not be the same pair, though."

"It's cool. How wild things can live in such an urban
area."

"Yeah. Pretty cool. They're both wild and free."

She looked at him, not understanding his point.

He was no longer watching the deer.

He was watching her.

Smile lines crinkled the edges of his eyes. He reached
for her hand and interlaced his fingers with hers. He
tugged her closer until her hips met his.

"What are you doing?" she asked, even though she
knew exactly what he was doing. What he wanted them
both to be doing. She looped her arms around his neck
and pressed her body even tighter against him.

Wild and free.

It was how Tony made her feel.

And for once, here on this isolated path where it was
only the two of them and the occasional animal passing by, she was determined to enjoy the feeling without
guilt or recrimination.

"Wild and free," Tony repeated, grinning. A light

breeze traveled down the path of the waterway, grabbed the tips of her hair and flipped them up. "Just like you," Tony said. "You are the same as those deer. Wild and free, despite the fact you live in a civilized, controlled environment. You shouldn't feel bad when your true nature yearns to break free. You should celebrate it. Not all the time, but sometimes. When it's safe. When you're with me."

He kissed her and she moaned, feeling her hunger and love for him filling her up.

Her passion boiled over like a Texas storm cloud, taking away her reason and giving her only pleasure until he broke off the kiss. She whimpered and touched her tender lips, wanting only his taste, his scent, his touch all over her.

"Let your wild child out," Tony whispered in her ear, then caught her mouth with his again.

Hot, passionate and wild, the kiss went on and on. She forgot about Justine, her father, her quest for the judgeship and her doubts about a future with Tony. All she knew was her love for him, here and now. She marveled at the feel of his mouth, his taste, the sound he made when he sucked in air and the feel of his heart beating against her own.

She was free. *They* were free.

Free to feel. Free to enjoy each other despite the years and the heartache that had separated them for so long.

But then Tony broke their kiss once again. Her knees caved and she sagged against him. Surprised by her sudden weight, he stumbled backward and tripped over a root. He caught himself by twisting, then winced as he righted both himself and her.

"I'm sorry," she cried. "I hurt you."

"It's nothing," Tony said. "Come here."

"Where—"

He led her to an outcropping of rocks beneath a large tree. They were completely off the path now. Secluded, but still close enough to hear someone if they came toward them. Slowly, Tony sat on a large flat boulder and patted the spacious area next to him.

Heat zipped through her veins.

She sat beside him and placed a tentative hand on his thigh. Did he want what she thought he did? Did he want to make love out here, out in the open, or would he be horrified by her attempts to take things in that direction? She was afraid of misreading him and as a result her touch was hesitant. Fleeting. He swallowed hard and placed his hand over hers. Picked it up and pressed it to his lips before placing it back on his thigh.

"Don't tease me, baby. I'm about to explode as it is."

His unexpected confession sent sensual quivers through her limbs. It made her tummy turn somersaults. "I wasn't meaning to tease."

Tony moved her hand farther up his thigh until her fingertips swept the length of him on the inseam of his jeans. "I want to be inside you. Here. Give me your wild side, Linda. Please."

Once more they kissed for several moments, rubbing their hands over one another's hair and bodies. She protested when Tony raised his head. He kept stopping. Why did he keep stopping?

"I won't stop. We won't stop. But I want you naked. Now."

She stopped protesting.

And reached down to take off her clothes.

While she stripped, Tony did the same.

They came together as wildly as Tony thought her to be.

She rejoiced in that wildness, but she also rejoiced in the other things he made her feel.

Beautiful. Sexy. Loved.

Linda felt bombarded by sensation, emotional and physical. She no longer knew where she was. The world ceased to exist. Only Tony was there. In her mind. In her heart. In her body. She felt a familiar pressure building inside her, but didn't fight it.

She embraced it.

Welcomed it.

When she came, she came looking into Tony's eyes.

Several hours later Tony dropped Linda off at their hotel and drove to the motel where Justine had said to meet him. Thinking positively, he was dressed to go to Club Matrix, but because he was prepared for the worst, he was also wired.

Yet another reason not to get naked with Justine.

As if he needed another reason.

As if the memory of being inside Linda would ever allow him to do such a thing. Ever allow him to want or love another woman again.

He shook his head to clear it.

He couldn't see Justine with thoughts of Linda clouding his head. He had to be careful. Very careful. If she was taking Rapture and had put a bounty on Linda's head, she was seriously dangerous. He took some comfort in the fact that Yee would not only be able to hear what he and Justine talked about, but that the other man was stationed around the block. He could be inside Justine's motel room in under a minute.

All Tony had to do was say the code word in enough time for Yee to actually get there. That, and pray that his instincts in choosing to again trust Yee were spot-on.

He knocked on the designated motel room door.

The motel wasn't a palace, but it wasn't sleazy, either. It was clean. Respectable.

Despite her attempts to blackmail him, maybe Linda was right. Maybe Tony could help Justine get back on the road to being clean and respectable, too. He'd failed to help Rory, and for all he knew it was Justine's grief at her brother's death that had sent her spiraling out of control. If he could help Justine, he would.

But he was not going to risk himself or his relationship with Linda to do it.

"Justine," he called when she didn't answer. "It's Tony. Open the door."

But she didn't answer.

Had she tricked him? he wondered abruptly. Had she lured him here knowing that would mean leaving Linda alone and vulnerable?

"What's going on, Tony?" Yee asked through the transmitter in Tony's ear.

"She's not answering," Tony said softly. He knocked louder. Called out again. "Justine!"

"Is there a problem, sir?"

A maid pushing a linen cart spoke from behind him.

He thought quickly. "I locked myself out and my girlfriend isn't answering. We got into a fight earlier and I'm worried. Can you let me in so I can check on her?"

The woman shook her head. "Sorry. I can't."

"Yee," Tony said.

"I got it," Yee said. "I'll check with the manager. Get a key and meet you in a few."

"Hurry." Tony didn't know why he said it. But once he did, urgency made him start pacing.

Soon, Yee showed up, key in hand. He pounded on the door. "Ma'am. This is the manager. Are you in there? I need you to answer me or I'm coming in. Ma'am?"

With a final glance at Tony, who stood to the side, Yee withdrew his gun and held it at the ready. He unlocked the door and slowly swung it open.

He didn't walk inside the room, though. He cursed, entered the room with his gun drawn, then almost immediately snapped, "The room's clear. Call an ambulance. I think she's OD'ing."

Tony swiftly entered the room and saw Justine. She was lying in the bed, pale and sweaty, her entire body trembling. Her eyes were open, however, and they were latched on Tony, her gaze desperate. Her dry cracked lips moved, but no sound came out. And even as he dialed for the ambulance, he knew what she'd been trying to say.

Help me.

Chapter 30

Tony stood looking down at Justine, who was sleeping again. She'd been in the hospital for almost forty-eight hours. It had been touch-and-go for her at first, but once the medical staff had stabilized her, her health was improving rapidly. Physically, it seemed, she was going to be fine.

Her mental health, however, was still in question.

She'd been in and out of consciousness, and Tony had rarely left her side. He couldn't. At first he'd been worried about her. Then it had become obvious that seeing him always caused her to have an intense emotional response. Initially she'd simply cried or screamed with rage. But then she'd started talking. And once that had happened? Well, he hadn't wanted to risk missing a single word she'd said.

Some of what she said didn't make sense, but a lot of it did.

Her words were a jumbled mess of love and hate, with her alternately thanking him for saving her and fighting for her brother, and cursing him for abandoning her for Linda. Other times she didn't seem to realize what had happened, and she'd ask whether he'd discovered the identity of the Rapture supplier or whether Guapo had been released from prison yet.

The real shocker had occurred almost twelve hours ago, however, when she'd confessed, quite gleefully, to twice hiring someone to kill Linda. She'd been responsible for both the shooting at the courthouse and the attempted attack on Linda at her house. She'd done it because she loved him, she'd said, and knew she wouldn't have a chance with him so long as Linda was around. When Tony had asked her the identity of the person she'd hired, she'd waved him off, saying that she'd met some guy at a bar and had been having sex with him to get him to do what she wanted. At his urging, she'd finally given Tony the guy's name and address. He'd already been picked up and booked into jail, and Yee was working on serving a search warrant on the Tortuga Boulevard house. Soon, Carl and Nicco Santos would be in jail, too, although the bust would in no way be linked to either Justine or Tony. In that way, at least, Justine would be protected, and hopefully in protecting herself, she'd keep Tony's true agenda a secret, too.

Tony was still struggling to accept it all, including his stupidity for not having seen Justine for what she really was and his guilt for having placed Linda in danger again despite all his good intentions to protect her.

"Hey," Linda said softly, squeezing his arm and making him jump.

He turned toward her. She'd been sitting in a chair several feet from Justine's bed, but had risen to stand beside him. It was the second time she'd come to see him at the hospital even though he'd told her he didn't want her here. It wasn't that Justine was a threat to her anymore—her hands and feet were manacled to the bed—but he didn't want Linda to hear the ugly things that Justine often said about her.

But when Linda had insisted on staying again, he hadn't had the strength to fight her. If she wanted to stay with him after everything he'd put her through, he'd just enjoy her while he could. In his mind, she'd be walking away from him soon enough.

"Stop it," she said. "I know what you're thinking. I can see it in your eyes. You're blaming yourself for all this, and I'm not going to let you do it. You are not responsible for what she tried to do to me and you're not responsible for what she did to herself. She had a drug problem, Tony, long before you and I ever saw each other again. You have to remember that."

He heard what she was saying. Logically, a part of him could even accept it. But emotionally? He hurt. More than he'd ever hurt physically. He felt like a failure.

As a cop.

As a man.

Maybe he couldn't do anything about the latter, but the former? Maybe he could still do something about that.

"You should get to work," he told her. "It's your first day back, remember? Now that we know Justine was behind the threats to you, you need to get on with your life. There's no sense in you sitting here waiting for her to wake up. And I'd really prefer you not be here when she does, anyway. Please."

"You still think she'll tell you something about the man who sold her the Rapture?"

"I don't know, but I need to find out. Maybe I was wrong about everything else, but I still think she loved her brother. If I can appeal to her on that level, who knows?"

Linda nodded and stood. Then she bent to lightly kiss him.

He closed his eyes. Breathed her in. Soaked in the feel of her and wondered how long this would last. Wondered when she'd realize that, just like Justine, he was still a drug addict and as such would always bring complications to her life. Complications she wanted no part of.

"Will you come by my house later? Around six o'clock? I'll be back from work then and there's something I want to show you."

"Sure," he said, giving her a tired smile.

After she left, Tony stared at his clasped hands and waited.

Less than an hour later he looked at Justine and found her gaze on him.

She was looking at him with a calmness and clarity he hadn't seen her exhibit the whole time she'd been here.

"Hey," he said softly and scooted his chair a couple of feet closer. He forced himself to smile.

"Hey," she said back, returning his smile. A few seconds of silence passed, then she said, "So do you know?" she whispered. "Did I...did I tell you what I've done?"

"That you tried to have Linda killed, you mean? Yeah, I know." Inside his rage was still building. He hated her for the danger she'd put Linda in. For the way she'd played him. But he'd been playing a part for so long, he almost felt like a different person. He needed information from Justine and showing his rage wouldn't get it. So he didn't show it. It was as simple as that.

"I did it because I love you, Tony. And I know you love me. You were willing to go to jail to protect me, weren't you?"

"Yeah," he said, leaning over and touching her arm. "I was."

She smiled and they were silent again.

Finally he said, "Do you still want to help me find the man who sold Rory the drugs that killed him, Justine? The drugs that almost killed you? Or was wanting to help me all a lie?"

She jerked her gaze to his. "No, it wasn't a lie. I—I used Rapture, too. Before Rory died. But I got it from him. I didn't know who he got it from."

"But you knew he got it from Club Matrix. And you know who's peddling it now, don't you?"

"I don't know him," she said. "I don't know his name. But—"

"But what?" he said calmly. Almost numbly. Which was exactly how he felt. Numb. Not like himself. But who was he really?

"But I know who might," she said.

He felt a spark of something ignite inside him. Excitement? Hope? "Who?"

"Linda."

Linda sat in her office with her boss sitting across from her, but her mind was still on Tony. She'd hated leaving him in that hospital room. Knew that guilt was eating away at him. But he was right. She'd needed to get back to work. To her life. She just hoped she'd be able to convince him that she wanted him to be part of it.

"What a mess," Norm Peterson said. "But I have to say, I'm glad for you, Linda. We'll contact that reporter as soon as things are squared away. Being involved with an undercover cop posing as a drug dealer is going to be a lot better for your judicial campaign than being involved with a drug addict."

"He *is* a drug addict," she said. "Whether he's a cop or not, that hasn't changed. But…"

Norm cocked a brow. "But?"

"But I have. At least, I've changed my mind about running for judge. I'm going to withdraw my name from consideration."

Norm sighed. "Because you're going to stay with him?"

"No. I mean—I want to stay with him. I hope he wants to stay with me. I hope we can make a relationship between us work this time. But if I have any chance of making that happen, I can't be concerned about my reputation and I can't expose my private business or Tony's to the public, especially given what he does for a living. I also…I also can't expose my father's private business to the public, either."

"We already talked about this before you ever put your name in for the bench. So long as you disavow your father, your campaign shouldn't be negatively affected by his past mistakes."

"I know. But I don't know if I want to disavow my father any longer. I've made some calls about seeing him. I want to talk to him and see what kind of possibilities exist there, too. I'm sorry if that disappoints you."

Norman stared at her for a few seconds, then smiled and rose. "It doesn't disappoint me, Linda. You're a great attorney. One I'm proud to have working for me. You do what you need to. Judge or no judge, I'll be behind you." He reached out a hand and she shook it.

"Thank you, Norm."

When he was gone, Linda sighed and picked up the phone. Twenty minutes later she had an appointment to see her father in prison. She really hoped Tony meant what he'd said about being willing to go with her, because she was planning on taking him up on his offer. Somehow, knowing Tony would be by her side made her feel as if she could face anything.

Linda rose, exited her office and was on her way to the watercooler when she saw Allie just leaving the main office and heading into the lobby. She hadn't talked to the other woman since Allie had caught Linda and Tony having sex at Club Matrix. She supposed she should get that first awkward conversation over with.

Quickly Linda made her own way to the lobby. "Allie," she called just as the younger woman was stepping out the back entrance to the parking lot.

The law student held the door open as Linda followed her out.

Tony stared at Justine and said "You're sure you saw the man who gave you Rapture before? In the courthouse when I was arraigned? And after I was released on bail?"

"I'm sure, Tony. He flirted with me both times. And then when I went to Club Matrix that night, when I was so angry with you for disappearing with Linda, he flirted with me again. He wanted to have sex with me. And when I jokingly said I'd do it if he gave me some Rapture…well, he had it. He gave it to me. We used it together. And then he said he knew who you were, and that if you were interested in paying him, he could arrange for you to get more."

"I was at Club Matrix, Justine. I saw one of Linda's coworkers there. But he has dark hair. You said this guy is blond."

"That's right. Blond. Handsome. Cocky. Annoying as hell. I swear, if he pointed his finger at me like a gun one more time, I was going to bite it off. I—"

"Pointed his finger like a gun?" Tony echoed. And just like that, he had a vision of himself sitting in his car, watching Linda and Neil Christoffersen talking as another man appeared and made the very gesture Justine was talking about. It could be coincidence, of course, but—

Tony stood and walked to the door.

"Tony? Wait! Where are you going?"

Pausing at the doorway, he looked back at Justine. He was still angry with her, but mostly he felt sorry for her.

"I—I remembered something. And I need to make a phone call."

"But you're going to come back, aren't you? You still love me, don't you?"

It should have been easy for him to lie. To say he loved her. But he couldn't. He loved Linda, and he refused to diminish those feelings for her by saying the words to this woman. So he said what he could. "I don't know what's going to happen, Justine, but you've done the right thing by telling me what you know. Thank you for that."

Chapter 31

As Tony drove to the District Attorney's Office, he tried calling Linda, but she didn't answer her phone, not her office phone or her cell. He tried again, this time calling the receptionist, who put him on hold. When the woman came back on the line, she said she couldn't find her.

"What about Neil Christoffersen?" he asked. "Is he there?"

"One minute."

A few seconds later Christoffersen answered his phone.

"This is Tony Cooper. I need you to answer this question for me. It's important. Life or death important, and I'll explain later. Do you understand?"

After a brief pause Christoffersen said, "Fine. But *if* I answer, it's because Linda trusts you. Not because I do."

"A few weeks ago, before I was arrested, Linda was

eating her lunch outside. You joined her. You were both sitting on a bench when a blond man stopped to talk to you. He made a gesture, pointing his finger like a gun, and when he left, you both laughed about it. Do you remember?"

"How do you know all this?" the other man growled. "Were you—"

"Do you remember?" Tony interrupted.

"Yeah, I remember."

"The blond man. Does he work with you?"

"Damn it, tell me why—"

"Does he?" Tony shouted.

"Yes he does," Christoffersen shouted right back. "Now tell me why you want to know."

"Because I have an eyewitness who says this man gave her Rapture while they were both at Club Matrix."

"Rapture. While he was at Club Matrix," Christoffersen echoed. "Oh, my God."

"What is it?" Tony asked, catching the peculiar tone in the other man's voice. The tone that sounded almost like acceptance. "You were there. Was this man there, too?"

"He was there the same night I saw you and Linda. He was the one who invited Allie and me to the club. He said it was his new favorite hangout. After we saw you there, I left. But they stayed. *He* stayed."

"What's his name?" Tony asked. "Is he there now?"

"His name is Brian Heald," Christoffersen said. "And is he here now? I don't know. Hang on while I check."

"Wait—" Tony shouted, wanting to tell the man to look for Linda instead.

But Christoffersen had already put him on hold.

Tony drove faster, cursing steadily until Christoffersen came back on the line.

"He called in sick. He's not here."

Tony felt a moment of relief. "Linda. Have you seen her?"

"She was in her office a while ago, but when I went looking for Heald, she was gone. Her cell was on her desk."

"Hey, Linda," Allie said as the door closed behind them. "How are you?"

Linda couldn't help it. The fact that Allie had seen Linda and Tony having sex in a public club made her face burn. She forced herself, however, to appear unconcerned. "I'm good, Allie. How are you?"

Allie shrugged. "I've been better. Look, I'm glad you stopped me. I've been meaning to call you and tell you…you don't have to be embarrassed about what happened at Club Matrix. I don't think any less of you. Okay?"

Without waiting for Linda's reply, Allie started walking again, obviously heading to her car.

Linda thought about the other woman's words. She should be relieved, shouldn't she? Part of her was. What she'd done had been reckless and it wasn't something she planned on repeating anytime soon, if ever. But she also found it a little odd that Allie would bring it up. Once again, she fell into step beside the law student.

"Do you go to that place often, Allie?"

Allie stopped beside her car, a little white Cabriolet, and shook her head. "No. That was the first time I'd been there. Neil, too."

"Are you two dating?"

Allie blushed. "I wish. Neil's not interested in me. But you already know that, don't you? Since he's interested in you," she said with a twist of her mouth. "I told Brian his plan wouldn't work."

Brian?

Brian-The-Jerk-Heald?

Linda sucked in a breath. "What do you mean?"

Allie unlocked her car and pulled open the driver's side door. She blew a strand of hair out of her face. "He goes to Club Matrix all the time. He went even before his wife left him. It's probably the reason she left to begin with. Anyway, he's the one who told me about it. He invited Neil and me to get some drinks there. Neil thought it was to celebrate Brian's divorce, but Brian was really trying to get the two of us together. Because he knows how I feel about Neil."

Linda narrowed her eyes. "Did he try to do you any other favors while you were there, Allie?"

Allie averted her gaze. "I—I—I don't know what you mean."

Realization made Linda's skin crawl. "Yes, you do. Did Brian try to give you anything while you were at the club? Drugs. Rapture. Did you take it?"

Allie flushed, giving Linda her answer.

"Oh, Allie, no."

"I'm sorry," she blurted out. She looked around as if wanting to make sure no one else could hear their conversation. "I know I shouldn't have. But Neil was so pissed off after he saw you and Tony. And I was upset. And Brian was there and he offered me something and I thought it would be just like taking a drink. That I'd just give it a try, you know?"

"Have you done it since then?"

Allie shook her head. "No, I swear, Linda. It was just the one time. I mean, Brian's kept offering but—"

"Shut up!"

Linda and Allie whirled and gasped in unison.

Brian Heald stood next to them.

But he didn't look like the Brian Heald Linda knew.
He looked frazzled. And dirty. And crazed.

And he had a gun pointed straight at them.

"You," Linda said to Brian. "You're the supplier Tony's been looking for."

Brian laughed. "I'm not a supplier, Linda. I'm just a user. And occasionally, a dealer, only I usually trade in sex not money. Unfortunately I picked the wrong person to deal to, didn't I?"

"Justine," Linda said.

Grinning, Brian said, "Bingo." Then his grin was replaced by a scowl. "I was hoping I'd get lucky and she'd die before they got her to the hospital, but that didn't happen, did it?"

"I don't know what you're talking about—" Linda began.

Brian shouted, "Give it a rest. I know, Linda. I know Tony Cooper's a cop. I was on my way to pay Justine another visit when I saw Tony there. With an undercover cop. Ash Yee. He's testified in my cases before. You can imagine how freaked out I've been, imagining what Justine's been telling him. Wondering if she's told the police enough to implicate me. But you'd know, wouldn't you? You've been to the hospital. So tell me. What do they know?"

"You're crazy." She glanced at Allie. "Get out of here, Allie."

"I don't think so," Brian said. "Fine. You won't tell me on your own? Then I'll have to make you tell me." He waved the gun at them. "Get in the car, Allie. Behind the wheel. Linda, get in the passenger seat. We're going for a little drive."

"No," Linda said, trying to sound firm when she was scared out of her mind. There was no way she was getting in that car with him. Doing so would be a death sentence.

Brian narrowed his eyes. "Now, Linda. Or I'll shoot you both right here."

"With our coworkers inside?" Linda asked. "You're going to shoot us? Kill us?"

"I'm going to do whatever I have to do, Linda. Make no mistake about that. Now do it or I'll shoot Allie in the head right now."

Allie whimpered and Linda said, "It's okay, Allie. Do what he says."

They watched as Allie slid behind the wheel and shut the door.

Brian kept his gun trained on Linda. "Now you. Go around to the other side."

Slowly she walked toward the passenger door. As she did, she kept a close eye on Brian. He was swaying on his feet, obviously either sick or under the influence of something. She wondered if it was Rapture and, if so, why the damn stuff hadn't yet killed him the way it had Rory and the way it had almost killed Justine.

"Is this why your wife left you? Because you're a drug user slash dealer slash man whore?"

"Shut up, Linda, and open the door."

Linda reached for the passenger door and opened it. As she did, she saw Brian frown. She almost wanted to laugh.

The Cabriolet was a two door.

If he was going to get in the backseat in order to hold a gun on them, he'd have to do it before she got in the car.

"This is ridiculous, Brian. Why don't you get out of here? Get a head start on the police."

"Shut up!" he screamed before he winced and grabbed at his head with his free hand. "You and your damn boyfriend. And here I thought he was just like me. A drug addict."

Linda lifted her chin. "He is a recovering drug addict. But he's nothing like you. Nothing," she spat. She glanced at Allie, who looked teary eyed and helpless.

Brian turned, placing his back to the open passenger door. "Don't try anything," he warned. "I'll shoot if you or Allie make a wrong move. I'm going to get in first, then you're next."

He eased back and stooped, clearly intending to settle into the backseat. Clearly not expecting her to make a move given he had a gun pointed at her. But he was going to kill them anyway. She knew that. And she'd just as soon take her chances right here and right now.

Linda did the only thing she could think of. With a mighty shove, she sent the car door barreling toward him and screamed, "Allie, get out!"

The door slammed against Brian's right arm with enough force that he screamed and dropped the gun. Linda dove for it and had just wrapped her fingers around the handle when Brian slammed his foot down on her arm.

She screamed in pain.

Vaguely she was aware that Allie had bolted out of the car and was racing back toward the D.A.'s office. Brian obviously realized the same thing.

Panic swept over his face.

"No," he said before turning his sights back on Linda. "You damn bitch. I'm going to kill you!" he shouted. Then he was on her.

Dragging her up by her hair. Hitting and kicking her.

It was just like the night Guapo's men had beat her, only then it had been a different parking lot and she hadn't known whether anyone was close enough to hear or help her.

That wasn't the case now. People were close. So close. Allie would get them.

But even so, Linda knew she couldn't rely on anyone else to save her.

So just as she had with Guapo's men, Linda fought for her life.

She clawed at Brian's eyes and screamed as loud as she could.

Ultimately her screams weren't enough to drown out the shouts of the others as they ran out into the parking lot and came to her aid.

She saw Neil running toward them. But before he could get there—somehow, some way, Tony was there.

He pulled Brian off Linda and wrestled him to the ground. Brian was flailing and kicking, but soon he was surrounded by a bunch of officers, all with their guns pointed at him. Instantly, Tony was at her side.

"Linda. My God. Are you okay?"

She couldn't talk. She gulped for air. But words weren't what mattered. Action was.

As she threw herself into Tony's arms, she knew he'd truly saved her. Not just now, when he'd pulled Brian off of her, but far earlier than that.

He'd saved her when he'd returned to Sacramento. When he'd returned to avenge Rory Maverick. And, she was sure, when he'd also returned for her.

Later that night Linda lay silently in Tony's arms. Even though they'd made love, even though Linda seemed happy, he was once again haunted by fears that sometime soon, she was going to add up all the heartache he'd caused her and kick him to the curb again. For all he knew, she was simply enjoying the sex and wasn't really considering anything long-term between them.

Slowly Tony eased himself away from Linda and stood. Silently he put on his pants, then padded to the kitchen where he poured himself a glass of milk and sat at her dining-room table. Instead of drinking the milk, however, he simply stared at it. He should simply ask her what she was thinking and feeling but—

"I love you, Tony. I always have and I always will."

At the sound of Linda's voice, Tony closed his eyes. Oh, God. The way her words mirrored his mental yearning almost made him dizzy. Now that she'd said the words, he didn't doubt she meant them. She loved him.

But she'd also loved him before. And it hadn't been enough to keep them together.

Maybe it never would be.

She was Linda Delaney. Prosecutor. Warrior woman.

And he was flawed. Too flawed.

He sensed her sit down beside him. Felt her reach out and lay her hand on his. "I've never said that to another man in my life, Tony. Not before you and not after you. I love you."

Tony turned his hand so he could clasp hers. "I know that. And you know I love you so much. But I'm scared, Linda. My addiction got in the way of our happiness once before. And that was before Guapo's men and Justine tried to kill you because of me. Someday, that's going to sink in and—"

"I don't blame you for their actions, Tony. I never will."

"How can you be sure?"

"I just am. I love you," she said.

When he didn't respond, she said it again. "Tony, I love you." As if repeating it would make his insecurities vanish. But it didn't.

"I love you, Tony."

"Damn it, don't," he said, suddenly standing and pulling away from her. "Don't love me. You shouldn't love me."

She stood as well, her voice calm. Sure. "I can't help it."

"I'm not worth it, Linda. You know that. I'm nothing."

Linda shook her head. "You're everything. I love you. Despite your addiction. Despite the problems and hard times we've faced. I love you and I trust you. God, Tony." Linda's voice grew harsh with emotion. "I let you go before. I know now it was a mistake."

"You're only saying that because you know I've remained clean. But there's no guarantee I won't slip up in the future, just like you thought I had before."

"No, there's no guarantee you won't, but I can guarantee this. I won't stop loving you, Tony. And I won't leave you. Not ever again. I'm standing here giving you my heart. Don't break it by walking away from me. I want a future with you and that's never going to change."

Could she be telling the truth? He mentally cursed at himself. Of course she was telling the truth. The question was, was she right? Could he allow himself to believe her? Could he allow himself to believe in them?

But what other choice did he have? He could either take a risk and try his best to keep her, try his best to deserve her or he could spend the rest of his life without her.

Cautiously, he stepped toward her. "I've been thinking about getting a pet. A dog. What—what do you think about that? You want to get one together?"

She smiled. "How about a cat *and* a dog?"

Tony laughed. And all of a sudden, he believed.

Chapter 32

As she stared at the stone entrance of Folsom Prison, Linda couldn't know how she'd react to seeing her father for the first time in over twenty years. She couldn't know if the love he'd expressed for her in his letters was enough to open a dialogue between them and enable her to move beyond his past weaknesses, as well as her own, to forge any kind of relationship, let alone one that resembled father and daughter.

Likewise she couldn't know that Tony had beaten his addiction forever, that he'd never give in to temptation and start taking pain pills again, or that other problems wouldn't threaten to drive a wedge between in the years to come.

There were no guarantees.

Except for one.

She wasn't perfect. Tony wasn't perfect. No one was. Not even Dom or Mattie, the woman who'd sent

Linda that fax encouraging her to trust her instincts about Tony.

Whether someone was a waiter, a prosecutor, a cop, a judge or a little girl, it didn't matter. They'd possess strengths and weaknesses alike.

No, love didn't guarantee a happily ever after. But it certainly made striving for one a lot more fun, and Linda was enjoying her reunion with Tony and his family to the fullest.

Taking a deep sigh, Linda tightened her fingers around Tony's. He was staring down at her, sharing his strength just as he always did. Just the way she gave him strength when he needed it.

After only a few more weeks of trying and with some help from Brian Heald, who had been more than ready to cut a deal, Tony and his team had successfully identified the major suppliers of Rapture in Sacramento. Now he was working as a regular patrol officer. According to him, he'd spent far too long hiding from who he was and he had no wish to go undercover ever again. Occasionally, he still had doubts about whether he was "good" enough to be a cop, but she reminded him everyday how silly his doubts were. Even if he'd never caught the Rapture suppliers, Tony's goodness and determination left her with no doubt that he made the world a better and safer place.

He made *her* a better person, too.

"You can do this," he said.

"I know. With you beside me, I can do almost anything."

"Almost?" he teased. He wiggled his eyebrows up and down. "That sounds like a challenge."

She snorted. "And you love a challenge."

He liked to tease her about her wild side, and that

occasionally resulted in them having sex in less than conventional places, but he was protective of her, too. It didn't matter that she'd withdrawn her name from the judicial campaign; he took care that nothing they ever did together could come back to shame her. It was his mission in life that she never feel shame again, and though she knew it wasn't something he could actually accomplish, she loved him all the more for trying.

He raised her hand to his lips and kissed it. "I love you more. Once an addict, always an addict."

She smiled, glad they could joke about something that had once brought them so much pain and still very well could.

Nope, there were no guarantees, but trying was everything, and so long as Tony tried to be the man she knew him to be, so long as she tried to be the best *she* could be, they'd be able to overcome any challenge that came their way.

The past month had been hard on him, but it appeared that finally the worst was over. She took some comfort in the fact that, even though Justine had tried to kill her, Justine had also given Tony the information to save her life.

Since Heald's arrest, Tony had visited Justine in the hospital twice, and in jail once. The last visit had been to say goodbye. He'd done what he could to help her, but that was over now. He insisted he couldn't maintain a relationship with someone who'd acted to end Linda's life.

Even so, Tony had made sure Justine received word that the Rapture supplier had been caught. Hopefully that would give her some measure of peace.

"So," Linda said. "There's something I've been meaning to talk to you about. Do you remember when

I left you at the hospital with Justine that last time? When I asked you to meet me at my house?"

He nodded. "You said you wanted to show me something."

"Things got a little crazy and I never had the chance to make what I wanted to show you."

"You were going to make me something? What?"

She hesitated, suddenly feeling shy despite the fact they'd been living together for well over a month and she was absolutely secure in their love for one another. But Tony was the bravest person she knew. She could be brave, too. "Cookies," she said. "I wanted to show you chocolate-chip cookies."

His brows lifted in surprise. "Uh…cookies, huh? Well, that's great."

She nodded. "I was going to make them even though they wouldn't be as good as yours. But I was…I was hoping you'd help me with that."

He continued to look confused, but as he absorbed what she was saying, understanding flashed across his face. Instead of smiling as she'd been expecting him to, however, he swallowed hard and suddenly looked nervous himself. Hopeful, but nervous. "What are you saying, Linda?"

"I'm saying that I want you to help me make chocolate-chip cookies. But only after you tell me your secret ingredient."

"Is that right?" he said cautiously. "Because I've always said there's only one way I'll tell you that secret ingredient. Or have you forgotten that?"

"Nope. I haven't forgotten. You said you'd only tell me once we were married," she confirmed.

She smiled at him and slowly, surely, he smiled back at her.

"Then I think, after we're done here, that we should definitely go shopping."

"For a ring?" she teased.

"For a ring, yes. And cookie ingredients."

* * * * *

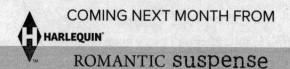

REQUEST YOUR FREE BOOKS!
2 FREE NOVELS PLUS 2 FREE GIFTS!

ROMANTIC suspense

Sparked by danger, fueled by passion

YES! Please send me 2 FREE Harlequin® Romantic Suspense novels and my 2 FREE gifts (gifts are worth about $10). After receiving them, if I don't wish to receive any more books, I can return the shipping statement marked "cancel." If I don't cancel, I will receive 4 brand-new novels every month and be billed just $4.74 per book in the U.S. or $5.24 per book in Canada. That's a savings of at least 14% off the cover price! It's quite a bargain! Shipping and handling is just 50¢ per book in the U.S. and 75¢ per book in Canada.* I understand that accepting the 2 free books and gifts places me under no obligation to buy anything. I can always return a shipment and cancel at any time. Even if I never buy another book, the two free books and gifts are mine to keep forever.

240/340 HDN F45N

Name	(PLEASE PRINT)

Address	Apt. #

City	State/Prov.	Zip/Postal Code

Signature (if under 18, a parent or guardian must sign)

Mail to the **Harlequin® Reader Service:**

IN U.S.A.: P.O. Box 1867, Buffalo, NY 14240-1867
IN CANADA: P.O. Box 609, Fort Erie, Ontario L2A 5X3

Want to try two free books from another line?
Call 1-800-873-8635 or visit www.ReaderService.com.

* Terms and prices subject to change without notice. Prices do not include applicable taxes. Sales tax applicable in N.Y. Canadian residents will be charged applicable taxes. Offer not valid in Quebec. This offer is limited to one order per household. Not valid for current subscribers to Harlequin Romantic Suspense books. All orders subject to credit approval. Credit or debit balances in a customer's account(s) may be offset by any other outstanding balance owed by or to the customer. Please allow 4 to 6 weeks for delivery. Offer available while quantities last.

Your Privacy—The Harlequin® Reader Service is committed to protecting your privacy. Our Privacy Policy is available online at www.ReaderService.com or upon request from the Harlequin Reader Service.

We make a portion of our mailing list available to reputable third parties that offer products we believe may interest you. If you prefer that we not exchange your name with third parties, or if you wish to clarify or modify your communication preferences, please visit us at www.ReaderService.com/consumerschoice or write to us at Harlequin Reader Service Preference Service, P.O. Box 9062, Buffalo, NY 14269. Include your complete name and address.

Diego unbuckled her harness as Vanessa clutched the helicopter seat's armrests. "What are you doing?"

He pointed across her, out the door. "You have to jump, Vanessa."

Oh, no. Absolutely not.

Clutching the door frame so hard her fingernails ached, she shuffled her feet toward the edge and poked her head out the side to stare at the green water below. Over the roar of the rotor blades, she shouted, "Are you crazy? How high up are we?"

"Fifteen meters. It's as low as I can get with these trees."

Fifteen meters was fifty feet. A five-story building. Her stomach heaved. "There could be barracuda in there, or crocodiles. Leeches, even."

"That's a chance you have to take. There's nowhere else to land. The rain forest is too thick and we're out of fuel. You have to suck it up and jump."

"What about you?"

"I'm going to jump, too, but I have to wait until you're clear of the chopper. And there's a chance my jump won't go off as planned. We're running out of time."

She knew she needed to trust him not to leave her, but it was hard. She'd never been this far out of control of her life and she couldn't stop the questions, couldn't let go of the fear that he'd abandon her to fend for herself. "How do I know you're not going to dump me here and fly away?"

"I thought we went over this. Did you forget my speech already?"

"No." But promises were as fluid as water, she wanted to add. People made promises all the time that they didn't keep.

"You gotta hustle now. We don't have much time left in this bird."

She stood and faced the opening, then twisted to take one last look at Diego. What if he didn't make it? What if this was the last time she saw him? "Diego…"

"Jump into the damn water or I'm going to push you. Right now."

She whipped her head straight. Like everything else that had happened in the past couple hours, with this, she didn't have a choice. She sucked in a breath and flung herself over the edge.

Don't miss
TEMPTED INTO DANGER
by Melissa Cutler

Available June 2013 from Harlequin Romantic Suspense wherever books are sold.

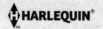

ROMANTIC suspense

CONFESSING TO THE COWBOY
by Carla Cassidy

Small town Grady Gulch has been held captive
by a serial killer targeting waitresses.

Mary Mathis may hold the secret to the killings,
but she risks losing it all if she confides in Sheriff
Cameron Evans, a man who has been captivated
by Mary. Will she confess to the hot sheriff
before the killer takes her as his final victim?

Look for *CONFESSING TO THE COWBOY*
by Carla Cassidy next month from
Harlequin® Romantic Suspense®!

Available wherever books and ebooks are sold.

Heart-racing romance, high-stakes suspense!